More Critical Praise for C.J. Farley

for *Zero O'Clock*

"An insightful, eye-opening, and inventive story. C.J. Farley has penned a novel that sheds an important light on real issues facing young people today."
—Angie Thomas, author of *The Hate U Give*

"Thoughtful, provocative, and pounding with the fast-paced beat of a sharp-witted adolescent mind, *Zero O'Clock* is the story of a Jamaican-American teen girl at the early epicenter of the COVID-19 pandemic in New Rochelle, New York. C.J. Farley has created an irresistible heroine in Geth Montego. Simmering with justifiable anger at everything from the cancellation of her senior prom to racial injustices and police brutality, Geth manages to overcome grief, anxiety, and confusion to discover a new sense of herself and her ability to create change."
—Karen Dukess, author of *The Last Book Party*

"*Zero O'Clock* seems to have a direct line into the mindset of a modern teenager. I enjoyed it immensely!" —Alex Wheatle, author of *Cane Warriors*

for *Around Harvard Square*

• Winner of the NAACP Image Award for Outstanding Literary Work (Youth/Teens)
• A 2020 Paterson Prize for Books for Young People Honor Book
• American Booksellers Association's ABC Best Books for Young Adult Readers

"[A] smart, satirical novel about surviving the racial and cultural tensions ratcheted up in the elite Harvard hothouse. Farley has created a marvelously engaging and diverse set of characters, at the center of which is a nerdy Jamaican American with a philosophical bent and his cohort of oddballs struggling to win a spot on Harvard's brainy humor magazine, which provides a springboard for Farley to dive into the ethics of comedy, among other subjects." —*National Book Review,*

"C.J. Farley's *Around Harvard Square* is a witty and artful narrative of a society on the crossroads of change . . . A must read." —*The Gleaner* (Jamaica)

"For anyone who likes satire, this quick-witted tale . . . catches a bundle of truths about a very particular and powerful corner of our world."
—*New West Indian Guide*

"*Around Harvard Square* [is] C.J. Farley's fun novel about an exceptional Jamaican student-athlete facing class and race issues to get a spot on an elite Harvard University humor magazine." —*New York Daily News*

"This former *Lampoon* editor, journalist, and now satirical novelist, has lots of insight into the discrepancies around race and gender that remain present in the comedy industry."   —CityLine (ABC TV Boston)

"*Around Harvard Square* brings social commentary to college life, approaching the issues in a humorous attitude . . . Farley makes the injustices more tangible to a younger audience who may be future students at such institutions, and he shows how little progression has been made in the educational system regarding institutional racism."   —*Prism Review*

"This coming-of-age novel, set in the '90s, follows Jamaican-American Tosh Livingston and his group of friends—Lao, Meera, and Zippa—on their quest to land coveted spots on the staff of the *Harvard Harpoon*, Harvard's humor magazine . . . The characters' clever dialogue challenges privileged and stereotypical thinking."   —*Publishers Weekly*

"In this throwback coming-of-age novel, an ensemble of freshmen on the margins struggle for self-definition amid the race and class complexities of Harvard . . . Through the whirlwind of their journey, they begin to question the purpose of jokes and the consequences of laughter—when it's not just about the joke, but also about who's making it and why (a significant, timely exploration as comedy culture today struggles to demarcate ethical boundaries) . . . [T]he diverse ensemble of core characters defy and refuse reductive stereotypes . . . [F]or those who would like to take a trip through the hallowed Harvard halls of the past, this goes out to you . . ."   —*Kirkus Reviews*

"Wry, sly, and ferociously funny, *Around Harvard Square* is not just the satire Ivy League college life deserves, but the one it's been waiting for."
                    —Marlon James, Man Booker Prize–winning author
                    of *A Brief History of Seven Killings*

for *Game World*

"*Narnia* for the Social Media Generation."   —*Wall Street Journal*

"Drawn from both video gaming culture and the rich tapestry of Jamaican myth and folklore, blending pointed social satire and mystical philosophy, this exuberant, original hero's journey is a real trip . . . Exhilarating, thought-provoking, and one of a kind."   —*Kirkus Reviews*

"Farley's middle-grade debut draws from Jamaican mythology and beliefs, as well as from other cultures, to weave a fast-paced, whimsical mixture of magic and action . . . [T]he setting lends itself well to memorable imagery and a fun experience."
                    —*Publishers Weekly*

C.J. FARLEY was born in Kingston, Jamaica, and lives in New Rochelle, NY. A graduate of Harvard University, Farley is the author of the acclaimed fantasy adventure novel *Game World* and the best-selling biography *Aaliyah: More Than a Woman*, which was adapted into a hit Lifetime movie. Farley's young adult novel *Around Harvard Square* won an NAACP Image Award and was named a 2020 Honor Book by the Paterson Prize for Books for Young People.

ZERO O:CLOCK

by C.J. FARLEY

BLACK SHEEP

This is a work of fiction. All names, characters, places, and incidents are the product of the author's imagination or are used fictitiously. Any resemblance to real events or persons, living or dead, is entirely coincidental.

Published by Akashic Books
©2021 C.J. Farley
ISBN: 978-1-61775-975-8
Library of Congress Control Number: 2021935108

Black Sheep
c/o Akashic Books
Brooklyn, New York, USA
Twitter: @AkashicBooks
Facebook: AkashicBooks
E-mail: info@akashicbooks.com
Website: www.akashicbooks.com

Special thanks to Iakowi:he'ne' Oakes for consulting on the manuscript, and to Emma Sinéad for creating the original emojis.

I WOULD GIVE ANYTHING to make old people remember what it was like to be a teenager. There were copters buzzing over our house for like forty-five minutes last night while I was trying to do my Mandarin homework. It might have been Fox News or the cops. I don't know and I don't care. All I know is that they give us way too much homework. I was up past midnight finishing it. I asked my mom how much homework she used to get when she was sixteen and she said she didn't remember. High schoolers today get so screwed when it comes to homework. Old people never remember what it was like for them and treat us like they never would have wanted to be treated when they were our age.

I skipped a grade back before middle school, so now I'm a year younger than a high school senior is supposed to be. My mom likes to say I'm young for my grade but old for my age. I don't even know what to do with that, so when she says it I try to pretend that I'm listening to really loud music on my earphones whether I've got earphones in my ears or not.

I should tell you I've got obsessive-compulsive disorder, or maybe I should say it's got me. I get in circles about certain things and it puts people off. Hell, it puts *me* off. I hate when I hear people in school make jokes about trivial stuff and compare it to OCD, like, *He's so anal about eating green Skittles, he's got OCD*, or whatever. OCD is serious and it's not like it is in movies or on TV. If you always brush your teeth and look presentable it doesn't mean you've got OCD necessarily, it just means you're not Post Malone.

My OCD got worse after what happened with my dad. It takes me an extra hour to finish my homework because I have to line up my pens and pencils and paper a certain way in a certain order, and if they're not lined up in that certain way in that certain order I have to start all over again. I can't leave or enter any building without clucking my tongue three times and touching my left eyelid twice. That's what you do when you have OCD—you have these compulsions or rituals you have to perform. But it's not just about handwashing or any of that. You get these thoughts or obsessions that you can't help thinking. They keep replaying in your mind and you have no control. It's like a sample of a song you don't want to hear and somebody else is the deejay. It is what it is.

I take clomipramine for my compulsions and everything but it pretty much gives me every side effect listed on WebMD. I get nausea, upset stomach, loss of appetite, blurred vision, constipation, you name it. What I don't go through is all the fun stuff you see in those pharmaceutical commercials on TV—friends giving me fist bumps after we win a race, smiling parents and siblings toasting me at a food-filled dining table, hotties holding me in their arms on candle-filled dance floors. I hate drug company ads. After all the fantasy images, some announcer speed reads through all the side effects I'm actually suffering like he's an auctioneer taking bids.

Did I mention I also suffer from anxiety attacks? They're a side effect of the clomipramine. My psychiatrist gives me Zoloft to treat them and that causes diarrhea, dizziness, drowsiness, fatigue, insomnia, loose stools, nausea again, de-layed ejaculation—which luckily I don't have to worry about cause I'm a girl—and xerostomia, which even though I got a 98 in English last semester I had no idea what that meant un-til I looked it up. I'll save you a google—it means dry mouth, which is just stupid because they could have just said that from the jump. All of this makes me kind of depressed, so I take Abilify for that, which, you guessed it, exacerbates my OCD. Big Pharma is a scam, I won't lie.

They're saying school will be closed for a minute because of this thing that's going around. Everybody was psyched about getting a flu break until we started receiving e-mails about distance learning and our teachers started going crazy on Google Classroom. You know how in that book *1984* they say that what's in room 101 is the worst thing in the world? Well, turns out what's in room 101 is Google Classroom. We might end up getting more homework with school out than we do with school on.

I texted my friend Tovah this past weekend about maybe getting together and seeing that new Pixar movie, but she was like, *I have too much work to do.* I did too, but that was the one movie I was willing to take a break to go see. Tovah's a hypochondriac and a germaphobe, which is a pretty terrible combination; and she's a workaholic on top of that, so I just figured she was gonna be about that homework life until the whole flu bug was over. Even before they began officially canceling classes, Tovah started pushing ahead in her coursework so she wouldn't miss anything even if the teachers did. We both stayed home like two nerds and neither of us got to see that Pixar movie. I was bummed about it. There's nothing better than going to the Ozy Theater on opening weekend. They serve you dinner right in your seats. It's a real meal too, not like horrible theater food. They don't even let people turn on their cell phones, which Tovah can't stand, but I love it because it's just fantastic to not have someone waving or poking or texting you for a couple hours. And they show old films there too like all the Miyazaki classics.

If you haven't seen Miyazaki's stuff, you have to. People call him the Japanese Walt Disney but that's racist and stupid because he's way better than Walt Disney. First of all, I'm pretty certain Mickey Mouse is just low-key blackface and I'm not okay with that. Miyazaki's movies have environmental and spiritual and antiwar themes. But they also have these moments that Miyazaki calls *ma* where there's no action at all and the characters just sigh or listen to the wind in the trees or stare at a running stream. Disney movies don't have moments like that. Without *ma*, everything is like a long hashtag you can't figure out because there aren't any breaks between the words. I saw Miyazaki's *Spirited Away* with Tovah at the Ozy Theater and after the lights came up we just sat there and hugged each other and cried because the movie is about the afterlife and I was thinking about my dad and we didn't care that all the parents there with real little kids thought we were like mental.

I'm still bummed we didn't get to see that Pixar movie. That's like the first Pixar movie I didn't rush to see on opening weekend. Except *Cars 2*. Have you seen that movie? The talking cars get caught up in an international spy ring? Even when I was seven I called bullshit.

It's not like I didn't do anything over the weekend. I did get a lot of homework done—I studied for a test we were going to have in Mandarin and a quiz we were supposed to have in AP Gov. We've been reading about FDR and the Great Depression and World War II. Ms. Swain told us FDR kind of saved America. Did he really though? I mean, of course the New Deal was awesome and I wish more people knew about the Second Bill of Rights that FDR proposed that included freedom from monopolies and the right to work and have housing and medical care and education. But I'm kinda tired of the whole great-man-of-history thing. FDR didn't storm the beaches at Normandy. FDR wasn't working in assembly lines in Detroit building amphibious trucks and flame-throwing armored cars. Yes, FDR was a great president and he helped create the whole postwar international framework that President Mad King is currently breaking apart like a bull in a LEGO store. But why isn't history more about the everyday people who do stuff and not just about the names with blue check marks?

Of course they're not going to ask us anything interesting like that on the quiz, just a bunch of stupid multiple choice questions about dates and names and definitions. Homework is such a waste of time. Teachers use it to pretend they're really teaching. Now it looks like we won't even have that quiz in AP Gov, or the test in Mandarin. They sent out an e-mail blast that we're going to be out of school for two weeks at least, and they canceled a bunch of quizzes and tests until they figure things out. I wasted all my time studying when I could have been getting my Pixar on.

Instead of sulking even more, I closed my window shades, put in my earphones, and turned up BTS. They're like my favorite band. None of my friends can understand why I like them. To tell you the truth, I don't even completely understand it myself. I know they're not what most people would call a cool band. I know they're not all whatever like Kendrick Lamar or XXXTentacion. I will sometimes check out vintage stuff if it comes recommended by a person I respect. My mom's crazy boyfriend is always listening to crazy stuff from decades ago like Public Enemy and the Fugees, and rock stuff like Nirvana and the Strokes, and obscure stuff like Jonathan Richman and the Modern Lovers. No thank you. My mom's boyfriend is like fifty years old, so he's pretty much stuck in the past like that prehistoric mosquito trapped in amber at the beginning of *Jurassic Park*. People in their fifties are funny because they're too young to realize they're really old.

BTS—there's just something about them. It's not exactly cool to like K-pop, but I love their music because it goes against what other kids at my school are into. I don't know any other Black girls in school who are into them. My friend Tovah follows them on social media and she's like the only person in school I can really talk to about BTS. She's not as into them as I am, but she doesn't shame me for liking them. When she had her bat mitzvah she put that BTS song "Wings" on the after-party playlist, partly because her dad's Korean and she wanted to have a nod to her culture, but also because she knew I'd lose my mind and actually get up and dance if I heard it.

I know all the band members' birthdays, and I watch all the videos they post on YouTube—not just the music videos, I also keep up with the documentary-style ones, and there are about a thousand of those. BTS makes a lot of videos where they're playing weird games and the clips are all in Korean and some of them don't even have subtitles. Korean game shows are really funny, and they have elaborate sets, like there was this one I saw that took place in what looked like a classroom and the point was for contestants to try to hit the teacher with paper airplanes. I love BTS but I have to admit watching all their videos is a huge time suck. I'd like to blame my obsession on my OCD though I think it's just that I really love this band. It is what it is.

There are seven members of BTS and I have a sticker of Jungkook on the water bottle I use whenever I've finished a run; I keep it on the nightstand next to my bed. Jungkook's got a sweep of hair that falls down just above his eyes, and he's got a sweet perky red mouth like a flower that I'm pretty sure he accentuates with lipstick. He is the youngest member of the group. He's like twenty-two which is only a few years older than me. He's the best singer in the band, IMO, and he has the most energy. He's also the only member of the group with tattoos—a tiger flower and a skeleton hand on his forearm, the date he joined BTS under his thumb on his right hand, the letters A-R-M-Y on his knuckles as a tribute to his army of fans, and his life motto—*Rather be dead than cool*—on his wrist. Don't ask me why I know all this. I would never care this much about One Direction or the Jonas Brothers. My left brain understands that boy bands are ridiculous, like fidget spinners or American Girl dolls or the fact that the *Twilight* franchise was ever a thing. But my right brain likes looking into Jungkook's cute dark eyes as I lie in bed.

I could hear the TV through my bedroom wall as I drifted off to sleep last night. My mom's stupid boyfriend was watching the Night King and his White Walkers talking about the virus crisis:

We have contained this. I won't say airtight, but pretty close to airtight.

You have fifteen people, and the fifteen within a couple of days is going to be down to close to zero. That's a pretty good job we've done.

Right now, at this moment, there's no need to change anything that you're doing on a day-by-day basis. Right now the risk is still low—but this could change.

Goodnight, Jungkook.

GOT INTO AN ARGUMENT with Diego about BTS. Diego's like six foot six and plays on the football team. He's a right tackle or a left tackle or a quarterback or something—what do I know about football anyway? Okay, I do know he's supposed to be the star quarterback. And I know that for a jock he's not a completely lost cause. He's in my Mandarin class for one, so he's not just trying to skate by with easy A's in Astronomy or Gym. And get this—he loves Broadway. I like Broadway too, like *Hamilton* of course, and *Dear Evan Hansen*, and I've been listening to the soundtrack for *Six*—we have tickets to see it next weekend. But Diego says he only likes "forward-leaning" Broadway by "geniuses" like Terrence McNally and Stephen Sondheim. I like Broadway like I said, but I had never even heard of Terrence McNally until Diego started going on about *Love! Valour! Compassion!* Of course I've heard of Sondheim because everybody's seen *Into the Woods* with Emily Blunt and Anna Kendrick and that late-night TV host who had BTS on once for *Carpool Karaoke*. Diego plays Broadway show tunes all the time at his locker at school and nobody bugs him about it because like I said he's six foot six and plus he led the team to the state championship this past year.

One thing I hate about movies and TV shows about people my age is that they have huge friend groups with kids who are always cracking jokes and who have personal problems that are neatly resolved by the end of the movie or the episode or the season. They also go to high schools that are big and colorful and clean and they have massive bedrooms that look like grand hotel suites. I like a lot of those movies and shows but I don't relate to those kids because they have everything in life they want except maybe enough charging stations on the interstate for their Teslas.

Meanwhile, I have like two friends total, a house one size up from a trailer, and when I walk into my English class at New Rochelle High School, it's entirely possible I'll be greeted by a dying mouse twitching on the floor.

Diego, Tovah, and I decided to meet up at the Starbucks in the strip mall near my house. School's canceled until the end of the month and the governor has created a "containment zone" to control the spread of the virus in my area. The *New York Daily News* ran a front-page story yesterday screaming: "NEW ROCH-HELL: Mile-Wide Swath of W'chester City Shut, Schools Closed, National Guard Deployed." I don't read newspapers because I'm not a million years old, but I see stacks of unsold copies of the *Daily News* and the *Post* in Starbucks all the time and pretty much all of last month the *Post* acted like the virus wasn't a thing. About a week ago the *Post's* front-page story was "My Mom Is Hotter Than Me! Daughter's Lament." Now the tabloids seem practically gleeful we're in a containment zone. Nobody has explained to anyone exactly what a containment zone is, but it sounds scary and nobody's supposed to be hanging out in large groups, which is fine by me because I don't have any friends other than Diego and Tovah.

Diego showed up wearing a *Thoroughly Modern Millie* T-shirt and going on about how this Broadway actress Sutton Foster was "a goddess on Earth" and far better than Kristin Chenoweth; meanwhile, Tovah was worried about whether it was safe to drink her usual extra-dry nonfat cappuccino because of the coronavirus and everything.

Passersby are always doing double takes when they see Diego and Tovah together. People who like to put other people in boxes can never tell what her racial background is, with her thin eyes, pale complexion, and blond hair. They are always asking her about her mom and dad in ways that they think are clever, but they're basically trying to 23andMe her and find out if she's half Asian and half whatever. Tovah likes to say she's not half anything, she's 100 percent everything, because people aren't math problems and they don't have to add up. She's also really short and Diego's really tall. Tovah jokes that she's fun-sized like Halloween candy, but if you know her you know just because she's petite doesn't mean you can mess with her because she gets super argumentative when she thinks she's right. Diego is more of a mountain than a man. He's big, but unlike a lot of tall guys he doesn't look stretched, he looks magnified. He's also got black hair and tan skin and chiseled features like he should be on Mount Rushmore.

Diego slurped his caramel frappuccino. "I heard they already shut down all the Broadway shows."

"They wouldn't do that!" Tovah said. "Geth, don't you have tickets?"

"Next weekend. You guys are going too, remember? We're seeing *Six*."

"I totally forgot," Tovah said. "I can't say I'm that into it."

"I hear the production on the West End was better," Diego added.

"Maybe we should skip the show and just stream the soundtrack," Tovah said.

"There were plagues in Shakespeare's time too, and the Globe Theatre was shut down for months," Diego commented. "There was no streaming to make up for it, though."

"I should make sure the performance hasn't been canceled. I got us cut-rate obstructed-view tickets, but I have zero money to waste."

Tovah shrugged. "I never saw *Hamilton* either. I just memorized the cast album."

"Seeing it in person is what makes Broadway Broadway. You can't just DVR it. You have to be in the room where it happens."

"Oh my god," Diego said, "I hope that pun was unintentional."

Tovah sipped cautiously at her extra-dry nonfat cappuccino which is basically pricey foam, but whatever. "I dunno. Is *Six* even supposed to be any good?"

"It's supposed to be a feminist show," I said. "It's about Henry VIII's wives."

Diego shook his head. "I still don't see how that's interesting. They were just his wives. They didn't actually do anything but get divorced or beheaded by him."

"That's the point," I replied. "History changes depending on who is telling the story."

Diego snorted. "There are objective facts. It shouldn't matter who is telling the story if the storytelling is accurate."

"So, in your opinion," Tovah asked, "what did we talk about today?"

"We mostly talked about Broadway," Diego answered.

Tovah frowned. "We mostly talked about whether this Starbucks is clean enough for us to keep coming to. Remember? We saw that barista use the bathroom and when she came out her hands weren't even wet!"

"And I would say we spoke mostly about BTS."

"I think we can all agree BTS sucks," Diego laughed. "No offense."

"Why do people always say 'No offense' after they say something that's clearly offensive?" I asked.

"Same with 'Don't take this the wrong way,'" Tovah said. "People always take it the wrong way."

Diego smiled. "Nothing any good ever follows 'I'm not a racist, but . . .'"

I laughed. "My favorite is 'I don't know what you want me to say.' Yeah . . . you do."

After what felt like a million cups of coffee, we finished up and headed into the parking lot. I did my OCD thing, clucking my tongue three times and touching my left eyelid twice. Diego and Tovah totally ignored it because they've seen it a million times before. But what was going on in my head was even worse than usual because I'd been applying to colleges. The whole application process is like getting a grade for your entire teenage life. I kept thinking about my application to Columbia and it kept repeating in my head like a sample and I tried to put it out of my head but I knew my OCD wouldn't let that happen and I was going to have to let it keep going like a computer program that's running in the background.

The day was clear and cool and there was only a single sad cloud in the sky. I lived a few streets away, and Diego and Tovah lived close by too. A woman brushed by me wearing a serious gas mask type deal, like she was heading into trench warfare in World War I. I recognized her as a particularly nosy neighbor. She once tried to get a traffic lady to ticket my mom because her car was parked too far away from the curb. We found out later from a Black family down the street that they were also told to Kurb their Kar by the exact same Karen. #KKKaren #ParkingWhileBlack. The nosy neighbor caught my look and shot me a look right back.

"If you knew what was good for you, you'd be wearing a mask too," she huffed.

I flashed a fake smile. "Thank you for your service."

The nosy neighbor in the gas mask walked away.

Diego laughed. "Those masks look dumb as hell."

"I don't know," Tovah said. "My mom is ordering some surgical masks on Amazon."

"Do they work?" I asked.

"If I see someone in a mask, I figure they're sick," Diego said. "So if by work you mean do they raise everyone's anxiety levels unnecessarily, then yes, they work."

Tovah's eyes narrowed. "What do you mean *unnecessarily*?"

Diego shrugged. "The president said there's nothing to worry about."

"You actually trust President Joffrey Baratheon?"

"It's not about trust, it's about logic. This is like the flu."

"The flu kills like ten thousand people every year."

"Then why aren't you more worried about that?"

"Because we have a vaccine for the flu. We don't have one for the new thing."

"Coronavirus," I broke in. "They also call it COVID-19. King Joffrey's speech about it is trending on Twitter."

Just then, someone shouted across the Starbucks parking lot: "Hey QB1!"

"Hey QB2!" Diego answered.

Quade jogged up to us carrying a football, which he dropped on the ground when he got close, and he and Diego exchanged an elaborate handshake. Quade is Diego's backup, but he always acts like he's being followed by a fancam. He is supposed to be pretty good, but Diego is like all-state and getting recruited by major colleges.

Quade's dad is COO of Ozy Theaters which has fifty outlets all along the East Coast, so he's a super-rich kid like the Frank Ocean song. His family has two houses, one in New Ro and another in New Hampshire, and whenever his mom and dad are out of town Quade throws parties that are legendary. Now and again, because his family is in the theater business, minor celebrities show up, like that guy who costars in that one show everyone used to watch two years ago before they started doing special musical episodes, or that girl who played a nanny on that Disney series but never had a real career after that. The kind of stars you identify more by what they used to do than what they're currently doing. But they are still stars, especially in New Rochelle. Quade sometimes sends signals that he's feeling some sparks between him and Tovah and he wouldn't mind getting with her, which is weird for me because I'm the only person on Earth who knows Tovah is gay. She came out to me in middle school which is when all the girls come out these days, and she told me not to tell anyone else and I never have and meanwhile she never has either. Now it's one of those things with her that I feel like we can't talk about unless she brings it up first. She has a lot of things like that. Like race, or religion, or grades, or college applications, or why she has this long unspoken list of stuff we can't talk about.

"A bunch of us are going to Mickey D's," Quade said to Diego. "Want to come with?"

"Nah, I'm good."

Quade glanced at me and flashed a lingering smile at Tovah. He was a nice-looking guy, if you liked six-foot-tall athletic types with a broad chest and piercing eyes. "They can come too."

"I have homework," I said.

"Are you gonna play football in college?" Tovah asked Quade.

"I'm gonna try."

"Do you know John Urschel?"

"Am I supposed to?"

"He's getting a PhD in math at MIT."

"Then I definitely don't know him."

"He used to be a pro football player. He quit after the NFL released stats linking football to that brain disease CTE. And did you know even Australian-rules football pretty much turns your cerebrum into jelly? Or, I guess, Vegemite."

I forgot to mention that Tovah's like this math genius who's going to be valedictorian. I also forgot to say that she's really bad at making small talk with guys who aren't Diego.

Quade turned back to Diego. "You hear back from UVA?"

"They want me to come for a visit."

"That's tight. Their QB just declared for the draft. You could grab that slot."

"I don't know. I got lots of places I'm thinking about. Naverton's been calling."

"Naverton? My dad went there."

I interrupted. "Much as I'd like to hear you guys talk about football, we have to bounce."

Tovah and I started to walk away, and Diego and Quade did a complicated goodbye handshake. "Diego—I'm planning a big party soon. You have to come. We will discuss this."

Quade started to walk off, but after he had gotten about fifty yards away, Diego picked up the football Quade had left behind and called out, "Hey QB2!"

Then he threw what looked to me to be a perfect pass that smacked Quade right in the ass just below the number 17 on his jersey. Quade turned, smiled, and picked up the football.

Once the boys were out of sight, Tovah turned to me. "If Quade or Diego had sisters, I would totally smash them. I'm not even kidding."

I smiled. "Diego's cousin Angela is cute, but maybe you should keep that between us."

When I got home the phone was ringing. I don't know why anyone calls our home phone. I have like never picked up our landline once in my life and I don't even know the code to get the messages or even if there is a code. Why do people even keep old technology like landlines around, anyway? When I was seven years old and Tovah was eight and she was the only girl who would hang out with the nerdy new kid who skipped a grade, we used to play with two soup cans connected by yarn. But it's not like we hung on to the contraption after we got our first iPhones.

The landline kept ringing. By the time I did my OCD clucks and touches and I thought about my Columbia application again, voice mail picked up and I heard my school principal's voice. I figured it was going to be something either really bad or really good because we only heard from her when there was a school shooting or a football state championship and nothing in between.

Dear Parents and Guardians,

The City School District of New Rochelle is pleased to announce that local community organizations have stepped up to help mitigate the food shortage that will be experienced by some students during the two-week closure of three schools in the state-designated coronavirus (COVID-19) "containment area."

We understand that some of our students are food-dependent on the district. As we await support from the state government to help provide these students with food support, we are very thankful to local organizations who have stepped up in this critical time.

Additionally, we will share information about the 2,822 students who are food-dependent with the governor's office. We anticipate that the National Guard will help distribute food to these students in need.

At this time, there have been no confirmed cases of COVID-19 in our schools. We are closing the three schools temporarily in compliance with the governor's directive.

Luckily for our students and parents, we have a robust system of teleteaching and students will be meeting regularly on Google Classroom and Zoom. Even as we persevere through this crisis, rest assured your sons and daughters will have plenty of schoolwork to enrich their free hours.

Thank you from myself, Principal Starch, and all of us at New Rochelle High School.

That's what's so stupid about my school. The world could literally be coming to an end and they'd still be giving us homework. I ended up having too much homework to watch the news about the Night King's speech. I spent forty-five minutes lining up my pens and pencils and paper a certain way in a certain order just so I could start. Someone sent me a TikTok of some of that Oval Office speech I missed. The president had this weird cocaine sniff and he sounded like a bad actor reading his lines at an audition. The kids in my eighth-grade production of *Bye Bye Birdie* were better. While I struggled with my Mandarian homework, texts started coming in.

Diego: *Did you see that the NBA is canceling its entire season? Some players tested positive for coronavirus.*

Me: *Don't care. I just hope Steph Curry is okay. He's cute* ♡

Tovah: *Did you watch the speech?*

Me: *Working on Mandarin*

Me: *Diego you should be working on Mandarin too*

Diego: *Tom Hanks and his wife tested positive*

Me: *Stop playing*

Tovah: *I saw that too. Life is like a box of chocolates*

Me: *????*

Diego: *A line from Forrest Gump*

Me: *I* ♡ *Frank Ocean*

Diego: *Not the song. The movie. Tom Hanks won best actor*

Later in the group chat, Tovah sent me a GIF of the president as Thanos with the Infinity Gauntlet on, poised to snap his fingers. The caption read, "House Democrats can push their sham impeachments all they want. The President's re-election is inevitable."

Tovah: *The GOP tweeted this out*

Tovah: *This is terrifying*

Tovah's always getting me wound up about politics right before bedtime. I mean, I want Roose Bolton out of the White House too, but I have homework to do and friends to hang out with and I can't let my disgust for him rule my life.

This is our last year in high school together and I want it to be special and memorable and everything. There's basically nothing we can do about Littlefinger until November and who knows if we'll even make it to November. Sometimes I wish

Tovah would focus her rage on somebody else who sucks that we can actually do something about, like R. Kelly or Sean Hannity. I've told Tovah this before. I can't let Walder Frey's ugly name pass through my lips even one more time, so until he's out of office or George R.R. Martin finishes that final book, I'm just gonna say the names of *Game of Thrones* villains instead. Kind of like the way the kids in Harry Potter refuse to say Lord Voldemort's name and call him You-Know-Who and He-Who-Must-Not-Be-Named instead. People say his name enough. I'm not gonna help him trend on Twitter, he's got Russian bots for that. I remember when I used to read those Harry Potter books when I was a kid, the one thing I noticed was that You-Know-Who tried to kill Harry Potter every year he was at Hogwarts but Harry and his friends kept coming back. Every year. They kept boarding the train at Platform 9 3/4 and unloading their stuff at Gryffindor or Slytherin or Ravenclaw or Hufflepuff and going out and playing Quidditch or whatever. You can't let evil Dark Lords ruin your school year.

I turned off my phone.

I stopped by Open Market before it closed so we'd have some food in the house in the morning. The place is located in a strip mall in Scarsdale which is a town full of homes owned by people who have homes in other towns too. There's something supersad about strip malls. I imagine that back in the day they were mom-and-pop stores with charmingly ampersanded names like Addington & Sons Country Time Candy Mart or Capt. R.J. Pepper's Insulation World & Toffee Co. International. Now the same stores anywhere are the same stores everywhere. The same grocery stores, the same restaurants, the same products, the same same. I don't know why I feel nostalgic for a time I never lived through, but I do. Nostalgia is actually one of my favorite emotions. You can float in it like a warm salt lake. You can feel nostalgia about anything, even times that are really bad, so it's like a kind of emotional money laundering. I think I like nostalgia even more than schadenfreude, which is this mean word about taking pleasure in the bad things that happen to other people. I learned about the word from a song in that musical *Avenue Q*. I would never feel that feeling about my friends, but there are some bad people in Washington I would love to schadenfreude. If I ever had a really good bout of schadenfreude and was able to look back on it with nostalgia, that would pretty much be heaven.

Open Market is one of those upscale supermarket chains where the prices are way high and all the brands are fancy and there are girls my age in aprons and retainers in every aisle handing out samples of crackers and tuna salad. Almost everything in the store is marked *gluten-free*, including things I'm pretty sure never had gluten to begin with. I actually don't know what gluten is or why people in rich neighborhoods seem to hate it so much. All I know is gluten seems to be in every food that I like and when I buy the version that's gluten-free it tastes like ass, so I'm thinking gluten must actually be one of the best things in the universe, like one of the Infinity Stones. Taking gluten out of a food is like taking Michael B. Jordan out of a movie. There's nothing you can substitute that can make it better than it was.

I go to Open Market for the fresh fruit—and because I've got promo codes. Ms. Swain told us in AP Gov that during the Cold War, President Eisenhower took Soviet Premier Nikita Khrushchev to a typical American supermarket and Khrushchev was so overwhelmed by the quality and quantity of the foods and products on display that he immediately realized the Cold War was lost. Imagine walking down the cereal aisle and seeing Frosted Flakes and Froot Loops and Cap'n Crunch and realizing you're not a superpower anymore. I wonder what Putin would think of Open Market. I mean, I learned in World History last year that Russia is basically a failed state. They have one industry—oil, which totally sucks and is turning our planet into Venus—and their economy is barely bigger than Los Angeles's. Sure, Russian literature is supposed to be brilliant, but it's not like Tolstoy, Pushkin, or Dostoyevsky have published anything lately. Saying Russia is a superpower is like saying Hawkeye is a superhero. The dude shoots arrows. The Hulk smashes skyscrapers. Maybe if Putin got a look inside Open Market he'd stop trying to steal American presidential elections and enroll his kids in Scarsdale High.

There's a lot of amazing produce at Open Market. It's like the Garden of Eden only you don't get kicked out for sampling the fruit. Of course, they have old-school classics like apples and pears and strawberries. Then they have more exotic offerings like cherimoyas from South America, which Mark Twain once said was the most delicious fruit he'd ever tasted. Mark Twain also used the N-word 219 times in *The Adventures of Huckleberry Finn* so I'm not necessarily okay with *everything* that goes in and out of that guy's mouth. Then there are rambutans from Malaysia. I have no idea what rambutans taste like, but they look like red golf balls with green hair, so, well, yeah. Then there's this weird yellow fruit that's shaped like a twisted claw called Buddha's hand which is actually pretty racist if you think about it. They also have all these West Indian fruits like mangoes and plantains and ackee and star apples. The sweet smells make me think of my dad and sitting around laughing on a lazy Saturday. Whenever I visit Open Market, Andy, the fresh fruit guy, is usually there in the produce aisles, restocking the cotton-candy grapes or straightening the bottles of natural fruit juices on the refrigerated shelves.

As I throw ten bottles of POM Wonderful 100% Pomegranate Juice into my cart, Andy turns around to greet me: "Shay kohn!" That's not how you spell that, but it's a Mohawk expression and that's what it sounds like. Andy always says "Shay kohn!" to me when he sees me at Open Market.

He's Native American and he says it's a traditional Mohawk greeting.

"How's it going?" I reply.

He winks. "There's a special on mandarin oranges."

I already have a cart full of cage-free eggs, cruelty-free frozen veggie burgers, POM Wonderful 100% Pomegranate Juice, and Tate's chocolate chip cookies. "Maybe next time. How are you doing?"

"Good, I guess. They're gonna start opening an hour later and closing an hour early."

"Why?"

"To give us time to double-wash all the produce." He holds up his hands and wiggles his gloved fingers. "They got me wearing these now."

I wave goodbye with my ungloved hand as I head to the checkout line.

Sally, the checkout lady, is at her register. "Did you see there's a special on mandarin oranges today?" She gestures to a large bin of oranges nearby.

"Andy mentioned it."

"You speak Mandarin, right?"

"How did you know that?"

"Remember that day you came in with that big friend of yours and I asked you about your chitter-chatter?"

She has a good memory. I had come there once with Diego to practice food words. "I don't think there's a connection between mandarin oranges and Mandarin the language."

"Actually, Chinese dignitaries used to wear these really bright yellow robes and that's where the name comes from."

"Really? I've been studying Chinese for years and I didn't know that."

"I once looked into taking a cruise to Hong Kong," she said. "Did a lot of googling and that was one of the random facts I picked up!"

"So how is a mandarin orange different from a regular one?"

"Andy tells me they have more vitamin A, E, B3, and B6! I don't know what those vitamins are good for, but I'm betting they're better than vitamin C. I have a couple mandarin oranges right here."

"They look rotten. And—ew, they're soft!"

"That's the way they're supposed to be. Have a taste! I won't charge you for tasting."

I peel the mandarin orange and bite into it. "This is pretty terrific."

"See? I wouldn't steer you wrong. And neither would Andy."

I put six oranges on the conveyor belt. "That cruise to Hong Kong sounds great."

"It was out of my price range—but I'm saving up for a cruise to Italy. A girl can dream!"

She finishes checking me out and I look at the receipt. "I thought the mandarins were on sale!"

"That *is* the sale price. You should see what they're charging for the star apples."

ONE OF THE DEALS with my OCD is I check door locks a lot. Sometimes three or four times, just to make sure I've locked them. I also check the stove to make sure I've turned it off. A couple times to be sure. Same thing with the water faucet in the bathroom. I'm always worried I've left it on and I'll wake up in the morning and the house will be flooded. So I get up two or three times a night to check. And yes, I do wash my hands a lot. I was doing that before the whole coronavirus crisis made handwashing a thing. I also make music lists.

<u>Geth's Social Distancing Playlist</u>
00:00 (Zero O'Clock), BTS
SICKO MODE, Travis Scott
Solo, Frank Ocean
Circles, Post Malone
Broken Clocks, SZA
Feels Like Summer, Childish Gambino
Paramedic!, SOB x RBE
Hard Place, H.E.R.
The Only Journey, L-Boogie
Far Away, Jessie Reyez
m.A.A.d city (feat. MC Eiht), Kendrick Lamar
God's Plan, Drake

Tovah forwards me and Diego a link of Euron Greyjoy from a press conference he had several days ago.

It will go away. Just stay calm. It will go away.

Me: *Seriously*

Me: *Could you stop sending me these? I already saw this one. He just says the same thing over and over* 🤡 🤡 🤡

Tovah: *You have to keep up with the news*

Me: *Not every minute*

Diego: *Maybe he's right*

Tovah: *You're not serious*

Diego: *Flu season only lasts a couple months*

Tovah: *Then it comes back*

Tovah: *That's why they call it flu season. It's seasonal*

Tovah: *Plus it's not the flu. This is a pandemic*

Tovah: *Can you imagine if the Vietnam War was seasonal? This is like that*

Diego: *You can't ignore the political dimensions of this*

Tovah: *Turn* 👏 *Fox* 👏 *Off* 👏

Me: *Can we please talk about something less stressful?* 😫 🗼

Me: *Like the fact Columbia is going to tell us all whether we got in or not on March 26. Roar, lion, roar!* 🦁

Tovah: *[Three dots appear then vanish]*

I should probably tell you that I changed the names in this diary. But I'm not gonna tell you that because I pretty much didn't change anything. The robocalls from my school and the mayor, those are pretty much verbatim, and screw them if they complain because they shouldn't have been robocalling me so much anyway. Everything I'm saying happened to me just the way I'm saying. I mean it's *my* diary, and I'm going to get into some stuff that's pretty personal. Like that one time in seventh grade when Tovah and I made out. It was after school and my parents were still at work and Tovah and I were on my couch in the living room watching that Nickelodeon cartoon series *The Legend of Korra* instead of doing our Social Studies homework, which is why she had come over on a school night. I still remember she took a Sour Patch Kid out of her mouth before we kissed and her lips tasted like lemonade made with too many lemons. I told her I liked boys and not girls and I was totally cool with her coming out and proud of her too but maybe we should keep this incident between us.

The whole "Night of the Sour Patch Kid Kiss" has kind of always made me feel closer to Tovah, like it was our special bond. Like she was Dumbledore and I was J.K. Rowling and I was the only one who knew robes and wands weren't the only things hidden in her closet. Or maybe not exactly like that since J.K. now has some weird hateration against trans people that's messed with my nostalgia for her books. I call Expelliarmus on that anti-LGBTQ+ bullshit. Anyway, maybe I should have changed all the names before I told you that story about Tovah, but I don't care because people should be able to do whatever and kiss whoever. So I told you what I told you. It's not like you're going to meet any of these people. I, however, see all these people on the regular. Just last month on North Avenue I ran into the mayor, who turned out to be this super-smart guy who told me this crazy funny story about how some mystery hacker was trying to steal the text and e-mail address of everyone in town. New Rochelle is supposed to be a city but I pretty much know everyone. There are some people I wish I didn't know. My mom's boyfriend's one of them.

I always hate books or movies where the stepparents are evil so I guess it's hypocritical of me if I start slagging off the guy who's auditioning to be my stepdad. But the way I feel is the way I feel. Like the way everyone should feel deep, grammatical disgust for movies with numbers embedded in the title, like *Se7en* and *2 Fast 2 Furious*. He's asked my mom to marry him twice and she's turned him down twice, I think because she knows I hate his ass. The fact is, the main thing that's really wrong with him is he's not my dad. Also that my mom hooked up with him in such a hurry after my dad died. I hate it that when the three of us walk around together, even though I look nothing like this guy I still have to tell people that he's not my real dad.

I hate phrases like that—*real dad*, or *whole milk* or *real reality*, as opposed to the virtual kind. There's a word for things like that but I forget what it is. Things that are the originals that you now have to qualify with an adjective because there's now an imitation or pretender out there. My mom started seriously dating this guy a year and a half after my dad died. The grass had barely grown in on his grave and they were on a couples retreat in Phoenix. I understand being lonely but you don't have to be thirsty. I didn't even ask if she had met Kevin, that's his name, before or after Dad died. I actually didn't want to know. And I don't even care that he's white, I really don't. And he's white-white, like he was telling me how great *Pet Sounds* by the Beach Boys is, and I could give a fuck about a Beach Boy. He's one of those white men who puts raisins in food and thinks it's okay to borrow a toothbrush.

Kevin's a freelance journalist, which these days basically means he's unemployed. He's always borrowing mom's car late at night cause his Kia sucks and I think he's secretly driving for Uber or going out and getting drunk or maybe both, which is not only really dangerous and pitiful but a sure way to get yourself a one-star rating. My dad died a hero. Kevin will never be my goddamn real dad.

I try to get away from the house and this situation as much as I can. There's no track practice cause school is out, but I've been running on my own to stay in shape. They're saying school will probably open back up sooner rather than later, and I don't want to go back to practice with a big Pop-Tart gut. I run down North Avenue and back which is about a six-mile route. When I get to North Avenue and Huguenot Street, I pause to take a puff from my inhaler and then I turn around. Sometimes I stop by places I used to go with my dad, like Cal's Barbershop. There's always people waiting at Cal's, and it's like an hour-long wait to get a cut, but my dad appreciated when I would wait there with him. Some of the customers in that shop wouldn't care if it was a ten-hour wait. They just sit around and trade stories about the way the neighborhood used to be, about how great the football team was back in the day, stuff like that.

I think really knowing a city is the opposite of navigating it on GPS. When you really know a city you remember what used to be there, not what's visible to the naked eye now. The New Ro old-heads live in a ghost city of shut-down pizza places and department stores that used to be right over there and neighbors who used to live right on that block before they moved out west. There are these faded advertising murals for hair products and soft drinks and butcher shops painted on the brick walls of older buildings in New Rochelle and I sometimes think that for the old-heads the ghost signs still appear to them in full color like they haven't aged a day.

So on my way home, I popped my head in the door of Cal's Barbershop.

Cal's has four barber's chairs, and they are always filled. Cal's station is against the far corner, and on the wall behind him is a sign that says *Black Wall of Fame* with photos of his favorite Black celebrities. There's a photo of Denzel of course, from that Spike Lee movie *Malcolm X*. Then there's a photo of the real Malcolm X. There's a signed photo of Barack Obama with Michelle, Sasha, and Malia. There's Shirley Chisholm, Thurgood Marshall, and Jesse Jackson. There's a page ripped out from *Essence* magazine with a drawing of Maya Angelou and a copy of her poem "Still I Rise." There's a poster from *Hidden Figures* and another from that movie *Glory*. There are a bunch of musicians—Stevie Wonder, Bob Marley, Aretha, Prince, Aaliyah, Lauryn Hill, L-Boogie, Drake, Luther Vandross, Beyoncé, and Jay-Z. There are athletes—Ali, Air, Bron, Kareem, Steph, Bolt, Venus, and Serena. I remember there used to be a Tiger Woods photo, but Cal took it down and replaced it with Ida B. Wells after he heard a podcast about her. I had to look her up on Wikipedia—Wells was a crusading journalist who fought against lynching. Cal can be deep like that. After Cal took a trip to the Studio Museum in Harlem, Chris Brown got his abusive ass bumped off the Wall of Fame by Jean-Michel Basquiat.

Cal, wearing his white barber's jacket, noticed me peeking through the door and smiled. "You coming in for a cut?"

"No, just saying hi!"

"I can give you a short natural if you want. Have you looking like one of them Black Panther bodyguards, you know what I'm saying?"

Two old men in the back were arguing over football.

"That team from 2003," said an old guy with a receding hairline, "that was the one."

"Nah, man," said another with light skin and freckles, "Diego plays both ways. Can't nobody fuck with that!"

"2003. That was Ray Rice and them boys. Won the state title. Ray only lost one game each season his whole time in high school."

"Didn't Ray Rice hit his girlfriend?" I interrupted.

"Why you gotta be bringing that stuff up again?" the balding old man said.

"Cause it's important."

"Can't every hero be perfect," the freckled man said. "Even Iron Man be fucking around. You see the eye he gave Black Widow? You think he ain't tap that ass?"

"I'm not asking for heroes to be perfect. I just don't want them to hit women."

"Cops be brutalizing us all the time," the freckled man argued. "They bust my nephew upside the head and he ain't done nothing but jaywalk. Why not focus on them?"

"We can talk about the cops. But we're talking about Ray Rice now."

"He did his time," argued the balding man. "How much longer you gonna punish him?"

"I'm not punishing him. But I'm not rewarding him either."

"You one of them #MeToo girls? Would you stop listening to Jay-Z because he cheated on Beyoncé?"

"Cheating is not hitting. But yes, I might consider it. Just like I stopped listening to Kanye when he started wearing MAGA hats and talking about how slavery is a choice."

Cal nodded in agreement and the two old men slapped hands.

"She got a point there," the balding guy laughed.

"And Diego is way better than Ray Rice on and off the field," I added.

Cal laughed—he knew that Diego and I are friends.

I headed out, running up North Avenue.

My next stop on my way home was Doreema's Health and Beauty Shop. Doreema is like a long crazy trip. She took a vacation to Mumbai five years ago and still wears a henna tattoo on her left hand that she has redone every month. She has photos from her travels hanging all over her shop. She's been to South Africa and France and Thailand. She loves music and always talks about how she'd love to take time off to work for the *Essence* Music Festival or something like that. I used to come here all the time with Mom, before I got my braids. And before my mom got Kevin. It was a real mother-daughter bonding thing. She'd get her hair straightened every two weeks, and I'd tag along. Now I only stop by every month or so to get my braids tightened and I come alone.

I popped my head in the door, fighting the urge to cluck and touch my eyelids.

"Hey, girl!" Doreema called out over the head of a cornrowed client. "You gonna sweat out those braids with all that running!"

"Running is why I got the braids!"

She was playing Champaign's "How 'Bout Us" on the store stereo and swaying her hips. Doreema always has a great playlist going. That was part of the reason I used to love coming here with Mom. It was a musical education. Doreema is only in her thirties, forty tops, but the songs she plays in the shop are all from the '70s. Funky, soulful stuff like Al Green's "Love and Happiness," Harold Melvin & the Blue Notes' "The Love I Lost," Patrice Rushen's "Haven't You Heard," Earth, Wind & Fire's "Devotion," and Minnie Riperton's "Les Fleurs." I learned a lot about soul sitting in that shop. I figured this was the music that Mom and Dad used to listen to when they were around my age.

Doreema glanced out the window. "There's a police writing tickets to anyone who double parks. They always be messing with the Black businesses on this block. And shouldn't you be in school?"

"School's out because of the virus, you know that."

"Mmmm-mmm. I guess I did know that. But I think there's stuff they ain't telling us."

"Like what?"

"Maybe it ain't viruses. Maybe it's artificial intelligence."

"What? You're crazy."

"Mmmm-mmm. Think about it. If you were an artificial intelligence, and you wanted to learn all about humans so you could replace them, what would you do?"

"I don't know. Check their Instagram?"

"They're already doing that. They got us living our lives online. Now, with all y'all home, you're on them phones more than ever. Now the machines can get you all figured out."

"So they can replace us."

"I'm telling you, it's the new slavery. White folks have been looking for someone to work those plantations ever since we left 'em. Now they got robots. What they don't understand is that robots ain't looking to toil in the fields, they looking to live in the big house. Mmmm-mmm!"

"You should start a podcast."

"Maybe I will. I tell you, I got it all narrowed down. This

COVID is either artificial intelligence, aliens, or dolphins. I never did trust them dolphins. Always look like they smiling."

"Now you're just playing. I gotta run."

"You ain't want me to tighten those braids?"

"I literally have to run. I'll be back, maybe next weekend. We'll probably be back in school soon and I don't want to go there looking all crazy!"

Even though it's only been days, it feels like I haven't been back in school for weeks—except in my dreams.

The clock on the wall says zero o'clock but I don't see anyone else in the halls. Sunlight is shining through the windows and the floors are polished and shiny. The bell rings signaling the start of eighth period but there's nobody to hear it except me. The doors of all the classrooms are open and the rooms are empty. The doors of all the lockers are open and empty. I start walking and I can hear my footsteps echoing, but then I realize the echoes aren't from my footsteps. Whoever is in the hallway with me is coming closer and I start to run.

The halls are too polished for traction. I'm wearing shoes made of mirrors and I slip and fall and get up and slip again. This time when I get up I am conscious of my own breathing. I can hear it in my ears. I'm suddenly aware of my racing heart, which is beating against the ribs of my chest like a prisoner in solitary pounding their fists on the bars. I am running full speed now, just like my track coaches taught me, pumping arms, stretching my stride, head down.

I turn the corner and I crash into you and I wake up.

I turned on my light.

Suga from BTS was looking right at me. That calmed me down.

I love all seven members of BTS equally, but I love them differently at different times. The group is divided into two parts—there's the rap line and the singing line. RM, Suga, and J-Hope are the rappers and Jin, Jimin, V, and Jungkook are the singers. RM is also the leader of the group and he speaks the best English so he's front and center when they do interviews in America. People who don't know what they're talking about say there are too many members in the group because there are seven, but I think that's just the right number. Everyone has his role in BTS so it all works out. The group wouldn't be the same if even one member wasn't in it. Kind of like that show *The Office*. You need Michael and Jim and Pam and Dwight and the rest or it's not the same. The saddest episode was when Michael left the show. Even though he was an arrogant self-centered jerk, you liked having him around.

Right now, I'm really feeling Suga. I put a sticker of his face on my nightstand water bottle so he's the last thing I see when I turn off the lights and the first thing I see when I turn the lights on again. I put it right over the sticker of Jungkook. Even though I'll always think Jungkook's great, I'm all about Suga right now. At that moment, the lights were on and I was looking right into Suga's eyes. It's a picture of him from four years ago when he had mint-green hair and was wearing big black-framed glasses with Pikachu-yellow lenses. He's always changing his look, all the BTS members do that, but I like this photo a lot. Suga is kinda quiet and low-energy but he's ador-able—like a cat. He's a little bit distant but not cold, like a campfire you see burning far away in the hills in the dark. He makes you wonder what he's really thinking, which makes you think about him that much more.

I fell back asleep looking at Suga.

WENT TO THE WEBSITE for the Brooks Atkinson Theatre on Broadway and what I figured was gonna happen had already happened. There was a message right at the top:

Please note: Due to public health and safety concerns, all performances of the Broadway musical Six have been canceled through April 12, 2020. For questions regarding refunds and exchanges, please contact your point of purchase.

I felt bad for the cast and crew and I wondered what they were gonna do for money. The actresses spent all this time rehearsing this show that got canceled so suddenly. Henry VIII divorced and beheaded his wives one by one but the coronavirus finished them all off at once.

I texted Diego and Tovah.

Me: *So much for Broadway* 😫

Diego: *I saw*

Diego: *I was about to text you*

Diego: *They canceled every show last week, not just Six*

Diego: *It sucks hard*

Tovah: *You can never fit in those seats anyway*

Diego: *I'm willing to endure the pain for theater*

Diego: *Broadway, movies, art are supposed to get us through times like these*

Diego: *We don't have sports to watch either*

Diego: *We do have video games*

Tovah: 😵

Me: *At least we have Netflix*

Diego: *Don't forget Quibi. That's coming soon*

Tovah: *It's the golden age of television* 🖵

Me: *I hope Pixar does the smart thing and releases Onward for streaming*

Me: *Even though it's still in theaters. So we don't have to watch Tiger King*

Tovah: *I don't get Tiger King. White people*

Diego: *You're half white*

Tovah: *I'm half kidding*

Tovah: *And I'm 100 percent Korean and 100 percent Jewish. No halfsies*

Tovah: *We should all binge Text Z for Zombie. It's that series about a woman who works in a call center in Nebraska who goes on the run from the cops. It stars that woman who was in that thing who dated that dude*

Diego: *With a pitch like that hell yeah*

Tovah: *It would be fun to do something together*

Tovah: *Doesn't it feel like the whole world is coming apart?*

Tovah: *We don't see anyone and nobody sees us*

Tovah: *I read 💀 doesn't have any friends*

Tovah: *He's shattered the country into little fractal bits that all look like him*

Tovah: *Now none of us have friends either*

Tovah: *When I give my valedictorian speech I'm kicking butt and taking names*

Tovah: *I've only been working on it for four years*

Me: *I gotta do some homework. You know it takes me longer cause I have to line everything up*

Kevin's not completely out of shape, but nobody's gonna look at his body and feel a need to test him for HGH either. And unfortunately, I've seen his body. He got comfortable walking around our house in just his underwear way faster than a middle-age man not named Brad Pitt ever should have.

Kevin was on the couch staring at his phone. Kevin is always on the couch staring at his phone. Old people like to complain about teens and their phones but they're the ones who haven't built up the antibodies to resist them. They went more than half their lives without streaming and texting and now they have it all and no training on how to not be on it 24/7. To us the stuff is old, but to old people it's magic. Kevin was mesmerized by some shopping app or whatever. He had basically only used Amazon for books but now he saw he could use it for life and that like every store was home delivering now. I think the idea you could have so much stuff delivered to your house was blowing his mind and he was pushing the limits of what he could get. "I can't believe they're out of toilet paper."

"Did you try CVS?" my mom asked, taking off her nurse's uniform.

"CVS, ACME, Harmons. They're all out. People are panic buying."

"Did you try Amazon?"

"The only toilet tissue they have is novelty shit with Obama's face on it."

"Are you kidding? People are sick."

"I'd rather wipe my ass with leaves than with the face of the only president in my lifetime who was worth a damn."

I looked up from the kitchen table where I was doing my Mandarin homework. White people gushing about Obama is the new "some of my best friends are Black." I loved the Obamas too, but pulling the lever for a Black man twice in eight years doesn't make up for four hundred years of slavery, oppression, segregation, not to mention the Kardashians' overuse of spray tan, which is basically low-key cultural appropriation. Drives me cray-cray. "Weren't you alive when Kennedy was president?"

Kevin laughed. "I'm not that old."

"LBJ?"

"Try Nixon. I'm a child of the Nixon administration. And every president since then, except for Jimmy Carter and Barack Obama, has sucked."

"What about Clinton?"

"Don't get me started on Clinton."

"Please," my mom begged. "Don't get him started on Clinton. I'm serious. Don't. Get. Him. Started. On. Clinton."

I didn't get to know Diego until sophomore year. Sure, I saw him around. He's hard to miss, like a sequoia. He was also in my Mandarin class, which is a pretty small class. Ms. Gong's a great teacher and a tough one and maybe because he was a transfer and an athlete she felt she needed to push him. We're not allowed to speak English when class is in session and she was always peppering him with questions that she knew would require him to use Mandarin words he was unlikely to know. One day during sophomore year, after a brutal session where Ms. Gong asked him to use the Mandarin words for "glucose," "hippopotamus," and "epistemological" in a sentence—the same sentence—he was waiting for me outside the class.

He sighed. "I feel like I was hit with an eleven-man blitz."

"No idea what you just said."

"I'm in that class with you."

"You've never talked to me like ever."

"I'm still kinda new. There are people I pass in the halls every day who I'm like, *I wonder what they're like?* But you can't just walk up to them and start talking."

"Of course you can. You just did it with me."

"I guess you're right. Mind blown."

"You know what's weird? When you actually know someone for years and you never learn their name. But after a while it's too embarrassing to ask."

"That's happened to you?"

"To my mom. She works in a big hospital. There are lots of doctors and nurses and you can't catch everyone's name, and if they spot your eyes drifting down to their name tag then they know you don't know who they are. Plus, when someone introduces themselves there's that second or two where you black out and you're not really listening cause you're just caught up in the moment of meeting them. Of course, that's when they tell you their name, and you miss it. I don't know why that's a moment that happens, but it's a moment that happens."

"You're really smart. The Mandarin program at my old school wasn't great, so I'm playing catch-up in this class. Do you think you could tutor me?"

"So is that the only reason you talked to me? Because you wanted something?"

"Well, yes, but I always thought you seemed interesting."

"What about me is interesting?"

"I heard you talking about Broadway. You hate jukebox musicals as much as I do."

"I don't need to pay to see people dance to Billy Joel. I can just go to the parking lot at MetLife Stadium and see it for free."

"And you had an interesting perspective on nontraditional casting," Diego said. "You were talking about how Dave Chappelle and Eddie Murphy were better at playing white people than white people were because they had an outsider's perspective."

"Race is totally a social construct. They need to cast more Black and brown people in roles that weren't written for us so we can help deconstruct the whole skin-color thing."

"That's why *Hamilton* is so good."

"Exactly! White people have been looking at the so-called Founding Fathers for years and not talking about the fact that Jefferson was raping Sally Hemings and Washington's fake teeth were ripped from the mouths of slaves. When you cast Black and brown people in those roles, we see the blind spots."

"I used to go to a Shakespeare summer camp. I played a Hispanic Macbeth. We even translated some of the lines into Spanish."

"I'm here for nontraditional casting," I said. "Except in the case of Scarlett Johansson. That white lady needs to never play a Japanese woman again."

"*Ghost in the Shell* really sucked."

"You should see *Aloha*. Emma Stone is supposed to be Hawaiian. She is whiter than the Beatles' *White Album*. Oh my god, that was tragic. Whitewashing is a whole nother thing."

"Movies like that are why I love Broadway."

"Why do you care about the theater? Aren't you a star fullback or something?"

"Quarterback, actually."

"What?"

"I'm the quarterback, not the fullback. That's a totally different position."

"Is the quarterback only 25 percent as good as the fullback?"

"Not usually, no. And definitely not in my case."

"I don't know football. But I'm sure you could find a better Mandarin speaker than me."

"I get good grades. This is the only class I'm in danger of failing."

"So drop it."

"I want to be able to get into a good college, not just a football factory. Mandarin makes me well-rounded. I'm just looking for help once a week."

I paused for a second.

"So?" he asked.

"I just wanted to wait until we're out of the moment."

"What moment?"

"The initial moment of meeting. So you'll remember my name. I'm Geth."

"I know your name. I'm Diego."

He smiled. He had a smile that lit up his whole face and made you smile back. Like when you plug in a Christmas tree. I'll never forget the first time he plugged in that smile.

* * *

I headed out to Garibaldi's to join Diego and Tovah for pizza. They met me out front. Diego was wearing his football jersey and Tovah was wearing a blue surgical mask.

"Why are you wearing that?" I asked.

Diego shrugged. "School pride."

"Not you—Tovah."

"Haven't you heard? There's something going around," Tovah said sarcastically.

"But you're always worried about something going around."

"That's so not true."

"Remember the time you thought you got chlamydia from licking a yogurt lid?"

"It's all bacteria."

"Masks don't help anyway," Diego cut in. "Look at the countries that have it the worst—China and South Korea. Don't they wear masks over there?"

"And how are you even going to eat pizza with that mask on?" I asked.

"Let me worry about all that," Tovah replied.

I performed my compulsions after we walked through the door of Garibaldi's and we all went to the counter. The place was empty except for a few people waiting for to-go orders. Tovah, Diego, and I ordered slices.

"Where is everyone?" I said.

Sal, the gray-haired Italian man who owns the place, smiled. "They'll be back. It's just a little flu."

I handed him money for the slices. "I read that it's a little more than that. There's a vaccine for the flu. There's no cure for this virus."

Sal laughed again. "The flu kills ten thousand people a year. I don't personally know a single person who has died from this new flu. The president says it's all under control."

"Don't tell me you believe any of that," Tovah said.

"I heard this on Fox News. The other side wants to use this flu to slow down the economy to win the election."

"This isn't about politics," Tovah pressed. "This is about two plus two equals four."

"This is about pizza," Diego said. "Let's just leave it alone for now, okay?"

The slices came out—sausage for Diego, pepperoni for me, no-cheese garden for Tovah.

Tovah lifted the bottom of her mask up to nibble on the edges of her slice. "Are you guys going to Quade's party?" she asked.

Diego tore into his slice. "I was going to skip it."

"He must be into you if he sent you an invite," I said to Tovah.

"I'm sure you're invited too," she said.

Diego shrugged. "I'm gonna skip it. You guys can go if you want."

"Come on, you guys," Tovah said. "You know Quade's parties are legendary. I heard he's planning some stuff that will blow everyone's mind." Her blue surgical mask was now stained with red pizza sauce.

"It looks like you just had a really difficult day in the operating room," I said. "Like a patient came in from a three-car pileup on the interstate and bled out."

Tovah waved me off. "Are you gonna go with me to the thing or not? Our senior year is sucking big time. Writing this valedictorian speech is kicking my ass. We need something fun."

I shook my head. "Parties are depressing. They're funerals without dead people."

Tovah stared at me. "You need therapy."

"I'm in therapy."

Diego swallowed the last of his pizza. "Let's just enjoy the corona break while it lasts."

* * *

Kevin was sitting in the living room in a Strokes T-shirt and a pair of tighty-whities doomscrolling on his laptop. He was drinking POM Wonderful 100% Pomegranate Juice and maybe the sugar had reached his brain because he was amped up more than usual.

"Did you hear?" he said. "There have been 2,800 coronavirus cases now reported in the US, with 58 deaths. New Rochelle alone has more cases than any other city in New York State—or the world, maybe, except for Wuhan, China."

I was at the kitchen table doing Mandarin homework. I had been sitting there for forty-five minutes lining up my pens and pencils and paper a certain way in a certain order. I was also thinking about how Columbia was going to tell everyone who had gotten in and who had gotten rejected on Thursday, March 26, and I would find out whether I had gotten into Columbia or if I had gotten rejected from Columbia on Thursday, March 26. My mind was starting to go into one of my OCD circles like when your computer sticks and that buffering symbol goes round and round in the center of your screen. I didn't respond to Kevin. I wasn't in the mood to talk to Kevin. I was never in the mood to talk to Kevin. On Thursday, March 26, Columbia was going to tell me whether or not I had gotten into Columbia. I went into the bathroom to check if I had left the faucet on and then I went back two more times before returning to the kitchen.

Kevin was still talking. "You know that neighbor of ours from down the street who's been wearing a gas mask? I saw her walking around with a yardstick. If anyone gets too close she sticks it out and tells them to maintain a six-foot distance. It's called 'social distancing.' 45 has screwed up the country so much, we can't even get close to each other. That's what he's been after all along—breaking down the social network. He's the real virus. The MAGA-virus. I need to tweet that out:

#Magavirus. I would love to see that trend. Will you retweet me?"

I was thinking about Columbia rejecting me or accepting me on Thursday, March 26. It was like my brain was caught in one of those clichéd time-loop movies but the rest of me was in reality. My OCD medicine wasn't helping much to get me out of this obsession circle, but all those pills I was taking to block these kinds of thoughts were making me sick in all the expected WebMD ways. I was feeling nauseous and my vision was blurring so much I couldn't read the Mandarin characters in my textbook. They seemed to march and fall off the melting page like ants in a Dalí painting. Kevin was still talking. I had to get him to stop the rant. "What does a containment zone even mean?"

"It means we'll all be working from home."

My next words slipped out like a mean tweet: "Or *not* working from home."

My mom was in the bathroom but she heard and called out, "Geth! Apologize!"

"What?"

"Don't play innocent! You know what you were implying!"

"We don't have to get into it," Kevin said quietly.

"God! I have no idea what anyone—"

"You were trying to suggest that Kevin was not working from home because he doesn't have a job!" my mom shouted from the other room. "Apologize for saying he is unemployed!"

Kevin blushed. "It's okay. I'm a journalist. Unemployment is part of the career path. I'm not ashamed of being between gigs. I actually have some good news on that score."

I felt a flush of heat. The comment had felt good when I said it, but the aftertaste was all selfish, like eating the last potato chip. I decided to give him a break. "What's the big news?"

"I got a job."

My mom let out a yell from the bathroom that sounded like

she was either really happy or her hand had gotten singed by a hot iron.

Kevin smiled. "Don't get too worked up yet. That's why I was holding off on telling you. They're still playing around with head count, and they haven't sent me the formal letter, but I'm supposed to start next month."

"What's the job?" I asked.

"Working as an arts reporter for *Newsweek* online. It's kind of a step down, since I used to be a senior reporter there back when it was an actual physical magazine. But it's also kind of a step up because I'm not working anywhere at the moment."

My mom came into the room and gave Kevin a kiss. "I'm so proud of you. The first time I met you I knew this was a man who was gonna help provide for me and my girl."

As Kevin leaned over to hug my mom, I noticed a stack of bills next to him, the top one stamped, *Final Notice*.

Tovah called me up. She never calls me. She always texts.

"Dude, I need you to take me to the doctor."

"What? Are you okay?"

"Of course not. Did you not hear me say I need you to take me to the doctor?"

"Last month you thought you had lymphoma and it turned out you were just lactose intolerant."

"And if I hadn't seen that oncologist, that McFlurry could have killed me."

"Shouldn't you ask your mom or dad? To take you to a doctor, I mean?"

"No, I need *you*. You know how my mom gets. She's on the same antianxiety meds you are. I think she has an even higher dose."

"Are you pregnant or something?"

"That would be a virgin birth. And I'm Jewish and I don't believe in that crap."

"Why don't you just take an Uber?"

"Ew. In a pandemic? Why don't I lick a pole on the 7 train? For real, I think I'm sick."

"Do you think you have the virus? What are your symptoms?"

"Jaundice."

"What's that again?"

"When your skin gets all discolored."

"You do not need medication for that. You need a swimsuit and SPF-15 or lower."

"I also have back pain and loss of appetite."

"These are not COVID-19 symptoms. Do you have a dry cough? Fever? Loss of taste?"

"Loss of taste? That's a coronavirus symptom? I thought that was a sign of liking BTS."

"That's not funny."

"Just joking."

"Why should I help you if you're gonna say stupid stuff like that?"

"I'm sorry. Seriously, I am feeling sick. I've been trying to get this valedictorian speech done. I'm going through all the best speeches I can think of and I'm trying to take the best parts from all of them. Like 'Four score and seven years ago' and 'a date which will live in infamy.'"

"Remember that public-speaking class we took last year? Don't forget 'I have a dream!' and 'Ain't I a woman?'"

"'Ask not what your country can do for you!'"

"'It is an ideal for which I am prepared to die!'"

"'What the hell is water?'"

"'We didn't land on Plymouth Rock, Plymouth Rock landed on us!'"

"'You have stolen my dreams and my childhood with your empty words!'"

"'Yo Taylor, I'm really happy for you, I'ma let you finish, but Beyoncé had one of the best videos of all time . . .'"

We finished together. "'One of the best videos of all time!'"

Tovah laughed and then sighed. "See? There's just too many and it's too much and I'm feeling sick. I'm only gonna get one shot at this speech. I've been working toward this for four forking years. I must have missed a hundred parties. I want everyone to understand my choices. This is my one chance."

"Tovah, it sounds like you're just stressed."

"I'm sick, I'm serious. Dude, I need to see a doctor. Can you give me a ride?"

Tovah and I had the same pediatrician. Yeah, I know, we're both high school seniors so it's a bit, I don't know if *creepy* is the word, but it's low-key weird. We had both been seeing Dr. Winklestein since we were babies. The waiting room in his office was filled with murals of cartoon characters—Bart Simpson, Doc McStuffins, Dora the Explorer, the Powerpuff Girls, Batman, Wonder Woman, and, in a sign of great taste, Aang from *Avatar: The Last Airbender*. I had been lobbying Dr. Winklestein for years to add a Miyazki mural, but no luck. I remember the first time I talked to him about contraception I was in a patient room with a huge picture of SpongeBob SquarePants. I guess that's probably the point when Tovah and I should have traded up to an adult female doctor. But Dr. Winklestein was the only adult other than our parents who had seen either of us naked, so we decided to keep it that way.

There weren't many other patients in the waiting room besides Tovah and me. There was an unshaven guy in a Rangers jersey who must have been forty, which is way too old to be wearing professional sports insignias unless you're on the team or coaching it. And there was a youngish mom with her teenage daughter both coughing quietly into their elbows.

Tovah was wearing her pizza-stained blue surgical mask, which she pulled down a bit to talk to me. "Thanks for coming. I'm pretty certain I have lupus. Or pancreatic cancer."

"You are such a hypochondriac. I hope this is for real."

"You hope I have pancreatic cancer?"

"When you put it that way it sounds bad, but yes. This waiting room is like a petri dish. If we aren't sick already, we will be."

Tovah went up to the front desk and came back with a mask for me. It was black with little yellow smiley faces all over it. "You good now?"

"You better have Ebola or something is all I'm saying," I muttered, slipping on the mask.

A nurse had Tovah pee in a cup, drew some blood, measured her vitals, and a radiologist took an X-ray. We went back to the waiting room and the youngish mom was still there with her daughter, still doing muffled elbow coughs.

"How old do you think that girl is?" Tovah whispered to me.

"I dunno. Sixteen or seventeen?"

"She has a great smile. If she doesn't die of COVID, I could see myself in a medium-length relationship with her. You know, something that has a good run for a few months. I'd cheat on her once with a Sarah Lawrence freshman, she'd have an online flirtation with a female lacrosse coach. We'd break up before the summer, but it would be mutual and for years we'd still totally smash when we weren't in serious relationships with other people."

"That sounds cool to me, but I don't know how the coughing girl will take it."

"I know. That's why I can only tell *you* these things."

"Just trying to be a good wingwoman."

"I know."

Thirty minutes later, Dr. Winklestein called Tovah in. She grabbed my hand and pulled me in with her.

Dr. Winklestein is one of those guys who is always smiling and joking around. He grinned when he saw us and handed us both lollipops, which made me feel like a toddler, but I still took off the wrapper and started licking.

"Are you girls related now?" he asked.

"Why do you say that?" I replied.

"She's only really supposed to have relatives in the room."

"I'm just her support system," I said.

"Well, you can help her celebrate the good news. We ran some tests, and you don't have pancreatic cancer."

Tovah looked crestfallen. "But what about . . ."

"You don't have lupus either."

"Then . . ."

"What you have is an allergy to pollen," Dr. Winklestein said. "That's annoying, but it has a far lower mortality rate."

Tovah leaned her head on my shoulder. "I'm sorry."

"You're apologizing for not being sick?" Dr. Winklestein said. "Don't."

"Maybe I'm just stressed. Usually stress is good for me. Like Turán."

"You'll have to explain that one."

"You never heard of Paul Turán?"

"Not ringing a bell."

"Hungarian. One of the world's great mathematicians. Extremal graph theory."

"No idea what that is."

"Turán's theorem is a foundational result in extremal graph theory: an n-vertex complete k-partite graph does not contain K_{k+1}, but every n-vertex graph with more edges must contain K_{k+1}. Anyway, the point is Turán came up with the idea during World War II when he was imprisoned in a forced labor camp in Transylvania. Stress helped him focus."

Dr. Winklestein unwrapped a lollipop for himself. "Sometimes it helps to talk to someone."

Tovah *had* talked to someone. She had talked to me. I knew exactly what Tovah was feeling. She was feeling Thursday, March 26. She was feeling Columbia. We had talked about it since we were kids. We were going to get a dorm room together in Carman Hall. We'd study together in Butler Library. We'd grab noodles at that ramen place on Broadway, and coffee at that Moroccan café on Amsterdam. We'd attend lectures at Havemeyer Hall, check out student plays at the Lerner Black Box, and grab dessert at the Hungarian Pastry Shop. And get a rabbit for our dorm room. Neither of us had ever had a pet, so we were going to raise a rabbit together. We'd name it Steinbeck.

"I know exactly what she's feeling," I blurted out. "We both applied to Columbia and we're waiting for the acceptance announcement on Thursday, March 26, and it's a bit stressful."

Dr. Winklestein looked at Tovah. "I can get you some names of people to talk to."

"It's the Columbia thing," I said. "We've been planning to go to college together ever since we were kids. We even have the name picked out for the rabbit we're gonna get."

Tovah was quiet for a beat. "I really did feel sick. I feel bad for wasting everyone's time."

Dr. Winklestein bit into his lollipop. "Don't apologize. These are weird times and everyone's internalizing what they're seeing on the news. Some people, it makes them feel worse. Other people, the bad news actually makes them feel better because all the dystopian stuff they see around them confirms their view of the world. How about another lollipop?"

CONNECTING WITH MY FRIENDS through a screen in the dark of my bedroom isn't how I pictured the second half of my senior year. But here we are.

This past Friday, I had a Zoom class for Calculus 2. It sucked because I didn't even see any of my friends. There's a school rule that because kids can't control their home environment, they don't have to have their cameras on during Zoom class. The school actually prohibits having your camera on. I guess that's so if you're living in a trailer park or your house is filled with exotic beasts like on *Tiger King,* you don't have to display what's really going on in your living room or bedroom or kitchenette or whatever to the world. I guess that's fair. But Tovah told me the real reason that the school told us to keep our cameras off is that they don't want to see into our homes because that makes them liable. If they see drugs or child abuse or a *Tiger King* situation and they don't report it, that's a lawsuit. So it's not about protecting us, it's about protecting the school district. Typical. But all this means is that I don't get to see people in my class on a regular basis. I just see black rectangles on Zoom with red slashes through the microphones. Teachers usually put everyone on mute so they're not talking over each other. So we're all invisible and silent. I'm not sure this is how Socrates thought education was supposed to go.

Calculus 2 was a hot mess. Ms. Alvarado didn't quite get the technology and couldn't log on. It's not even really technology at this point—Zoom is like an appliance, like a toaster or a fridge. Not being able to use it is low-key embarrassing, like not being able to dispense ice or make toast. Because she wasn't on Zoom to manage the situation, nobody was muted and everyone was just blabbering. Some kid started sharing that Borat movie and after that it was *Lord of the Flies*–style chaos, but worse because thanks to technology everyone had their own conch that gave them the right to speak and they were all doing it at once. And the whole time I didn't see any of my friends. All I saw was my own face reflected in the dark screen.

Tovah: *Did you see this tweet?* 😂 😂 😂 *"I just went to a crowded Red Robin and I'm 30. It was delicious, and I took my sweet time eating my meal. Because this is America. And I'll do what I want"*

Diego: *I don't get it*

Tovah: *The tweet is from a conservative commentator or something. She was railing against being shamed into not eating in restaurants because we're supposed to be social distancing. I was hate-watching a segment on Fox*

Me: *Social distancing should not be a Republican or Democratic issue*

Tovah: *Everything is red or blue. That's the whole point of this crisis.* 👹 *has politicized everything. Even eating at Red Robin*

Tovah: *I'm not going into restaurants even for takeout*

Tovah: *If everyone socially distances we can stop the spread*

Tovah: *If some people are assholes it's not gonna work*

Tovah: *It's like global warming. We all have to be on board or we're all screwed*

Diego: *We're screwed*

Me: *You need to get a cable package that doesn't include Fox News*

Diego: *I found a way to get my mom to turn off Fox*

Tovah: *How?*

Diego: *We go to church*

Tovah: *I don't know what to say to that* 🙃

Me: *I do. See you at church later Diego* ⛪

Diego: *Will do* 🤍 🕯️ ⛪

Tovah: *I'll be at home thinking about the importance of Jewish tradition if anyone cares* ✡️

* * *

I don't know if I believe in God, but my mom believes in church. She drags me to service with her every Sunday. She had breast cancer a few years back and had a double mastectomy to make sure it never came back. She had never been religious before—I was never christened or baptized and we don't even have a Bible in the house—but after her cancer went into remission she said it was a miracle and started going to the New Rochelle Covenant Church. It's a small place, more of a storefront than a church, and it only draws about twenty-five people even on big religious holidays like Easter. Brother Anthony, the leader of the place, has a scar on his left cheek from a box-cutter fight he got in before he found Jesus. I don't even know why my mom picked this place—I think it was kinda random and she just let herself get guided by the Holy Spirit. Or maybe it was Yelp. But the people are nice and everyone knows everyone else, so it works for me.

Diego usually comes with his mom. He's not too religious but I know his mom is really into prayer and all of it. She somehow managed to escape Cuba and Castro and Communism and she says it was a miracle. She and my mom talk a lot about miracles and it's really annoying. I don't believe in miracles. If God sends deserving people miracles, where was he/she/they during slavery? Where was God during Jim Crow? Where is God now during COVID-19? The miracle I'm waiting for is for God to explain how any part of this world he/she/they created makes sense. But maybe that's too big an ask. I mean, if God didn't let Gandhi or Greta Thunberg in on the secrets of life, the universe, and everything, is he/she/they really gonna tell me, a high school senior in New Rochelle, New York?

Brother Anthony was preaching about Moses today. "Remember them plagues that God sent to Egypt?" he said. "Remember why he did it? He wanted to free people in bondage from a cruel oppressor. Hold on now."

The two dozen people in the pews called out or raised their hands or did both.

"I went to C-Town and they had run out of toilet paper. Hold on now. I went to CVS and the shelf where the hand sanitizer used to be was all cleared out. Deader than the Dead Sea. Hold on now. What did God say in Exodus 7:5? 'And the Egyptians will know that I am the Lord when I stretch out my hand against Egypt and bring the Israelites out of it.' God is sure enough sending the plagues again. This time, he don't want those in bondage to leave. This time, he wants Pharaoh to get packing! Hold on now!"

After the service, the church serves as a food bank and Mom and I usually stay to help pass out hot meals to the homeless; Diego and his mom sometimes help out too. There are usually more homeless than there are churchgoers. A lot of the homeless are entire families, which I find disturbing every time I see it. Disturbing, but amazing. It must take a lot of inner strength to stay together as a unit when you're on the streets. But I can't stop thinking about how tough it is for the kids not having a house or steady meals or school friends to look forward to every day.

The free meal today was curry chicken with potatoes and bread. Local restaurants often donate the food, so it's usually pretty good. One time we even had tacos. I'm glad the food is good because I'd feel like a fraud serving people stuff that I wouldn't eat myself. Some weekends, Diego and I can't resist and we take a few bites, but only after everyone has had seconds. We also do it for quality control. One weekend the turkey was moldy and Brother Anthony went out and bought Burger King for everyone. All the homeless kids, even the ones who always look depressed, were smiling and laughing that weekend as they tore into their Whopper Jrs. It was pretty cool. Burger King tasted better than Five Guys that night.

Working at the food bank gives me a chance to spend time with Diego. He was a hard one to figure out, like when you see something random trending on Twitter like #LavenderOctopus-Love and you have no idea why. I scooped out a helping of curried chicken for the first woman in line. "When do you think school will open again?" I asked Diego.

He put a scoop of mashed potatoes and a slice of white bread on the woman's paper plate. "No clue. They said at least till the twenty-sixth."

"We should watch movies about school to fill the time."

"Too bad the Ozy Theater is closed."

"But Netflix is always open," I said. "Can you imagine having to stay home for a month when our parents were kids?"

"I guess you'd have to do something terrible, like read a book or something."

I laughed. "I'm glad there are so many places to stream movies, but enough already."

"There's so much it's hard to choose. Do you know there's already a Lil Peep documentary? He died at twenty-one. Why are there so many lil rappers anyway?"

"Lil Jon, Lil Tjay, Lil Wayne . . ."

". . . Lil Yachty, Lil Tecca, Lil Uzi Vert. Do you want to advertise how tiny you are?"

"Spoken like a guy who's six foot six."

Diego shrugged. "Maybe I'll just watch *Mean Girls* again since I can't see the musical."

A boy with a gap-toothed smile looked up at me. "May I have extra curried chicken?"

I smiled. "Of course you can, Ray! How's your basketball game going?"

"I can almost dunk!"

Ray had been saying that for six months. We bumped fists. He was an eight-year-old kid with a sad backstory. His dad had been arrested last year because they thought he was selling pot. The cops didn't find anything on him, but they beat his ass and charged him with resisting arrest. It was bullshit, but he lost his job, his apartment, and the family was kicked onto the street. And now corporations sell CBD products at Walgreens. I gave Ray his extra helping.

"Movies about high school always seem like they're by old people trying to relive their glory days," I said, jumping back into my discussion with Diego. "You ever notice how many of them were period pieces even when they came out? *Dazed and Confused* is about the '70s but came out in the '90s. And *Freaks and Geeks* is about the '80s but came out in the '90s. There's this weird lag time that makes them irrelevant to the kids who watch them."

"*Mean Girls* is just funny."

"That's another thing I hate about teen movies. They're always about high school cliques. The jocks, the stoners, the geeks, that sort of thing. We don't have cliques like that."

"They're racial cliques. The Black kids mostly sit at their own table, I sometimes sit with them or the Latino kids, and the white kids have theirs."

"Why don't you ever sit with the football team?"

"I'm only QB1 on the field. Off the field, I'm doing me."

"Are you gonna play for Naverton?"

"I don't know. Quade has been sweating me about it. They've been recruiting him too. His dad went there so he's a legacy. Naverton's his best shot at a QB job."

"If you both go to Naverton, he'll be your backup again."

"I guess so. Do you think you and Tovah will end up at Columbia?"

"We've been talking about it forever. We're going to room together, get a pet rabbit, and we're gonna name the rabbit Steinbeck. You know, my dad wanted to go to Columbia."

"I didn't know that."

"He used to tell me there were only three things keeping

him from going there—grades, money, and the Columbia admissions office. He ended up attending a community college instead. But he always wanted me to go. He talked about it all the time."

Little Ray was back again. All he had to do was give me that gap-toothed grin and I scooped him another helping of curried chicken.

"Thanks!" he said, and started to walk away. Then he turned back and looked up at us with his wide eight-year-old eyes. "Who's gonna give me dinner when you guys are gone?"

I smiled at him. "I'm not going anywhere, Ray."

"I'm only gonna leave if you dunk on me," Diego said.

Ray stomped one of his feet. "I'm gonna dunk on you with two hands!"

"Oh yeah?" Diego answered playfully.

Ray stomped his foot again. "Yeah! I'll fuck you up and shit you out, you punk-ass trick!"

Diego grimaced. "Okay, you took things a little far, young brother, but I like the energy."

Once everyone was served, Brother Anthony led us all in a prayer. Diego and me and my mom and Diego's mother all circled up, held hands, and bowed our heads.

"'For whoever wants to save their life will lose it, but whoever loses their life for me will save it,'" Brother Anthony recited. "You understand the words I'm saying to you? Hold on now!"

A fox was rooting through our garbage.

The fox used to live only in the darkness. You'd hear about him, but nobody ever saw him, at least nobody you knew. If your garbage was left in a plastic bag instead of a garbage can, the fox would tear into it, leaving an unholy mess, spreading trash from the driveway to the street. But if you put the garbage in a trash can, it was safe. It was too much work for the fox and it would look for more vulnerable targets down the street. Everyone knew that the way to stop this driveway robbery was to keep your house in order.

But Mr. Fox had been getting bolder. Maybe because nobody did anything about him for ripping open the trash bags. Maybe because some people didn't believe there was a fox since they had never personally seen it. Maybe because residents had been fighting for tax cuts and one of the first cuts had been in animal control, so now the taxes were lower and the animals were uncontrolled. Maybe because people started arguing that if we were going to take steps against foxes, shouldn't we also take measures against dogs?

Mr. Fox brought friends. First, it was other foxes, who worked the garbage cans in teams and opened up even the sturdiest bins—the steel ones with latches—and ripped open the bags inside. The stench of the open garbage brought racoons who would battle the foxes for refuse. After feasting on the spoiled spoils, the victorious racoons would spew black steaming heaps of racoon shit on doorsteps, in driveways, and across front lawns where toddlers left their tricycles. A couple of my friends heard stories of a bear lumbering down the block, drawn in by the stink stirred up by the foxes and racoons and the trash. Or maybe it was the bear that had tipped over the steel cans to kick off the whole disaster. Some people said the bear was tame, others said it was rabid, but everyone who saw it said it was big and strong enough to open dumpsters and toss around crates full of empty vodka bottles.

There were so many animals in the neighborhood that the foxes started showing up in the daytime to beat the traffic. In the morning we were shocked to see the chaos in the streets that had spread while everyone was sleeping. What was next? Giant pandas? We thought it couldn't happen here. We were wrong.

So Mr. Fox was going through our trash today. I had brought the garbage out for pickup, but Mr. Fox had gotten to it first, toppling over the unlatched can, tearing open the white kitchen trash bag inside, and chomping down on the remains of an apple pie I had baked from scratch. I picked up a rock and threw it at the fox, who looked up at me and, sensing I was no threat, went back to finishing up his brunch. I'm sure he had his own stories in his head justifying what he did. Maybe he told himself he was some sort of fox patriot and was just defending the way of the wild. Maybe he told himself that humans are weak and wasteful and they deserve to get what they get. I don't think he believes any of the stories, not down deep, but the lies get him through his day and distract him at night. He never has to look at his own reflection in a river or a lake because those are far away. I have a bad feeling the fox is going to keep coming back. I just hope he doesn't bring the bear or the giant panda.

Tovah: *Caesar was killed on the Ides of March*
    Diego: *What are you talking about?*
    Tovah: *A dictator taken down for abusing his position. Ring any bells?* 😂
    Me: 💀 *is probably monitoring everything we say*
    Tovah: *It is a far far better thing that I do than I have ever done*
    Tovah: *It is a far far better rest I go to than I have ever known*
    Tovah: *A Tale of Two Cities*
    Diego: *We all read the same CliffsNotes*
    Tovah: *Rebellions are built on hope*
    Tovah: *Rogue One: A Star Wars Story*
    Diego: 😨
    Me: *Violence never solves anything. I saw that firsthand with my dad*
    Tovah: ♡ *Sorry*
    Me: *I didn't mean to take down the room*
    Diego: *He just said I take no responsibility at all*
    Me: 😵
    Diego: *You know who*
    Tovah: 💀

Me: *Stop watching Fox News*

Diego: *My mom has it on all the time. Not everything on it is bad*

Tovah: *Yes it is*

Me: *Let's not argue about this*

Tovah: 👺 *said anyone can get the tests. He said the tests are perfect. But nobody can get the tests. You know who can get the tests? Tom Hanks and his wife can get the tests*

Diego: *Tom Hanks is a Democrat*

Tovah: *You're missing the point*

Tovah: *My cousin has COVID*

Me: ♡

Diego: *Sorry. How old?*

Tovah: *22. He'll be okay I hope. They didn't even do the test. He couldn't get a test*

Diego: *Then how do you know he has it?*

Tovah: *Dry cough, 103 degree fever, chills. He had it. There are no tests.* 👺 *wants to keep the numbers down*

Diego: 🍑

Tovah: *Why did you send that?*

Diego: *Finger slipped*

Tovah: *What did you mean to send?*

Diego: *That's what will keep you up tonight* 😉

Me: *Have you guys heard from colleges yet?*

Diego: *A bunch of coaches said I'm in a bunch of places*

Diego: *I haven't decided yet* 🙁

Me: *Tovah you want to do that Columbia thing with me on March 26?* 🛡

Me: *We can check if we're in at the same time together*

Me: *It'll cushion the blow*

Tovah: *[Three dots appear then vanish]*

Me: *I gotta do a supermarket run*

Tovah: *Buy me* 🧻 *if you see any*

Diego: *Are you running short?*

Tovah: *Because of all the bullshit from Fox News*

Tovah: 😆 😆 😆

* * *

My mom was doing the graveyard shift at the hospital so Kevin and I decided to drive to Open Market together. While he idled in the driveway in his Kia, I had to get out of the car three times to check the lock on the front door, and twice to check the faucet in the bathroom. This is my secret OCD struggle. I know in my head that I've checked everything, but there's this feeling inside that something isn't quite right and the feeling won't go away until I check and make it right. Think about the hungriest you've ever been. How long could you keep yourself from eating? That's how powerful this drive is inside me. Resisting it isn't like a diet, like going paleo and giving up legumes. I don't even know what a legume is, so I don't know why I said that. Resisting my compulsions is like starving myself. The urge is primal and irresistible, greater than gravity, greater than masturbation. Sometimes when I get that OCD feeling, I give up and decide it's not even worth going out if I'm gonna have to come back five times. Other times, like now, I feel like I have to feed the feeling so I can do what I was going to do or my OCD will be more in control of me than I am. So I went back and forth and checked the faucet and the front door and washed my hands a couple times up to the elbow until everything felt right and I could leave. Another skirmish in the long-running civil war of me against myself.

When we hit the road, Kevin played some really loud '90s-type rock in the car. You know the way white folks do.

"Nirvana?" I asked.

"Rock on. What do you think?"

"Did you really just say 'Rock on'?"

"I know. It felt bad coming out of my mouth."

I looked out the car window. Kevin was at that tragic stage of middle age where all the stuff he thought was cutting edge was actually classic rock.

"I nearly met Kurt Cobain once," he said. "I was covering

the *Nirvana Unplugged* concert for *Spin*. It was one of my first assignments."

"What's *Spin*?"

"A rock magazine. It's still around."

"What's *Unplugged*?"

"Are you serious?"

"I'm seriously asking."

"MTV had these concerts where bands would play with acoustic instruments."

"What's MTV?"

"Now you're just trolling."

"Unplugged rock makes no sense. Aren't loud electric instruments kind of the point?"

"Can I finish my story? So after the show, I walk up to Kurt to shake his hand. But Courtney Love—that's Kurt's wife—steps in front of me and she's holding their newborn baby, Frances Bean. I didn't want to get into the middle of family time, so I walked away figuring I'd talk to him later. I never did because six months after that Kurt killed himself."

"What's the point of that story?"

"I dunno. Maybe that you have to take advantage of every moment in life. Kurt used to sing about how he'd rather be dead than cool. What's that about?"

"Jungkook has a tattoo that says that."

"Jungkook's a friend of yours?"

"Yes. That's exactly who he is."

We pulled into the parking lot of Open Market. I performed my compulsions at the door and slipped on my smiley-face surgical mask. Kevin pulled the top of his black turtleneck over his mouth and nose and we both went into the store. The vibe of the place felt a little different than usual. There was a sign near the front saying that the staff was taking extra cleaning precautions because of the pandemic and any workers who came in contact with infected people would immediately be placed in two-week quarantines. There were no girls hand-ing out samples today. Half the shoppers were wearing masks, and almost all the workers were too. There weren't very many shoppers but the shelves were pretty empty. They were run-ning low on milk, on orange juice, on pastas. Of course there was no toilet paper in the paper goods aisle. The whole shelf was bare, how I imagine store shelves in Russia were like during the days of the Soviet Union. I wonder what Putin would say about American supermarkets if he saw this place now. Maybe he would smile and think he and Khrushchev had finally won their Cold War against capitalism and Cap'n Crunch and American abundance.

"Number 45 has really made America suck," Kevin murmured.

I agreed, but I didn't want to talk politics, least of all with him.

I got some of the supplies I needed—some of those ready-to-cook meals that make you feel like you're a chef, Cheerios, ten bottles of POM Wonderful 100% Pomegranate Juice, and a package of Tate's cookies. All they had left were the wheat chocolate chip kind, but I figured how bad could they be? They had a lot of weird products like that. The kind of stuff nobody would buy unless the regular stuff was sold out. It was like all the good products had been taken in the Rapture and we were left to choose from the grocery store items that had been left behind by God. Maple syrup with ghost peppers. Radicchio-flavored La Croix. Hamburger sushi. I'm sure somewhere in heaven, God was like, *Leave the sinners and the meatless nonfat chicken nuggets. We don't need that shit in paradise.*

I went to pick up a couple mangos to make me feel like I was eating healthy.

"Shay kohn!" Andy called out to me. He was wearing a red bandanna over his mouth and nose and only his dark eyes and the tops of his smiling cheeks were visible.

"How are things?"

"You know. My daughter's going to Penn State so I gotta pay the bills."

"Congratulations!"

"Thanks. You must be applying to college soon, right? You look about that age."

"I'm waiting to hear from my top schools right now."

"I'm sure you'll do fine. What are you looking for?"

"Well, I really want to go to Columbia."

Andy laughed, holding his belly. "I mean, what are you looking for in the fruit department?"

I smiled. "Do you have any mangoes?"

"Shipments have been sparse. No mangoes, no grapes, no oranges."

"Is this because of COVID?"

"Well, they told us not to say, but yes. A lot of workers aren't showing up and it's slowing things down."

"Are you thinking of taking some time off till this all blows over?"

"People who can take time off or work from home have it easy. I can't sell oranges from my couch!"

"Where do you live?"

"I live in the Avalon apartments near the train station. Some of my relatives live on the Mohawk reservation up at Akwesasne. They're really having a hard time."

"What's going on?"

"They closed down the casino at the reservation so a lot of people are out of jobs. None of this would have happened if we lived in the old ways. We would have had no contact with infected people and been living off the land. Global warming would have been stopped too!"

Kevin and I went to the checkout lines. Sally, the checkout lady I always saw when I shopped there, rang us up.

"How are things going?" I said.

"They're going," she replied smiling.

"They're not making you wear a mask or anything?"

"I've had the flu before."

"This is worse than the flu."

"I hear it'll go away as soon as the weather warms up."

"I hope so, but I don't know if there's any evidence it will."

"The president says Google is working on some things. I'm not worried."

Kevin interrupted: "Sally, is it? I'm Kevin."

"Are you Geth's father?"

"Her mother's boyfriend, actually."

"Well, glad to meet you, Geth's mother's boyfriend!"

"Sally, if COVID-19 is a hoax, why are you out of sympathy cards? Is the greeting card industry in on the hoax?"

Sally gave him a look as blank as an all-occasion greeting card.

"So is Hallmark an organ of the Deep State?" Kevin continued. "Maybe those Hallmark Channel movies are the modern-day equivalent of Leni Riefenstahl propaganda pictures."

Sally's eyes narrowed. Her face took on an expression meaner and harder than I had seen on her before. Was this her real face? Which one was the mask? "Do you personally know anyone who's gotten sick?" she hissed at Kevin. "I sure don't. It's fake news. I had two cousins blown up in Iraq fighting a fake war. The entire lamestream media was in on selling that scam. You tell me—did they ever find those weapons of mass destruction?"

"I was totally against the Iraq War."

"Do you ever get deliveries? Instacart?"

"Sure."

"Then you're paying someone to take your risks. Just like my cousins paid the price for you in Iraq. Why are you on your high horse telling us what we should be thinking when—"

"Don't you get it? 45 doesn't believe in any of the things you do."

"I know the system is broke and we need someone who will shake it up."

"He doesn't have a program. He doesn't make good-faith arguments. It's all whataboutism and gaslighting and flat-out lies. He just wants money and power. He could give a shit about you. It's crazy that—"

"So what do we owe you?" I broke in.

Sally's twisted expression straightened out like a reflection in a pool after ripples pass over the water. She glanced at the register and smiled. "That'll be $243. Just insert your card!"

After we loaded the car with our groceries and got inside, Kevin sighed. "I'm sorry I kinda lost it in there."

"It is what it is," I replied.

"It's just other white people drive me so crazy. They say crazy shit because they have no Black friends, and they never talk about race so when they do they have the racial sophistication of toddlers. You ever see that movie *Nell* where Jodie Foster plays a girl who grows up in the wild and creates her own weird language? White people are like racial Nells."

"Never saw the movie. You have to refresh your references. You're like an operating system that hasn't updated for ten versions in a row."

"Sorry. I've got a lot on my mind waiting for my new job to start and everything."

"Noted. Hey, you said something back in the grocery store. What's *whataboutism*?"

"The other side does it all the time. Instead of trying to address what you're saying, they point out something else that they think is wrong, so you start arguing about that. It's bullshit."

"And where does that term *gaslighting* come from? I hear it all the time now."

"There was this movie back in the 1940s starring Ingrid Bergman called *Gaslight*. She played a wife whose husband is secretly a murderer trying to steal her family's hidden jewels.

Every time he goes to the attic to look for them, the gaslights in the house dim because he's diverting the gas to the lights upstairs, but he tells her the dimming is all in her head. That's where the term gaslighting comes from—a psycho murder thief telling you that your problems are imaginary when really he's creating them to defraud and destroy you."

"What's the point of arguing with people by throwing around terms from black-and-white movies? You're not going to convince anyone."

"Yeah, yeah, I know. The thing is, there's really no point in arguing with people like 45 because they don't believe their own arguments. They're just shit-talking to distract us and frustrate us while they loot the country."

"You seem pretty frustrated and distracted so I guess it's working."

"I guess so. I think people like your grocery clerk friend Sally have been cheated by the system for so long, they're willing to follow anybody who looks like they're gonna pull a Daenerys Stormborn and break the wheel. Plus, a lot of them are just completely racist. Anyway, it sickens me to see regular people get fooled into joining Cult 45."

"Cult 45? Is that another dated reference?"

"Colt 45 is a beer that the original guy who played Lando . . . never mind. Let's head home."

I still can't believe how much homework I have. It's like my stupid teachers are trying to prove they're teaching by making us really grind it out. I have to admit all the busywork keeps me from worrying about everything else that's going on, but I'm pretty certain my teachers didn't plan that. They're not that smart.

We got assigned *The Plague* by this dead French writer Albert Camus. It wasn't on the reading list at the beginning of the year but my English teacher Ms. Gray said she was making the change and "calling an audible." Diego is in my Zoom class and he knew I wouldn't get that phrase so he texted me that "calling an audible" is like a football term about when a QB changes the play right before he gets the ball. Our school is so football-oriented it's ridiculous. Anyway, the book we dropped to squeeze in *The Plague* was *War and Peace*, which is like a million pages long, so I was like hell to the yeah. I like to read, but I'm not trying to commit suicide by book.

The Plague wasn't that bad. I mean, it's about awful things, but it's pretty easy to read and it's really short. The lead characters are pretty much all men, which I thought was seriously screwed up. The narrator doesn't have a name at first but by the end you find out he's a dude too. The book is about this small town that gets the plague, hence the title. First they notice all the rats dying. Then people start to die. At first the leaders of the town don't want to alarm anybody so they put up all these notices that nobody really pays attention to and that don't really come out and say that the disease is really contagious and could kill everybody. The book takes place in the 1940s but nothing in politics has changed much since then.

There's this priest in the book, Father Paneloux, who gives a sermon that basically says people shouldn't fight the plague because it's the judgment of God. He eventually gets sick and dies clutching his crucifix. I read that some of the big megachurches in Florida are still holding services even though everyone is telling them they need to stop because of COVID-19 and everything. I guess not much has changed when it comes to religion either.

They really need to start assigning us some books by BIPOC authors. And women authors. And women BIPOC authors. Like Octavia E. Butler. She's this Black female sci-fi author. I haven't read her stuff yet, but I will, and if I had to for school, I definitely would. I told Ms. Gray we need to read more BIPOC books.

She said, "Tell me a book by Mr. Poc and I'll consider it."
This is what I'm dealing with.

After I finished my reading for the day, I rewarded myself with
Tate's chocolate chip wheat cookies and binge-watching something stupid but fun. I had reached the end of the season for
this reality show about baking cupcakes and I couldn't think
of what to watch that would cheer me up more than cupcakes,
and so I started *Text Z for Zombie*. It's one of those shows that's
designed like television crack where you have to keep watching. Each episode is only thirty minutes long and ends in a
cliffhanger. Mavis, a mild-mannered woman working in a call
center, overhears government officials talking about a secret
law enforcement germ project that will turn Black people into
zombies. They say it's like stop-and-frisk multiplied by the
Tuskegee experiments. The Tuskegee thing was something I
was only vaguely aware of, but I knew it was something racist
and awful. Mavis is biracial and had never thought of herself
as Black, but she feels a moral obligation to try to stop the program. So she races across the country to intercept the only vial
of the deadly zombie germ. I got through three episodes before
I started to nod off. The show wasn't bad but the Tate's chocolate chip wheat cookies were horrible. The Radicchio-flavored
La Croix, however, was surprisingly refreshing.

I got an e-mail from Ms. Gray:

> *Try to avoid tautological phrases in your writing. A tautology is
> defined as the saying of the same thing twice in different words (ex-
> amples: "they arrived one after the other in succession" or "a man's
> got to do what a man's got to do"). That's generally considered bad
> style.*

Her e-mail pissed me off. I started to write this reply:

I guess I use tautologies all the time but my mind just goes in circles sometimes. I disagree that tautologies are bad writing. Didn't Lincoln say "With malice toward none, and with charity for all"? That's pretty much a tautology. Didn't Yogi Berra say "It's deja vu all over again" and "You can observe a lot just by watching" and "It ain't over till it's over"? People quote him all the time and I've never seen him play baseball even once so it's all because of what he said, not what he did. There's actually this player from the Negro Leagues named Satchel Paige my dad told me about who I like more than Yogi and who has even better quotes like "How old would you be if you didn't know how old you are?" and "Age is a case of mind over matter. If you don't mind, it doesn't matter." I think if you can get people to understand what you're saying without actually saying it, then you've moved beyond words and that's a good thing. I listen to this South Korean band named BTS and most of their songs are in Korean and I still get what they're saying. I think Lincoln and Yogi and Satchel were eloquent in their own ways and everyone understood their words in a deeper way than words. Maybe moving in circles can actually get you someplace sometimes. Like a rocket that orbits Earth before slingshotting into outer space.

My dad always told me to save an angry e-mail for a few minutes before actually sending it. So I waited. After a few minutes, I moved my e-mail into the trash. There's no arguing with some people. It is what it is.

'VE BEEN THINKING A LOT MORE about touching and breathing, which are things I never had to think about before. I just did them. I try not to touch my face but that's pretty much as impossible as eating a single Dorito. It feels weird to even use the singular form of that word since in practice it's always plural. Because of my compulsions and everything, I touch my face every time I enter or leave a room. Now if I touch my face because I have a scratch or I'm just thinking, I feel guilty and a little anxious and I go wash my hands. Touching your face is a natural thing to do when you're thinking—just check out that statue *The Thinker*. Now that we're not allowed to touch anything, even ourselves, *The Thinker* looks thoughtless.

So now I wash my hands a lot, which means my skin is really dry and ashy even though I use lotion a lot too. My mom says there's a chance the virus can be on packages, so just to be sure we wipe our mail down with baby wipes which may not kill the virus but it makes us feel better at least and all our bills and collection notices smell like the top of a newborn's head. I basically assume the virus is everywhere and on everything. I never touch doorknobs or doorbells or doors in general. I act as if there's something scary behind every one of them like in *Monsters, Inc.* And there's no way I would go into a public bathroom, especially one that has one of those hot air hand dryers that blows superheated germs around the room like somebody shouted "Dracarys!" I always thought those blowers were gross even before the virus crisis hit.

Tovah: *What day is today?*
   Diego: *Monday*

Me: *Blursday*

Me: *Zero o'clock on a Blursday*

Me: *Every hour is terrifying*

Me: *I feel like we're living history right now so I'm looking back on every day*

Me: *even as we're living them. That makes time seem faster and slower*

Tovah: *The days are melting together like cookies placed too close on a sheet*

Diego: *That's because we don't have practice or appointments*

Tovah: *I have nothing but appointments. There's all this valedictorian shit they want me to do. A million administrators have to approve my speech. I have a Zoom meeting every day*

Diego: *Zoom sucks balls. Some kid who dropped out of school dropped into my chemistry Zoom today. He started mouthing off and shit*

Me: *Why didn't the teacher just mute him?*

Diego: *She did but the mute doesn't hold. You can just unmute yourself*

Tovah: *Zoom does suck balls. I forgot I was on camera and I smelled my pits*

Me: 😆

Tovah: *Dude, I haven't taken a shower in three days*

Me: 😫

Diego: 😫

Tovah: *So? I don't see anyone*

Me: *You see us*

Diego: *Texting isn't seeing. It's barely communication*

Tovah: *So are you going to that party?*

Me: *Quade's party? He's still having it?*

Diego: *He keeps DMing me*

Me: *That's crazy. You're not supposed to have*

Me: *Large gatherings anymore. They just announced*

Me: *That*

Diego: *He's gonna have like hundreds at the party*

Me: *Everyone's gonna get coronavirus at that thing*

Diego: 👏

Me: *That's so irresponsible*

Diego: *Quade says people our age can't get coronavirus*

Me: *That's so not true*

Me: *I saw someone on the news who was our age who got sick*

Diego: *They probably had an underlying condition*

Me: *Why did you ask about Quade's party?*

Tovah: *I kind of want to go*

Tovah: *It would be different*

Tovah: *It's not like anyone asked me to the prom yet*

Tovah: *I've missed every party for four years*

Tovah: *Everyone is talking about it*

Me: *Everyone is talking about Quade's party? Dude, the Dow*

Me: *dropped 3000 points today. Didn't you see the White House press conference?*

Tovah: *I can't watch* 👹

Me: *You're the one who is always talking about him*

Me: *Forwarding me shit I don't want to read*

Me: *One of the reporters asked* 👹 *to rate his*

Me: *handling of the coronavirus and he said 10 out of 10*

Diego: *My mom would agree*

Tovah: *You have to get her away from Fox News*

Diego: *She thinks the virus started because Chinese people were eating bat soup. She heard it on* 📺

Tovah: *I know she's your mom*

Tovah: *No disrespect but that's racist*

Tovah: *No disrespect*

Diego: *Got it*

Tovah: *You speak Mandarin. You study Chinese culture*

Diego: *She gets angry when we talk about stuff like that*

Tovah: 👹 *has been telling Fox viewers coronavirus is a hoax*

Diego: *I think he actually said the Democrat hype was the hoax*

Tovah: *Let's not split orange hairs*

Tovah: *That's the problem. He can say anything and then he just says the plain meaning of what he said is not what he meant*

Tovah: *That's why I like math. You can't argue with math. You can't argue with the numbers of bodies in refrigerated trucks in Manhattan*

Tovah: *Now 💀 admits there's a pandemic*

Tovah: *Now his White Walkers are saying we have to flatten the curve*

Me: *What's that mean?*

Tovah: *You know those charts showing the COVID-19 cases going up? They don't want everyone in the hospital at once*

Tovah: *So if everyone socially distances themselves we won't all get the virus at the same time and there won't be a big bump up of infections. The curve will be flattened*

Me: *I gotta bounce. I gotta finish The Plague*

At the end of *The Plague*, the sickness ends and the whole town parties. Then the narrator of the book reveals that he's really a doctor and he warns that plagues never really go away, they just kind of lurk around to come back later. Which is a really depressing thought.

Even though the book is called *The Plague*, the last line actually strikes a Spielbergian note of positivity. It says the author, Dr. Rieux, decided to write the book because he didn't want to be the kind of person who didn't speak up and he wanted to bear witness for all the sick people and to catalog all the injustice and he declares that in the end terrible times teach us there are more good things about people than there are bad things.

I wonder if that's true. People are murderers, polluters, child abusers, rapists. They call seniors at home to fool them into giving up their PayPal passwords. They attend MAGA rallies and lock immigrant children in cages. They cheat on their wives and husbands, they gamble away their kids' college funds, they drive drunk and distracted and high and run over schoolchildren crossing the road. They put on uniforms and call themselves cops and beat us and shoot us and say we're the lawless ones. People suck in ways that I can't even imagine.

There are some lines in the book that were so good I underlined them. Like when the narrator says, "The evil that is in the world always comes of ignorance, and good intentions may do as much harm as malevolence, if they lack understanding." Ignorant people who think their hearts are in the right place are the worst. They're the motherfuckers who try to touch your braids in the supermarket because they just heard a podcast about Juneteenth.

There's this other line where the narrator says, "But again and again there comes a time in history when the man who dares to say that two and two make four is punished with death." There's a line in 1984 like that where the protagonist Winston writes in his diary, "Freedom is the freedom to say that two plus two make four." CNN is running chyrons tracking deaths and infections from COVID-19 and the Night King has been raging that the numbers are a lie. Math is the final battleground of truth. If you can't speak up when things don't add up, you're screwed.

In History class last year we read about John Stuart Mill and utilitarianism, which is basically the philosophy that if some action results in more positive action than negative, you should do the action that results in the most positivity. So if your car is out of control and there's a fork in the road and you have to run over three nuns on one side or one nun on the other, you should run over that one nun. But that whole formula seems off to me. Maybe you have to challenge the entire question. Why does anyone have to get run over? Why did the manufacturer make such a lousy car? Maybe someone should take a hard look at toughening automobile safety regulations before any nuns get run over. Right and wrong is about more than numbers, it's about something deeper. It's not just about utility, it's about justice. That's bigger than 2+2=4. Does any of this make any sense? I'm trying to figure out how all this adds up!

This line in *The Plague* stayed with me as well: "I have no idea what's awaiting me, or what will happen when all this ends. For the moment I know this; there are sick people and they need curing."

TURNED ON CNN AND KING'S LANDING was holding a press conference. I watched it for a second just to see if there was any national emergency stuff I needed to know. When they cut to the anchors after it was all done, one of them said that the Mad King had called COVID-19 the "Chinese virus" and that some of his aides were calling it the "Kung Flu." I turned off the TV. That kind of anti-Asian bullshit is gonna get my friend Tovah bullied at school. That is, if we ever go back to school. I put on my running shorts and my running shoes and took a swig from my water bottle. I did my compulsions and started my run. I had to get out of the house.

I headed down Quaker Ridge Road and then Pinebrook Boulevard and past the basketball courts. I don't like basketball but some of the boys who play there on the regular are kind of cute. Don't judge me. They know what they're doing. They play with their shirts off and it's not hot enough weather to do that yet. They spray their faces and chests with water from their water bottles way more than they need to and they stand there glistening and dripping and pretending they don't notice that you're noticing how good they look. Boys are gross. Especially the ones who know how fine they are.

But today nobody was on the basketball court—there was just one guy in a yellow hazmat suit spraying down the surrounding asphalt. All the nets had been tied up so you couldn't shoot a ball through them. There was yellow police tape all around the court like it was a crime scene and someone had died and maybe someone had for all I knew. When the guy in the hazmat suit saw me, he stopped for a second and looked right at me like he was an astronaut on Mars spying an alien life-form. We stared at each other but his face mask was mirrored so I couldn't see his face, all I could see was the reflection of the taped-off basketball court and the tied-up nets and the sprayed-down asphalt and my own image looking back at me. That went on for a beat. Then the hazmat guy went back to spraying.

Kevin was grinning at dinner. I knew he wanted to announce something but I didn't want to give him the satisfaction, so I didn't make eye contact with him so he couldn't start talking.

He blurted out something anyway: "I've got an assignment."

"That's great," I said.

"From *Newsweek*. I don't even start until next month, but they want me to hit the ground running so they have me working on a story. A big story."

"You look like you want me to ask you what the big story is."

"Are you asking?"

"Not really. But for the sake of speeding this along, yes."

"You know L-Boogie?"

"The rapper? Nobody's heard from her in years. She ghosted the world."

"Exactly. She's like the Thomas Pynchon of hip-hop."

"The guy who was a guest on that episode of *The Simpsons*?"

"That, and he wrote *Gravity's Rainbow*, one of the greatest novels of the twentieth century."

"What's that book about anyway?"

"I don't know, I've never read it."

"Then why mention it?"

"It's one of those books no one reads but everyone talks about. Like *Infinite Jest* or anything by William Gaddis. The point is, Pynchon's really reclusive—like L-Boogie."

"People got love for her though. Rappers sample her and the samples she sampled."

"It's like an M.C. Escher lithograph."

"M.C. Escher? Is he an old-school rapper?"

"Yes, that's exactly who M.C. Escher is."

"I was joking. I know Escher. The birds, the staircases, the hands drawing each other."

"Here's what I was trying to say—I think L-Boogie lives in New Rochelle."

"How do you know that?"

"I don't know for sure, but I have a source. And if it's true, I'm going to track her down and do an interview."

My mom called out from the kitchen: "That's wonderful, honey! You're going to make a splash at *Newsweek* online."

"I'm going to get this interview sorted, and then start the job," Kevin smiled. "I just hope once I find her, she wants to talk."

"So she's been hiding in the suburbs?"

"That's what OBL did."

"Remind me who he is again?"

"You must know this. The guy behind 9/11. Osama bin Laden."

"Yeah, yeah, yeah. I knew that. You should have just said his entire name."

"They searched for him for a decade and it turned out he wasn't in some cave or military fortress—he was living in the suburbs in Pakistan. Don't they teach you this stuff at New Rochelle High School?"

I got quiet and he knew he had gone too far. "Don't fucking put down my high school," I shot back. I was surprised how angry I got and how quickly the rage erupted out of me. I felt volcanic and Kevin was Pompeii. "People have literally died to protect that school."

Kevin shook his head. "I'm sorry. You know that's not what I . . ."

My mom walked into the room. "Geth, you're overreacting."

"Maybe *you're* fucking underreacting. How about that?"

I went into my room and slammed the door. I slipped in my earphones and turned up BTS. I played "Burning Up (Fire)," which is one of their loudest songs. I was angry, but part of me just wanted to stick it to Kevin whenever I got a chance. I wanted to stick it to Mom too. Kevin couldn't begin to feel what I was feeling. But Mom should have understood. She just wanted to move on so quickly it made me sick. My dad wasn't a comma in a sentence where you pause and then blow right through, he was an exclamation mark! I didn't want to lose this feeling of overwhelming loss because it felt like losing Dad. Loss was all I had left. He was a goddamn hero and you don't leave heroes behind a year after they die to hook up with Kevin. You just don't. You just don't. My dad used to always give my mom gifts. Books and flowers. Serious books about technology and sociology and beautiful flowers like lilacs and hydrangeas. He said they balanced each other out. He was so thoughtful and romantic. That's so rare. So rare. But my mom told me that she just couldn't hang onto her feelings after Dad died. She still loved him and everything, but she couldn't love him in the same way. She said love was something that was alive and she could only love someone who was among the living. She was so sorry but she couldn't apologize for her heart because it wasn't in her control.

I don't believe that. I don't believe any of it. Love isn't an emotion—it's a decision.

Through the thin walls of my bedroom, I could hear Kevin watching the news on TV.

There is something to this lack of ability to connect. Don't hug. Don't kiss. Stay six feet away. We are emotional beings. And it is important for us, especially at times of fear, times of stress, to feel connected to someone, to feel comforted by someone.

I haven't seen my daughter in over two weeks. It breaks my heart. And this concept of maybe I can't get next to her because of this virus. There's a distance between me and my daughter because of this virus. It saddens me to the core. And it frightens me to the core.

And that plays out a thousand different ways. You put all this together. It's a hard time. It is a hard time on every level. It is a frightening time on every level. At the same time, it is this much time. Is it three months? Is it six months? Is it nine months? I don't know. But it's this much time. We will get through this much time.

Good Afternoon,

Tomorrow I will be holding a live class (via ZOOM) on the analysis questions you are working on today. The invitation is below. For the gentlemen who were in attendance during our last class, you know there was vulgar language and disrespectful behavior. This week you received an e-mail from Mr. McCourt regarding this matter. If you cannot behave properly, please do not attend. You may not disrupt someone else's education. Furthermore, I was appalled by the behavior as were all the administrators who saw the video. It was even more unfortunate that someone tried to use the names of other students and damage their reputations.

Parents, please remind your children that they need to act appropriately while attending online classes. If they cannot attend the live session for any reason, they will have access to the recording later on so they will not miss the lesson.

Thank you.

ZOOM MEETING
Ms. Gray is inviting you to a scheduled Zoom meeting.
Topic: Eng B - Period F
Time: March 19, 2020 11:30 a.m. Eastern Time (US and Canada)

Join Zoom Meeting
Meeting ID: 672 879 9779
Password: newroproud

I went out to Alvee's Caribbean Sandwich Shop to grab some takeout for lunch.

Alvee's kind of looks like that Edward Hopper painting *Nighthawks* of those lonely people at an old-school diner. I remember my art teacher, Ms. Swanson, pointed out to me that it's kind of a famous detail that the diner in the painting doesn't have an exit to the outside, making the scene seem claustrophobic and existential and everything. Alvee's has a door to the street. And in the daytime, it's not depressing-looking at all—there's lots of light and Alvee, with his long dreads and sly smile, is always friendly. He immigrated from Jamaica and his dream was to run a restaurant. He used to manage that McDonald's on North Avenue and he saved up enough cash to open this place, serving gourmet sandwiches with a Caribbean spin.

The restaurant smells amazing. The aroma of curry chicken and jerk chicken and jerk pork is always in the air. The sweet scent of fried plantain and sugary festival and tasty coconut cakes swirls through the small shop. Alvee always has something delicious frying or baking or stewing.

"You want the usual?" Alvee asked as I walked in.

"Make it three of them." He knows my usual is the curried chicken salad sandwich with plantain chips on the side. I was getting one for myself now, one for my mom, and another I could store in the fridge and eat later in the week. Kevin could get his own damn sandwich. I was feeling kind of dizzy and drowsy from my medications but I knew I had to eat so I just wanted to get the food and go home. "Not a lot of customers here today."

"I'm not doing dine-ins," Alvee said. "Nobody was coming in anyway."

"I'm sorry to hear that. I can come back—"

Alvee held up a hand. "If yuh cyaa get turkey, satisfy wid John Crow!"

"What does that mean?"

He winked. "You don't speak patois? I thought you were Jamaican!"

"My dad was born there, you know that."

"What I just said is an old Jamaican folk saying. It just means if you can't find a turkey to eat, you should look for the next best thing."

"So you're saying you have to be wise about your opportunities."

"Now you've got it. Dine-in is on hold, but takeout is up 300 percent. I had to hire two new delivery girls. There they are now."

Alvee's daughters, Lisa and Erica, two tall identical twins with dreads even longer than their dad's, walked through the door.

"Hello!" I said, giving each one an elbow bump. "I didn't think you'd be in town."

"Spelman sent everyone home for the semester," Lisa said.

"We figured we'd make some spending money working for Dad," Erica added.

"You won't do that sitting around talking," Alvee complained, setting two bags on the counter. "This one goes to Scarsdale, that one to Mamaroneck! De race no fe who can run, but fe who run a de end!"

Kevin was sitting around in his tighty-whities watching CNN when I got home.

"Ewww," I said. "Is it too much for you to wear pants?"

"I'm doing Zoom meetings all day. Nobody dresses beneath the waist for Zoom."

"I don't even want to think about that."

"Check this out—the stock market is now lower than it was when the Fraudster-in-Chief moved into the White House. His four years in office have been a complete con. He's like that fix-it-up chappie Sylvester McMonkey McBean in that Dr. Seuss book. He pits the Sneetches against each other and charges them to get more stars upon thars and once he's got all their money he packs up and leaves."

I had to shut down his rant before it started. I decided to sacrifice some of my food. "I brought you a sandwich."

"From Alvee's? Rock on!"

"That sounds even worse outside of a musical context. Please stop."

Kevin winked, took a sandwich, and turned back to the TV. "45 keeps talking about the virus being from China. The real virus isn't from abroad, it's from him. America has faced down public health crises before like swine flu and Ebola. What makes this different is the fact that just like he did in Ukraine, he moved to protect his political interests first instead of trying to preserve, protect, and defend our country. What's different is we don't trust him to manage the crisis going forward. The real virus is the Magavirus!"

He was on his soapbox again and I wasn't about that. "When do you start your job?"

"What job?"

"The *Newsweek* job."

"I was going to tell you. They rescinded the offer."

"What?"

Kevin looked away from me. "I know, it sucks. But now that the fix-it-up chappie has fucked up the perfectly working economy that Obama gave him, people aren't hiring and they're canceling new hires they were bringing in. If I had even started two weeks ago . . ."

"Why didn't you sign the contract the minute they offered you the job?"

"I-I-I wanted to finish the L-Boogie story first. I figured there might be a book in it."

"You could have written the book while you worked the new job."

"Books take a lot of time—it's hard to do one with a full-time gig. Plus, if I were a *Newsweek* employee, they'd own the IP."

"What's IP?"

"Intellectual property. The movie or book or podcast rights."

"Are you kidding me? Have you even done the interview?"

"I haven't tracked L-Boogie down yet, but it's going to happen. She's supposed to text me. Why are you sweating me?"

"Because my mom was counting on you getting that job. She's working extra shifts at the hospital . . ." My voice choked up. I turned away and went into my room.

I hoped he choked on his curry chicken salad sandwich.

Tovah: *Dude. Did you see that comment on the video from The Ingraham Angle?*

Me: *Did hell freeze over?*

Tovah: *???*

Me: *Why else would I be watching the The Ingraham Angle?*

Tovah: *She's definitely not an acute angle*

Tovah: *I'm gonna forward this to you*

Me: *Please don't*

Tovah: *"MAGAsweetie279: Literally only two people a day are dying from China flu. More red-blooded Americans die daily from auto accidents, heart attacks, and regular flu and NOTHING gets said by the lamestream media, not a thing. Get a grip ladies and gents. The pure asininity of folks stirred up by Dems and the lamestream are the real issue here, not the flu, which essentially is what this is."*

Tovah: *What MAGAsweetie279 doesn't get is that epidemics expand exponentially (like $y=2^x$, or 1,2,4,8,16...) not linearly (like $y=2x$, or 0,2,4,6,8...)*

Tovah: *Just one guy in New Rochelle infected dozens of people, but even if one infected person infects 2 people a day things spiral*

Tovah: *Day 1, you have 1 sick person*

Tovah: *Day 2, you have 3=1+2*

Tovah: *Day 3, you'd have 7=1+2+4 (the 2 from day 2 each got 2 more people sick)*

Tovah: *Day 4, you'd have 15=1+2+4+8*

Tovah: *So by the close of the month, day 31, you'd have forking two billion people sick. This is how zombie movies work*

Me: *The number I worry about is that there are 278 other MAGA-sweeties out there*

Me: *I seriously don't want to talk about 👺 or his White Walkers*

Me: *I have too much going on*

I watched that BTS video "Spring Day" on my iPhone. BTS is much deeper than people give them credit for. I didn't even see all the depth when I was first getting into them. The first time I watched "Spring Day" I thought it was about a bunch of pop stars who go to this place named the Hotel Omelas and throw a wild party and then leave on a train and go walking in the wilderness. Then I read in a K-pop Twitter thread that the group was really into "The Ones Who Walk Away from Omelas," which is this short story by Ursula K. Le Guin, who also wrote the Earthsea fantasy series. The short story is about this town with all this abundance and wealth where kids approaching their teenage years are shown this little girl suffering in a windowless basement and they are made to understand that the prosperity of the community is rooted in keeping that child in abject poverty and misery. Every resident of the town faces the choice that they can stay and continue the party or just pick up and leave. It's kind of a metaphor for capitalism or utilitarianism or living in a fascist state or something. I wondered why none of the Omelas residents who leave ever think to take that little girl with them. But the minute I read the story I understood there was way more going on in the BTS video than was on the surface. Even the train was a reference to *Snowpiercer*, that dystopian sci-fi movie about a train that never stops and passengers in the back try to fight their way to first class. The movie was directed by South Korean filmmaker Bong Joon-ho, who later won a bunch of Oscars for *Parasite*, which was another movie about wealth and class inequalities. There are all these images in "Spring Day" that I can't quite figure out, like there's a giant mountain of clothes in a couple scenes that's maybe about childhood and a pair of sneakers hanging by laces from a tree that maybe symbolizes loss. There's just so much going on with BTS that it's hard to get to the bottom of it all. You could lose yourself.

Another robocall:

This is your mayor, with an update for today. Here's what's new:

At the governor's direction, all nonessential businesses will close by the end of the weekend until further notice. By contrast, markets, groceries, pharmacies, gas stations, and other essential businesses will continue operating, as will restaurants for takeout and delivery service. For a full list, visit the State's website at esd.ny.gov.

If you were tested for the virus at Glen Island, you can now get your own test results more quickly by following instructions on the county website at: health.westchester.gov.

Parks will remain open only for solitary recreation, such as walking and hiking. But starting tomorrow morning, playgrounds will be closed, and fields will remain closed for any group sports and activities.

Now, a reminder about previous messages:

Social distancing is effective in slowing the spread of the virus, so let's each do our part, especially to protect the most vulnerable residents. We continue urging all residents to stay home as much as possible and limit physical interactions with others.

City Hall remains closed to the public, but all essential municipal services, including sanitation, will be maintained. Some city departments can still be reached by phone and many services can be accessed online.

This is an unprecedented challenge, but we can face it together by staying informed, using common sense, and supporting our neighbors.

Thank you for listening. We'll keep you updated. And additional information is always available at newrochelleny.com/coronavirus.

* * *

Tovah: *Dude. More than 14,200 people have tested positive in the US and 187 are dead and 🐙 isn't taking responsibility*

Tovah: *At all*

Me: *I'm bored talking about him*

Tovah: *Did you see this quote from Senator John Cornyn: "China is to blame because the culture where people eat bats and snakes and dogs and things like that. These viruses are transmitted from the animal to the people, and that's why China has been the source of a lot of these viruses like SARS, like MERS, the Swine Flu, and now the coronavirus"*

Me: *Who the fuck is John Cornyn?*

Tovah: *Asshat Republican Senator from Texas*

Tovah: *As if there's another kind of senator from Texas*

Me: *I just don't think it's worth it to talk about Republicans anymore. Anyone left in that party is a Nazi*

Tovah: *You sound like me circa six months ago*

Tovah: *You told me back then that the Nazi analogy went too far*

Me: *That was before they started literally killing people. I really*

Me: *don't want to talk about this*

Tovah: *Did you see the video of the kids partying in Miami Beach?*

Me: *No*

Tovah: *I'll send you a clip*

Me: *Please*

Me: *Don't*

Tovah: *Did you see all those people on the beach? White people are so stupid*

Me: *Tovah you're white people*

Tovah: *I'm 100 percent Korean*

Tovah: *I'm 100 percent Jewish*

Tovah: *I'm not like those other white people. White male evangelicals are like 99 percent in favor of the Mad King. They all hate gay marriage and affirmative action and evolution and science. It's a cult. I'm a reformed Jew. I believe in the 10 Commandments and eating Chinese food for Christmas dinner. Everything else in the Torah is up for discussion*

Tovah: *Anyway going to Miami Beach for spring break is stupid. And it's not even really spring yet*

Tovah: *I would like to someday go on Lesbian Spring Break*

Me: *???*

Tovah: *aka Dinah Shore Weekend in Palm Springs*

Tovah: *It's a golfing event that became a music fest when they realized how gay it was*

Tovah: *It's the largest annual lesbian event in the world*

Tovah: *20,000 lesbians in one place*

Me: *If you went to that people in school would know*

Me: *It would be like if JK Rowling had Dumbledore go on Grindr*

Me: *Which is totally fine but keep that in mind*

Tovah: *Dumbledore on Grindr is* 🔥

Me: *I gotta go eat*

Kevin told this joke at dinner tonight.

"Have you heard this one? I read it online. Four physicians from different countries walk into a bar. The French doctor declares, 'Where I come from, medicine's so advanced we took part of a man's intestines, put it in another man, and in six weeks he's looking for a job.' The Swedish doctor snorts. 'In Stockholm, we took part of a brain, put it in another man, and in four weeks he is looking for a job.' The Russian doctor slaps his hand on the bar. 'In Moscow, we took half a heart from a woman, put it in a man, and in two weeks he is looking for a job.' The American doctor laughs. 'We've got y'all beat. Four years ago, we took a man with no guts, no brain, and no heart, put him in the White House, and now our entire country is looking for a job!'"

Oh my god. I'm locked in captivity with an actual dad who tells dad jokes.

Around midnight I heard a ping. Somebody had thrown a stone against my window.

I pulled back the curtain. Diego was in the shadows of my back lawn. This was weird but welcome. He didn't typically just pop by in person, and when we did hang out it was almost always with Tovah. With the quarantine in effect, his visit was even more unexpected.

"You could have just tapped on the glass," I said. "I'm on the first floor."

Diego moved into the light. "This seemed more theatrical. You want to hang out?"

"Why didn't you text like a normal person?"

Diego looked down at his shoes. "My mom took my phone. I'll get it back soon, I hope."

"What are you, twelve years old? I was wondering why you weren't on the group chat."

"My mom thinks 5G is a mind-control network created by Bill Gates and Hugo Chávez."

"Hugo Chávez? The former president of Venezuela? Isn't he dead?"

"You clearly haven't read Hillary Clinton's e-mails."

"Oh my god. You have got to get your mom off right-wing media."

"Come down. I can tell you about her lizard people conspiracy theory. Spoiler alert: they're satanic pedophiles!"

I couldn't stifle my laugh. "Did you get the robocall? We're supposed to social distance."

"I'll stay six feet away from you, I promise."

"That's what she said."

"What?"

"It's kind of a joke. Whatever you say, I reply, 'That's what she said.'"

"Why is that funny?"

"It just is. Like *Chappelle's Show*."

"Just come."

"That's what she said."

* * *

I tried to play it cool but I was excited about slipping out with Diego. The outing felt a little dangerous because technically there is a curfew and there are stories about cops picking up kids on the streets after dark. They are letting white kids off with just a warning but if they catch a Black girl and a Hispanic guy they will probably Rodney King the hell out of both of us and maybe throw in a little Trayvon Martin too.

The whole thing felt like *Romeo and Juliet*, but not some boring production, more like the movie version with Leonardo DiCaprio and Claire Danes, with gun battles and crazy camera angles and fireworks in the sky. All sorts of questions raced through my brain. Did Diego swinging by to see me mean that he wanted to be more than friends? Did he want to ask me to the prom—that is, if we still had a prom? I hadn't even allowed my brain to go there before, but this visit opened up the floodgates in my mind. Something was up, I just didn't know what. #LavenderOctopusLove

We went to the hidden playground. It's supposed to be open to the public but the local homeowners placed it behind a grove of trees and tucked the entrance behind a bunch of bushes so pretty much the only people who know the way in are from the neighborhood. The gate to the playground was locked and there was a sign that said the place was closed until further notice because of the coronavirus, but Diego picked me up as easily as that lift in *Dirty Dancing* and boosted me over the fence and then jumped up and climbed over after me.

I smiled. "I should hang with big strong football players more often."

"There are advantages."

"Besides breaking and entering, what are the others?"

He winked. "My jersey can double as a nightgown."

The playground was lit only by moonlight. There was a

basketball hoop, swing set, and jungle gym. I sat on one swing and Diego sat on another, leaving one swing between us.

"Social distancing?"

"Social distancing."

We began to slowly swing. I didn't know where this was going but I love the beginnings of things. I love the first lines of books and the trailers they show before movies and the stiffness of a sneaker right out the box and biting into a crisp apple. We were definitely starting something. There was crazy electricity and I could feel it was gonna last all night. It's like when you get a new iPhone and it can hold a charge forever.

I broke the silence. "So what's up?"

"I needed to get out of the house," Diego replied.

"Did your mom have Tucker Carlson turned up too loud or something?"

"She's not just watching Fox. She's all into OAN and News-max too."

"I've never even heard of them. Are those conservative channels?"

"Oh yeah. They're all in the MCU."

"The Marvel Cinematic Universe?"

"The MAGA Cinematic Universe. Each channel promotes some story arc of conspiracies or grievances. If you don't watch all of them, it's like trying to follow the whole Marvel saga starting with *Avengers: Endgame*. The experience has to be 360 to block out contradictions and counterarguments and inconvenient facts. But this isn't about that."

"What then?"

"My mom was reading from the Bible."

"Doesn't she do that all the time?"

"She was doing it out loud. First Corinthians, chapter six, verses nineteen and twenty."

"I don't have those ones memorized. How do they go again?"

"'Do you not know that your body is a temple of the Holy

Spirit, given to you by God? You are not your own, for you were bought with a price. So glorify God in your body.'"

"Does this have something to do with football?"

"See? This is why I like hanging out with you. Maybe you don't understand football, but you understand *me*. My mom left Cuba with nothing. She believes we've got to use every tool we have to succeed. I don't know if I want to play football in college, and my mom doesn't even know what an extra point is, but she's convinced it's a crime if I don't use my God-given gifts."

"What's an extra point?"

"It's a football thing."

"Why would you not play football in college? You've got a million people recruiting you."

"I can get in just with academics. My grades are good. I might even get an A in Mandarin."

"Thanks to my tutoring. But why would you quit a sport you're so good at?"

"I play football, but I'm not a football player."

"I don't get that."

"Two-a-day practices. Away games. Lifts. Film sessions. Positional meetings. Speed and agility workouts. It takes over your life. If I did play in college, I'd maybe go to Naverton."

"The ninth ivy?"

"Yeah. So I could play, but maybe have a life too. The Ivy League isn't as intense when it comes to football. And if I didn't like it, I could just drop out."

"When did you start feeling this way about football? I thought you loved it."

Diego stopped swinging. "Guess how tall I was at the beginning of freshman year?"

"You didn't go to New Ro then so I have no idea."

"I was five foot six. I was vice president of the drama club and I was also backup kicker for the varsity football team. I would get bullied every day by other players. They used to call me 'Broadway Joe,' which when I googled it was actually pretty clever. One day after morning practice they stripped me naked and locked me in a locker in the science hallway. They opened it up just before homeroom when the halls were crowded. I ran naked all the way to the school nurse with kids laughing and spitting spitballs at me."

"Holy shit. I'm sorry."

"That was my last day at that school. I grew six inches that year while I was homeschooling. I ate and lifted weights like a maniac to bulk up. Nobody was ever going to bully me or anyone I knew again. Then I transferred to New Ro. I've grown even taller since."

"You're like Captain America. They give him this super-soldier serum so he's got a small guy's heart in a big guy's body."

"More like Captain Latin America, I guess."

"Do you talk to anyone about what happened?"

"The team has a psychologist, so I talk to her about stuff."

"The football team has a shrink?"

"Technically, she's a sports psychologist, but we never talk about on-the-field stuff. It's pretty great because I could never afford it otherwise. So that's why I don't see myself as a football player. It feels like I'm playing a part, like Hedwig or Tevye or Henry Higgins."

"Those are great parts. If someone was going to give me a free ride for playing one of those roles, I would take it."

Diego laughed. "I knew I could talk to you about this."

I actually didn't know what to make of any of this. Football was the last thing I wanted to talk about. I had been hoping Diego would bring up the prom because there was no way I was going to bring it up first. Now that he hadn't, I was feeling some kind of way. They were probably going to cancel prom, but there was a chance they could hold it later in the summer or something and it would be cool to be asked. But was he even thinking about asking? What was it going to take to get him to start thinking about me outside the friend zone? I'm glad Diego considers me a shoulder to cry on, but why isn't he thinking about the rest of my body?

MOM CAME HOME LATE from her shift at the hospital. I was lying on the couch watching BTS videos on my phone. The band's album *Map of the Soul: Persona* is way deeper than critics give it credit for. The lyrics are based on the theories of this psychiatrist named Jung, who I thought was Korean, but was actually this Swiss dude. Jung believed the mind is divided into different parts, including the persona (the mask we show the world), the shadow (which is all the parts of ourselves we hide and push away), and the ego (the self the conscious mind believes itself to be). In this one BTS video, if you pause at just the right moment, you can see a Jung quote written in the background: "I am not what happened to me, I am what I choose to become." I thought about the stuff Diego had told me last night. Football is his mask. And maybe the way he really feels about his mom and about those players who abused him at his other school, those are all in his shadow. But if that Jung quote is right, we all have a chance to choose who . . .

My mom collapsed onto the easy chair with a loud sigh.

She picked up a book titled *Medical Apartheid* and then put it down.

She turned on the TV and then turned it off.

"I wish we had a Peloton," she sighed.

"One of those stationary bikes?"

"They are so much more than stationary bikes. They have trainers who take you on virtual group rides. You can bike around anywhere in the world—Hong Kong, Italy, France. It's like having a virtual vacation machine in your house. A vacation machine that keeps you fit."

"Where would we even put it?"

"We could put it behind the couch. They look great, like athletic sculpture."

"Aren't they like two thousand dollars? How would we even afford that?"

My mom sighed again. "What day is today?"

"Monday. No, Saturday. I actually have no idea. Zero o'clock."

My mom pulled off her hospital scrubs. Then she pulled on baggy sweatpants and a pink and green T-shirt marked *AKA 1908*. She stretched in her seat. "All the days are blending."

"Rough night?"

"Day and night. I worked a sixteen-hour shift."

"Oh my god."

"Can you get me some wine, my little pom-pom?" That's what my mom calls me because of my love for pomegranate juice. "Just use the big mug we use for milkshakes."

I got up and grabbed the wine bottle and poured her a big mug of red.

She drained most of the mug, put it down next to her, and began to cry.

I hugged her. "Is there anything I can do?"

"I'm sorry," she said, wiping her nose with a tissue. "I'm just tired of walking into rooms and seeing sick people. I know that sounds crazy because I'm a nurse, but these are sick people I can't help because there's no cure for what they've got."

"I'm so sorry, Mom."

"I don't want to lay this on you, my little pom-pom."

"It's okay."

"See, usually, dying people are with their families. But the COVID protocol is there are no families in the ICU because we don't want them to get infected too. So we have all these patients who are probably going to expire and they're completely

alone. Their last moments on Earth and there's not even someone there to hold their hands."

"But you're there."

"I'm not. We're getting assigned twenty patients per nurse.
The most I've ever worked before this was ten. And I'm doing
this six days a week! It's too much. Most of these patients are
intubated and bedbound. They can't breathe for themselves,
they can't go to the bathroom by themselves. They're alone
and they're scared and there's no cure for what they've got."

"I'm sorry, Mom," I said again.

"Before all this happened, when I had a patient who was
alone and about to expire, I would always make sure I was
there for them. I would monitor their vitals and if they were
about to pass, I would sit by the bed, hold their hand, look
them in the eyes, and sing them a song."

"What would you sing?"

"You really want to know?"

I nodded.

"I don't know if I should tell you."

"Come on."

"It's a private moment. A really private moment."

Mom got up. She gave me a hug.

"I'm going to bed, pom-pom. I have another shift at 4:45 a.m."

"That's four hours from now."

"I wish I had a Peloton," Mom sighed. "Good night,
pom-pom."

There was only a little red wine left in her mug but she
took it with her to bed.

I put in my earphones and kept listening to BTS.

We got a robocall in the morning:

Dear Parents and Guardians,

I regret to have to inform you that I, Dr. Laura Starch, the principal of New Rochelle High School, have tested positive for the coronavirus (COVID-19). I received my results at 9:20 a.m. I was tested on Tuesday, March 17, 2020. According to my doctor, I must be quarantined for two weeks from that date. The vice principal will be quarantined too, given her very close proximity to me through this crisis.

Both the vice principal and I will remain at home through the quarantine period and will continue to commit to the work we are doing in the district.

My symptoms are mild and I feel blessed to have the support of family, friends, colleagues, and the Board.

I am sharing my results with you because it impacts me and the vice principal, who have been point people for many in the community.

I will ask my staff to use their best judgment in terms of being tested and self-quarantined. The district's work will continue and we remain committed to the success of each student.

In these uncertain times, work and routine are pathways to serenity. I've instructed all teachers to double the amount of homework assigned to their students. I'm sure the additional coursework will come as a welcome distraction to your sons and daughters.

I am at home, supported, and will begin the journey to recovery.

Thank you for your time and stay safe and healthy.

Tovah: *Dude. Are you following @steak_umm on Twitter?*

Tovah: *I don't even like red meat and I'm thinking about going vegan*

Tovah: *I don't even like the concept of Steak-umm*

Me: *What are Steak-umms?*

Tovah: *Frozen slices of steak that you can microwave or fry or whatever and make into sandwiches. Latchkey kid shit*

Me: *What's a latchkey kid?*

Tovah: *Something I heard my mom say*

Tovah: *The @steak_umm account is dropping truth bombs and I'm here for it*

Tovah: *I'm fascinated how companies turns our likes into love*

Tovah: *I know it's corporate crap cooked up by some Don Draper type but it's so working*

Tovah: *"@steak_umm friendly reminder in times of uncertainty and misinformation: anecdotes are not data. (good) data is carefully measured and collected information based on a range of subject-dependent factors, including, but not limited to, controlled variables, meta-analysis, and randomization*

Tovah: *"@steak_umm we're a frozen meat brand posting ads inevitably made to misdirect people and generate sales, so this is peak irony, but hey, we live in a society so please make informed decisions to the best of your ability and don't let anecdotes dictate your worldview, ok?"*

Me: *Okay going to sleep*

Tovah: *One more*

I thought it was some more Steak-umm shit. Or more political garbage to get me riled up before bedtime. But when I clicked on the link Tovah had sent, a live video feed came up of a deejay spinning old-school vinyl records. The deejay was wearing a mirrored face shield and you couldn't see their face or even if they were a boy or a girl or Black, brown, or white. The masked deejay was playing cool old songs like Marvin Gaye's "I Want You" and Barry White's "Can't Get Enough of Your Love, Babe" and Prince's "I Wanna Be Your Lover," but they were also mixing in newer tracks that had that old-school feel like Amy Winehouse's "Back to Black" and H.E.R.'s

"Comfortable" and L-Boogie's "You Must Change Your Life."

I was up and dancing from the first song. I could see people that I knew from school sending in requests and encouragement in the comments at the bottom. I was alone in my room but I didn't feel alone. It felt like we were all alone together and the walls of my bedroom were a dream and we were all outside under the same stars moving to the same beat. I floated on the music the way seagulls ride the wind, hovering like graphic-novel thought balloons over a stretch of sandy beach. I thought about how many things were slipping away. It was hard to remember what day of the week it was or what time of day it was. Nobody knew where anyone was anymore because everyone was on Zoom or FaceTime and they could be anywhere. Blursday was every day of the week. Zero o'clock was every hour of the day. All I knew for certain was this groove grooving on and on and my feet moving beneath me.

A distorted voice spoke over the beat: "Why do you think they're releasing those reports on UFOs? Don't you think the middle of a pandemic is a weird time to declassify shit like that? Mmmm-mmm. Maybe aliens are behind all of it and they're depopulating our planet to make space for them to move in. But I don't think the answers to our questions are on other planets. I think the answers are right here on Earth. It's all a human distraction. People in Washington don't want us to keep our eye on the ball. They want us sick and broke and isolated and frightened. Because that's how capitalism works. That's when capitalism works best. The unemployed worker is the perfect worker to employ. They're willing to do anything for anyone at any time at any price. That's why jobs are going down and tech stocks are going up. Wall Street could give a fuck about Main Street. None of this had to happen. None of this should have happened. But all of it needed to happen, are you feelin' me? We need to keep together, y'all. Like the man said, if we don't hang together we gonna hang separately. It's all about the Benjamins. One love. One beat. That's the only way we'll get to the truth . . ."

I didn't care about what was being said. I only cared about what was being played. I only cared about what I felt. By the time the deejay finished the set, I was sweaty and smiling.

Me: *That was amazing. What was that?*

Tovah: *The masked deejay. They'll be back next week*

M OM WANTED TO GO to church today but the church was closed.

"Honey, they're all closed," Kevin said. "Except the crazy ones."

Mom shook her head. "You think they're all crazy."

"I heard one of those crazy megachurch pastors quoting Hebrews 10:25: 'Let us not give up the habit of meeting together, as some are doing. Instead, let us encourage one another all the more, since you see that the Day of the Lord is coming nearer.'"

"Why in the world do you have that memorized?"

"I'm a lapsed Catholic, you know that. I think Stephen King has it right. Did you see what he tweeted? It was something like, 'If going to church may kill people and you still want to go, you're not in a church you're in a cult.'"

"Really? Theology from the guy who wrote *Cujo*?"

"He also wrote the *The Stand*. Religions have been founded on lesser books—"

I interrupted: "Mom, I think your church is digital today."

New Rochelle Covenant was streaming online. Brother Anthony was alone at the pulpit. The choir director was behind him, six feet away. The counter on the screen on my laptop said there were only four people watching. So, not counting us, there were only three people.

"I wonder who the other three are?" Mom said.

Kevin laughed. "The Father, Son, and Holy Ghost."

"This is actually sad," I said.

"My ex-wife has a kid who got into Native American religion," Kevin said. "He told me this story about the Great

Tree of Standing Light in the Sky. He's a little weird but it seemed to ground him. A little spirituality can be soothing. Marx called it the opium of the people."

"I thought opium was the opium of the people," my mom said. "Anyway, I don't think Marx meant that as a compliment."

"Kevin has an ex-wife?" I whispered to my mom.

She shushed me with a finger to her lips.

Brother Anthony started his sermon: "The reading today is from First Corinthians. 'Listen, I will tell you a mystery! We will not all die, but we will all be changed.' Hold on now. Great words don't just speak to their times, they speak for *all* times. We are in a pandemic! Some of us will die. Hold on now. But all of us will be changed. The word of the Lord."

"I wonder who's going to serve the homeless today," I said.

"If I know Brother Anthony, he'll do it all by himself," Mom responded.

"Should we go down to help?"

Kevin shook his head. "No way. Your mom puts herself in enough danger at the hospital. There are other ways we can give back."

"Like?"

"Some of the money we get from the government we can give to the church."

"What money is this?"

"Money we need. They're talking about sending people what they're calling stimulus checks directly from the government. All these goddamn idiots on the other side have been roasting Bernie Sanders as a socialist for years and now they want to put the whole country on welfare."

"You think that's a bad thing?"

"It's a great thing. When we get a check, I'll make a donation. Then we'll pay some bills."

Brother Anthony was wrapping up his sermon and the head of the choir came to the front of the church to perform.

There was no choir. He started to sing Kanye West's "Ultra-light Beam." I still like that song even though I hate Kanye now.

I hoped little Ray with his gap-toothed smile got an extra helping today.

It was a cool, bright afternoon so I went for a run.

I ran by the barbershop. Cal is never open on Sundays, but today he was sitting on a lawn chair outside his shop sipping on a glass of lemonade and reading an old copy of *Ebony* magazine. When I got to six feet away, he put down the lemonade and tied a kente cloth handkerchief around his nose and mouth.

"Are you actually open today?" I asked.

"Closed until further notice," Cal explained. "Barbershops are nonessential businesses. It's essential for me, because I got to pay my rent. But I guess for everybody else, it's optional."

"I heard the government might be sending out checks."

"The check is in the mail. I'll believe that when I see it."

"What are you doing out today then?"

"Just trying to hustle up some concierge business."

"What does that mean?"

"Ain't you heard of concierge medicine? That's when the doctor visits you at home and charges you twice as much as he does at the office."

"So you're going to give haircuts door-to-door?"

"It's either that or just wait on that government check. And I don't like waiting on anybody. That's why I went into business for myself from the gate."

"I'm sorry about this, Cal."

"You got nothing to be sorry about. And I ain't mad at 'em. They should have done this whole shutdown sooner, far as I'm concerned."

"Really?"

"It's just good business. You take a little trim now, you don't take a big haircut later. The issue I have with it is this is just gonna be another scam. When they start cutting them checks, the money is gonna go to the big boys who get traded on the stock exchange. Wall Street goes up, Main Street goes down. Ain't no money gonna trickle down to Black businesses like mine. What's that they say? When the white man gets a cold, the Black man gets pneumonia. So if white folks are catching COVID, we better start digging graves, you know what I'm saying?"

I ran by my school next. New Rochelle High looked like a war zone. There were military vehicles parked outside, like jeeps and things like that. Some tents had been pitched on the football field. Gun racks were set up on the tennis courts. There were soldiers stomping around wearing masks over their mouths and noses and carrying automatic weapons.

I slowed my run and texted Tovah.

Me: *There's like a military takeover. I think the Night King is marching to Winterfell*

Tovah: *Dude. Calm down. I'm supposed to be the political crazy*

Tovah: *That's just the National Guard*

Me: *What?*

Tovah: *We're under quarantine, remember?*

Me: *How is the National Guard supposed to*

Me: *help us? This is like*

Me: *Schindler's List*

Tovah: *You can't say that. I'm the one who's Jewish*

Tovah: *You get to say the N-word in rap songs and I get to make the Nazi analogies. Just because we're under quarantine doesn't mean we have to let the whole social order fall apart*

Tovah: *And yes, it's exactly like Schindler's List*

Me: *Are you serious?*

Tovah: *Of course I'm not serious*

Tovah: *We're not looking at an Anne Frank situation with one group specifically trying to annihilate another group*

Tovah: *Worst case scenario this virus is not going to kill off everybody in their teens and twenties. It's horrible and it's the Mad King's fault but it's not the end. This is not Schindler's List*

Me: K

Tovah: *This is more like The Plague. We both just read that book. You have to keep track of which dystopian novel we're actually living in real time*

Tovah: *We still have 1984 and The Handmaid's Tale to live through*

Me: *Oh my god I just spotted a Humvee on North Avenue*

Tovah: *We could be moving into a Hunger Games situation*

Tovah: *May the odds ever be in your favor* 🖐 ⌁ 🦵

I started to sprint. I wanted to run away from all of it. I definitely didn't want to confront it. I had seen where confrontation got my dad. You had to keep running. Maybe you couldn't get away but it would take problems longer to catch up. My dad once told me something Satchel Paige said: "Don't look back. Something might be gaining on you."

I ran for another two miles until I came to Cemetery Road. It's a quiet street, with an old church on one side and a small graveyard on the other. I used to run down this street all the time, under the shadows of sugar maples, red birches, and white oaks. Marigolds, milkweed, and honeysuckles bloom in ditches on either side of the asphalt. There's a breeze that blows across the street, and on hot days it puts zip in your step during a long run. But I never go down that road anymore. When I reach there, I know it's time to stop and turn back.

I had taken my meds, but after my run I was feeling anxious.

I used my asthma inhaler but couldn't catch my breath. I sucked down some water from my water bottle but my throat still felt dry and my skin was hot. I opened the front door of my house and did my compulsions and washed my hands then went into my bedroom and lay on my bed. I got up to check the front door lock. Then I got up two more times to check the lock again. Then I checked the water faucet in the bathroom twice. Then I lay back in my bed.

Everything seemed hopeless. There was no end in sight. That was the worst of it. I felt like I was on one of those science-fiction shows where they enter an alternate time line and everything is different but all the actors are the same, just in slightly different costumes and maybe now one has a mustache. I didn't like this time line. I didn't like my old time line either. I just wanted to go somewhere else. Not backward or forward, just maybe sideways or diagonal. I wanted to move like a knight and all I could do is shift single spaces straight ahead like a pawn. I didn't know where I wanted to go. My eyes filled with tears. I got up to wash my hands.

I couldn't get to sleep so I turned on the TV. This guy named Dr. Larry Brilliant was talking to some reporter from *Wired* magazine. Dr. Brilliant was the consultant to that movie *Contagion* that basically predicted all of this. Dr. Brilliant also has the name I bet Bill Nye the Science Guy wishes he had. Who gave him the title "The Science Guy" anyway? Einstein was Einstein and even he didn't call himself the Science Guy. The movie *Contagion* had been trending all week, which was maybe why Dr. Brilliant was on TV. I don't know why you'd want to watch a movie about a pandemic when you're in the middle of one. That's like being on a sinking ship and streaming *Titanic*. The current tragedy you're living is not entertainment. I kept watching as Dr. Brillant spoke:

People say Contagion *is prescient. We just saw the science. The whole epidemiological community has been warning everybody for the past ten or fifteen years that it wasn't a question of whether we were going to have a pandemic like this. It was simply when. It's really hard to get people to listen. I mean, the current president pushed out the admiral on the National Security Council who was the only person at that level who's responsible for pandemic defense. With him went his entire downline of employees and staff and relationships. And then the current president removed the early warning funding for countries around the world.*

But did we get good advice from the president of the United States for the first twelve weeks? No. All we got were lies. Saying it's fake, by saying this is a Democratic hoax. There are still people today who believe that, to their detriment. Speaking as a public-health person, this is the most irresponsible act of an elected official that I've ever witnessed in my lifetime. But what you're hearing now, to self-isolate, close schools, cancel events, is right. But is it going to protect us completely? Is it going to make the world safe forever? No.

I turned the channel to Text Z for Zombie. I totally forgot I was bingeing this show.

There were ten episodes and I was only up to episode four. Mavis meets up with Adele, a crusading podcaster who agrees to help her expose to the world the existence of the germ that turns Black people into zombies. But before Mavis and Adele can finish recording, police try to arrest them. Turns out turning Black people into zombies is priority number one for police departments across the country. The two women hit the road, dodging feds and cops and state troopers, and gradually getting to know each other. Adele, who looks white, turns out to be biracial, but she's always seen herself as Black. Mavis and Adele eventually fall in love, and Mavis embraces her Black heritage as the romance heats up. The show is an over-the-top sci-fi soap opera with some lesbian-tinged Blaxploitation thrown in and I couldn't stop watching. And at least it wasn't another show about a goddamn time loop.

Me: *Are you guys watching*
Me: *Text Z for Zombie?*
Tovah: *No spoilers I'm only on episode 3*
Diego: *I can't believe Mavis kills Adele in the end*
Me: *Arrrrrghhhhhhh*
Me: *Argghhhhhhhhhhhhh*
Tovah: *Arggggghhhhhhhhhhh*
Diego: *Just joking I'm still on episode 1*

Kevin saw me listening to my social distancing playlist and he texted me this: *I'm not totally out of touch. My ex-wife has a teenager. I know what music kids like*

I think he's trying to get me to like him but it's not going to work.

Kevin's Social Distancing Playlist
One, Aimee Mann
Alone, Together, The Strokes
Decks Dark, Radiohead
Tears Dry on Their Own, Amy Winehouse
So Far Away, Carole King
Go Your Own Way, Fleetwood Mac
Quicksand, David Bowie
Someday We'll Be Together, Diana Ross & the Supremes
Pure Imagination, Fiona Apple
Don't Stand So Close to Me, The Police
Between the Bars, Elliott Smith
Eleanor Rigby, The Beatles
I Just Don't Know What to Do With Myself, The White Stripes
My Queen Is Anna Julia Cooper, Sons of Kemet
Truth and Dread, L-Boogie
This Must Be The Place (Naive Melody), Talking Heads
In Between Days, The Cure

Boulevard of Broken Dreams, Green Day
We Are Nowhere and It's Now, Bright Eyes
Not the Same Anymore, The Strokes
Here Is No Why, The Smashing Pumpkins
Stay Away, Nirvana

Most of the stuff on his playlist is rock and roll. Once I gave some of the songs a good listen, I started to like the Strokes, the Cure, and the Talking Heads, but I didn't really get Radiohead or the Smashing Pumpkins, at least the first couple times. I already loved Diana Ross & the Supremes of course, and I'd heard the Carole King song when I saw *Beautiful* on Broadway a couple years ago. Maybe some of the other tracks would grow on me. Like there was also this crazy reggae hip-hop jazz number by a group I'd never heard of before called Sons of Kemet. All this stuff starts out all edgy and weird and it ends up totally mainstream. *Hedwig and the Angry Inch* started out as this edgy off-Broadway show about a genderqueer punk rocker straight outta East Berlin. I saw online that they were doing a *Hedwig and the Angry Inch* musical episode on *Riverdale*. To paraphrase something Ms. Swain told us in AP Gov: History repeats, first as tragedy, then as commodity.

I took an online science test today.

> *Question: How does Milgram's quote in paragraph 8 of the passage you just read help you to better understand his experiment?*
> *Answer: Milgram's experiment studied to what extent people would follow orders. In the experiments, the participants were instructed to shock the learner whenever they got a question wrong. The results of the experiment showed that a high percentage of the people, 65 percent, would hurt someone in order to comply with an authority figure. At the end of the article, Milgram explained why many of the participants in the experiment shocked the learners all the way:*

". . . even when the destructive effects of their work became pa-
tently clear, and they were asked to carry out actions incompatible
with fundamental standards of morality, relatively few people have
the resources needed to resist authority" (paragraph 8). Milgram's
quote further develops our understanding of the findings of his experiment by showing that regular, everyday people would comply
with an authority figure, even if it meant going against their own
moral values and harming others. Even though many of the partic-
ipants were ashamed that they were hurting the learners, they still
continued to shock them. I kept wondering what the shocks looked
liked and felt like. Could you actually see the shocks like a lightning
bolt in the air? Did they feel like knives cutting into the skin? The
results of Milgram's experiments were surprising and disturbing
because they showed that people would continue following orders
even if they were tormenting others in the process.

**Question: Which answer best describes the main theme of the
passage you read?**
A. Science can tell us a lot about the real world and we ignore
   it at our peril.
B. People are willing to hurt people they don't really know.
C. People are capable of terrible things if the wrong leader
   commands them.
D. None of the above.
E. All of the above.

THEY CANCELED GRADUATION.

We'll still get to graduate. They'll send everyone diplomas in the mail or some shit. But we won't get to wear caps and gowns and file through an audience of our parents and grandparents. We won't get to walk the stage in high heels and shiny shoes. We won't get to blow kisses to teary-eyed relatives sitting in folding seats in the crowd. We won't get to throw our caps into the air and hug each other and make plans for that big party on the beach with all the friends we've had for the last four years and drink warm beer and dance to old hip-hop songs and make memories we'll carry for the rest of our lives. And Tovah won't get to give her valedictorian speech. The one she's been writing since middle school.

I texted Tovah. I called her. I even put on my smiley-face surgical mask and swung by her house. There was still the chance they might hold prom later in the summer or something even though graduation was off. I knew that wasn't much consolation, but still. Anyway, she wasn't answering texts. She wasn't responding to calls. And she didn't come to the door.

I've been watching more TV than I have my whole life.

Actually, I don't really watch TV, I just stream. But the couch in front of the TV is the most comfortable spot in the whole house and I was getting bored sitting in my room looking at my iPhone. So I ended up lying on the couch in the TV room seeing what was on. There was a doctor on CNN talking about the coronavirus.

The coronavirus is named because of all the spikes it has jutting out. It's like the Jesus virus. It's like a crown of thorns.

I changed the channel.

No! Don't go in there! You don't have to die! No one has to die at thirty! You could live! Live! Live, and grow old! I've seen it!

Logan's Run was on, this cheesy sci-fi movie from the '70s. It's about a dystopian world in the twenty-third century where everyone is young and beautiful like Lana Del Rey and everything is a paradise like in a Coldplay song. The secret of the place is that once you turn thirty you are secretly killed to make room for the next generation of young and beautiful people. Basically it's like Hollywood is for women, but in the movie it's like that for men too.

We've been outside! There's another world outside! We've seen it!

There's something amazing about old movies with crappy special effects, because even when the effects are laughably terrible they feel homemade and human and special. Someone had to build those effects, someone had to test them, and actors and stuntmen and crew had to put themselves at risk to pull them off. Some coder sitting in his basement and programming the new *Star Wars* film—that just doesn't have the romance of Hollywood to me. It's like me going to high school on Zoom. When everything is done on a computer, nothing feels at risk.

Life clocks are a lie! Carousel is a lie! There is no renewal!

I turned the sound down because I could hear Kevin and my mom arguing. I wanted to make sure he wasn't being abusive or anything. In some sick way I kinda wish he had a drinking problem or anger-management issues so I could have an excuse to stage an intervention with my mom and convince her to kick him out. But no such luck. The truth is, when Kevin and my mom do argue, it's pretty one-sided. She screams and he responds in a kind of inhumanly calm NPR *All Things Considered* voice that enrages her even more. Their squabbles are actually more entertaining than most podcasts, and they're commercial-free. I muted *Logan's Run* so I could hear every word.

"We're in the middle of a goddamn pandemic!"

"That's exactly why he's coming."

"I didn't even know he existed until six months ago."

"I'm pretty certain I mentioned him well before that."

"I think I would remember if my boyfriend told me he had a son."

"Stepson. He's not my biological child."

"Then why—"

"My ex is not capable of raising a child on her own. She's an artist. A free spirit."

"A heroin addict."

"Recovering. You can be a great parent and be a recovering addict."

"Really? Let's call Philip Seymour Hoffman's widow and see how that's working out."

"Heroin is not her problem."

"Are you listening to the words coming out of your mouth right now?"

"My ex's problem is she doesn't believe in rules. That works in her art, but not in life. Not with a child. Especially now, with COVID and everything, he needs a house with rules."

"Has he even had a COVID test? I need time to wrap my head around—"

Brrrrrrrring!

My mom's voice was sharp. "You're kidding. Is this mother-fucker at the door right now?"

"I'm surprised, but not surprised. This is how my ex does things."

"Kevin, this isn't fucking funny. We're supposed to be self-isolating. What if he brings—"

Brrrrrrrring! Brrrrrrrrring!

I called out: "Guys—do you want me to get that?"

My mom and Kevin opened her bedroom door.

"Geth . . ." Kevin began.

I put up a hand. "I heard everything."

"We don't have to let him stay if you . . ." my mom began.

"We can't just turn him away," I said.

"You're right," my mom mumbled.

"So where's this kid gonna sleep?" I asked.

Kevin cleared his throat. "I was thinking we could put a divider in your room."

I laughed bitterly. "This just gets better."

My mom shot Kevin an angry look. "There's no way . . ."

Kevin rubbed his forehead. "I just don't see another way."

I turned to Mom. "Really? You're gonna put the junkie's son in my room? What if he's like a perv or a rapist? I feel like this is the start of a Netflix true-crime doc."

My mom looked at Kevin. "There has to be another way."

Kevin was still rubbing his forehead like a genie might pop out with some ideas. "There's no other way right now. But I'm working on the L-Boogie article. If the money comes through . . ."

My mom's eyes opened wider. "So she agreed to talk to you?"

"Not yet." Kevin looked crushed. He kept rubbing his own forehead. I almost felt sorry for him.

Brrrrrrrring! Brrrrrrrrring! Brrrrrrrrring! Brrrrrrrrring!

I got up from the couch. "I'm going to get that before he breaks the door down. What's his name anyway?"

Kevin spelled it out. "K-a-r-h-a-k-o-n-h-a. It's pronounced like 'Gall-hah-goon-hah.' It means 'hawk' in Kanyen'kéha."

"Kanye what now?"

"Kanyen'kéha. It's another word for the Mohawk language."

"So your stepson is Native American?"

"I'm going to let him explain all that."

Kevin set up a screen in the middle of my room—a shower curtain hung on a coat rack—and he and my mom left me alone with our new house guest. He was a weirdo, which is okay I guess since I'm weird too, but I was a little freaked out about actually falling asleep with him only three feet away from me since a shower curtain hadn't turned out to be that great a deterrent to the guy in *Psycho*. I also had no idea if he had been self-isolating or not and if he was bringing COVID into our home. I felt guilty for even thinking that. This whole social distancing thing had me feeling emotionally distant from everyone. I kept thinking about that nice warm feeling I would have when I was serving homeless families food at the church. That glow I would feel inside when little Ray looked up at me with that gap-toothed grin and asked for another helping like he was Oliver Twist. Now I feel jumpy when I see strangers. I'm anxious when I see people coming toward me without masks. I had to fight the urge to contact trace my new housemate to find out who he knew and where he'd been to make sure he wasn't a viral threat.

I tried to smile. "So your name is Karhakonha?"

He didn't answer. He had yet to acknowledge my existence. He hadn't arrived with any luggage, just a rectangular box strapped to his back. My mom had given him a pillow and a sleeping bag, and told him to find a comfortable spot on the floor. The box, the pillow, the sleeping bag, and the comfortable spot seemed to be the only things in the world this kid had.

"What's in the box?" I asked.

Again, no answer. He just looked blankly around the room. He had large black eyes and long black hair that was tied into a high ponytail like Ariana Grande.

I kept going: "Well, my name is Gethsemane. But everyone calls me Geth. If you have any questions, just ask me. We might be cooped up together like this for a while."

Karhakonha pointed to my sticker of Suga on my water bottle. "You like BTS?"

I smiled. People always say music is the universal language, but BTS proves it. Korean is only really spoken in South Korea and North Korea and BTS have managed to score Korean-language hits all around the world, from America to Japan to Australia to South Africa. BTS has this amazing network of K-pop stans who track the band's concert dates and music releases and public appearances, and they tie the fans together wherever they are. Now this stranger I had been prepared to schadenfreude the hell out of for disrupting my already shitty home quarantine situation was going to bond with me over our shared love and respect for Bangtan Sonyeondan aka Bulletproof Boy Scouts aka BTS.

I started to gush: "I love BTS. It's weird, I know, because I'm not a boy-band kind of girl. I don't like One Direction or anything like that. I don't even like a lot of pop. I listen to SZA, Drake, Childish Gambino, stuff like that. I'm getting more into the Strokes and the Cure. But I just love BTS, I'm not gonna lie. Their music is way more meaningful than most people—"

"BTS sucks!" Karhakonha said this so loudly and abruptly that I stopped short.

My voice sounded small when I replied, "What?"

Karhakonha laughed a honking laugh. "You should peep your face, bro! You're capping! That's dumb funny. Anyways, where's your bathroom?"

I pointed the way to the bathroom and he went in and slammed the door.

What the hell? Who goes into someone's home for the first time and says something shitty about someone's musical tastes? I could feel tears coming to my eyes but I wasn't going to let this idiot make me cry. He didn't mean anything to me. Why should I care about his opinion? BTS played concerts to packed stadiums full of tens of thousands of people all around the world. They had given a speech in front of the UN. They've been on the cover of *Time* magazine. I never read *Time* magazine but I knew that was a pretty big deal. The demonstrable fact was BTS definitely did not suck. What did this stranger know about their music?

I went over to what was now his side of the room. He had put the only thing he arrived with, that flat rectangular box, on the floor. There were wires coming out of it. Scrawled on the outside of the box were these words: "This Machine Cures MAGAts."

Karhakonha didn't come back out of the bathroom until much later that night and I didn't care. I wanted to get as far away from him as I could, even though at most that would only be a few feet away. I had actually been enjoying a lot of things about isolation. I didn't have to deal with anyone if I didn't need to. I didn't have to grapple with what a steaming pile of shit the whole world had become. Now I had some jerk in my face and there was no escape. I wanted to be a solo act again. Even the members of BTS needed time by themselves. Every member of the group has put out solo stuff. Separation stops them from breaking up. I know loneliness can hurt the worst at a party or a concert or something, but isolation can also give you the space to figure out your shit, like Whatshisface Thoreau when he went to Walden Pond or Beyoncé when she left Destiny's Child.

I guess I'm not talking about isolation, I'm talking about solitude, which I see as more refined, reflective, philosophical. It's hard to get the most out of solitude when you have a roommate. Solitude is like masturbation—being alone isn't a requirement, but it helps. I slipped my earphones into my ears and my blanket over my head and clicked on the link to the masked deejay. But I didn't need to dance. I just wanted to listen and get taken away.

The masked deejay was playing all these songs that I've heard rappers sample, like Timmy Thomas's "Why Can't We Live Together" and Otis Redding's "Try a Little Tenderness" and The Royal Jesters' "Take Me for a Little While" and Diana Ross's "I'm Coming Out" and Sister Nancy's "Bam Bam." The deejay was mixing in some of the rap songs by Jay-Z and Kanye and Biggie that sampled those same tracks. The set was connecting the present to the past, showing how what had happened was happening again in a different way.

The deejay's distorted voice rode the beat: *"Black folks are dying from this disease at a higher rate than the majority population—be clear about that. We're 13 percent of the population and 58 percent of the death. They say the disease isn't that deadly unless you got an underlying condition, like heart disease or diabetes. Guess what? We got all those things. Mmmm-mmm. We're also the ones working all those so-called essential jobs like nurses and bus drivers and grocery baggers. The jobs are essential but society treats the workers like they're disposable. And you and me are disposable too, more disposable than that TP you can't find no more. The underlying condition that makes you susceptible to this disease is being Black in America. I don't even like calling it a disease. A disease is curable, it goes away, you feel better. This is a mutation. It's permanent. It's changed something about us and America. We got to change too. Mmmm-mmm. We gotta be like the X-Men and become supermutants if we want to save ourselves. We need to evolve. We need to think different thoughts and learn different jobs . . ."*

As she/he/they cued up the next record on the turntables,

I caught a flash of her/his/their left hand. I thought I saw the shadow of a faded henna tattoo. Just like Doreema, the beauty shop owner.

I got a text from Tovah.

Tovah: *My life is a dog's breakfast*

Me: *???*

Tovah: *Aussie expression. Means I'm a mess*

Me: *I'm so sorry you won't give that valedictory speech. That sucks*

Tovah: 😖 😳 😫

Tovah: *But enough about me how was your day?*

Tovah: *Maybe that will take my mind off my train wreck life*

Me: *Things are sucking here too*

Me: *My mom's boyfriend's crazy stepson is isolating with us and*

Me: *they're making me share a room with him*

Tovah: *That sucks*

Me: *Totally doesn't even begin to describe it*

Tovah: *The dance party doesn't make shit better but it doesn't make it worse*

'M DREAMING THAT DREAM about school again.

The time is zero o'clock. The halls are empty again. The footsteps are growing closer again. But this time I don't run away. I walk toward the sound. I am not alone, I'm far from alone. I hear screams in front of me. I hear footsteps coming at me. The footfalls are fast and frequent like someone is fleeing. I keep heading toward the sounds. My breathing is rapid and I take one deep breath to slow it down. My heart is racing and I try to ignore the blood pulsing in my temples. I turn the corner and I see myself standing in the hallway.

I'm holding a gun.

I wake up.

Diego: *Today is the worst day ever*

    Tovah: *I'm not giving my valedictory speech*

    Tovah: *I had finally cracked the code on how to give a speech*

    Tovah: *I spent four years prepping*

    Tovah: *Is it worse than that?*

    Diego: *I'm sorry about that*

    Diego: *I guess it's relative*

    Me: *Did you hear back from colleges?*

    Me: *Columbia regular decision candidates find out this Thursday March 26*

    Tovah: *[Three dots appear then vanish]*

    Diego: *My bad news is Terrence McNally died*

    Tovah: *That's terrible*

    Tovah: *Who is that again?*

    Me: *He wrote Love! Valor! Compassion!*

    Diego: *He was a Broadway genius*

Diego: *He died of COVID*
Me: *That's terrible*
Me: *How old was he?*
Diego: *81*
Me: *That's not as terrible as I thought*
Diego: *My mom won't let me play music from his shows in the house*
Me: *Why?*
Diego: *Gay characters*
Me: *That's crazy*
Tovah: *That's wrong*
Diego: *I know. She grew up in Ciego de Ávila*
Diego: *That's in Cuba*
Tovah: *There are gay people in Cuba*
Diego: *I know that but she doesn't*
Tovah: *No disrespect Diego but your mom's gotta turn off Fox News. Really*
Diego: *Same sex marriage is still illegal in Cuba*
Tovah: *God*
Diego: *I actually don't want to talk about this anymore*
Me: *We should talk about something else*
Me: *Tovah you want to Zoom on Thursday and we can find out about*
Me: *Columbia together?*
Tovah: *[Three dots appear then vanish]*
Tovah: *Geth how is your houseguest?*
Diego: *You have a houseguest?*
Diego: *I thought we were isolating*
Me: *It was news to me too*
Me: *He's my mom's boyfriend's stepson*
Me: *His name is Karhakonha*
Me: *First thing he did was insult BTS*
Tovah: *No wonder you hate him*
Diego: *Even I have made my peace with BTS*
Diego: *I like that song Boy in Love*
Me: *Boy with Luv. I could do without Halsey but it's a great song*

Tovah: *Is BTS the only reason you don't like your houseguest?*

Me: *He carries a box around with him that is full of wires*

Me: *The outside says "This Machine Cures MAGAts"*

Tovah: *That's like what Woody Guthrie wrote on his guitar*

Diego: *The guy who wrote This Land Is My Land? He knew the president?*

Me: *That's impossible. He lived in like the Dust Bowl*

Tovah: *Woody Guthrie in the 1940s wrote a song called Talking Hitler's Head Off Blues*

Tovah: *He got so worked up about the fight against facism he wrote on his guitar "This Machine Kills Fascists"*

Diego: *The guitarist for Rage Against the Machine has a slogan on his guitar too*

Diego: *Tom Morello*

Diego: *Arm the homeless*

Me: *How do you know any of this?*

Tovah: *Vox Explained. So good*

Me: *I saw the one on K-pop*

Tovah: *Of course*

Tovah: *Guthrie knew the 💀 BTW. Or his dad Fred. He was such a horrible landlord that Guthrie wrote a song about him*

Tovah: *It's all about what a racist the Mad King's father was because he wouldn't rent to Black people*

Diego: *My mom's dream is to live in Mar-a-Lago*

Tovah: *Don't tell me that*

Tovah: *💀 probably wouldn't rent to her*

Tovah: *But King's Landing has vacancies*

Tovah: *So does Mordor*

Me: *Gotta go*

Me: *I have to go shopping with a disturbed person*

Me: *Text me if you want to log on to Columbia 🛡*

Me: *and find out together if we got in*

Kevin said he couldn't go with us to the store. "I'm expecting a call from L-Boogie."

"Don't you have a mobile phone?" I said. "That's where the mobile part comes in handy."

"I don't want to be out of service range or something. This is really important."

"I don't want to go to the store either," I said. "Can't we just have it delivered like a normal family?"

Mom shook her head. "I've been trying to get a slot on Instacart for a week. Plus the fridge is bare. No milk, no fruit, nothing."

"I noticed," Karhakonha muttered.

Kevin threw his arms into the air. "He speaks!"

Karhakonha frowned. "Why you gotta be so extra? Did you bring me here to starve me?"

"I brought you here so you wouldn't end up killing yourself and your mother."

"Wait—what?" Mom said.

"Let's not get into this now," Kevin said.

"It sounds like we need to get into this," I said.

Karhakonha's voice rose: "You all are capping. I shouldn't even be here. Back in the day, Mohawk tribes were matrilineal. Women owned the family's land and decided what to grow on it, and when a man got married he moved in with his wife's family. If we were living that Mohawk life, I'd be with Mom."

Kevin shook his head. "Let's not get into this now."

Karhakonha's eyes looked far away. "I'm lost in the woods. That's what they call all of this on the rez. The woods. They say, 'Don't get lost in the woods.'"

"Kevin is right—let's not get into this now," Mom suddenly agreed. "Let's get you guys ready to go to the grocery store. We'll talk about this later."

We dressed up like we were going into surgery. Or into war. Or out zombie hunting. Kevin gave Karhakonha an old dust mask with leather face straps. "I'm glad I saved it," Kevin said.

Mom gave us both some antibacterial wipes and latex gloves and she wanted to give me her N95 mask from work that she said was the top of the line, but I told her that was crazy and she needed it for her shift. I put on my smiley-face surgical mask. "It's raining outside," Mom warned. "Don't get the mask wet or it'll diminish its effectiveness."

I did my compulsions before leaving the room while Karhakonha watched me.

"What are you doing? You're capping."

"Mind your own business."

"You can't touch your face like that, you'll get the virus. So cringe!"

"Screw you. Your mask makes you look like Bane in *The Dark Knight Rises*."

Before climbing into Kevin's Kia, I went back and checked the lock on the door three times. Then I went inside to check the water faucet in my bathroom twice.

All the way to the supermarket, we drove in silence, except for Karhakonha's sniggering.

When we got near Open Market, Karhakonha spoke up: "Let's go to Tradesman Tom's."

"We're going to Open Market."

"It's right across the street."

"Can you not read? Someone died of COVID at Tradesman Tom's. It was on Twitter."

"You're buggin'."

"A checkout lady died. Working at a grocery store now is like fighting in Vietnam."

"She died? For real? Was there an underlying condition?"

"Why? You want to rule out that it could happen to you?"

"This shit is worse than they are letting on."

"No shit."

"Just swing by Tradesman Tom's."

It was only nine a.m. and there was already a line at Trades-man Tom's that wrapped around the block, like people were waiting for BTS tickets or something. Most of the people were wearing masks of some sort—surgical masks, colorful home-made masks, scarves wrapped around their noses and mouths. They were also keeping six feet apart. Nobody was talking or even making eye contact. There was a weird collective shame that we had all allowed it to come to this.

"I can't believe the line is that long to get into a store where people have died," I muttered. "There's a body count and peo-ple still want their groceries."

"Can we just go there?" Karhakonha pleaded. "Tradesman Tom's Organic Watermelon Fruit Spread is mad nice. I'm not even kidding."

"No way. I'm not waiting in that line."

I drove down the street and pulled into the Open Market parking lot. It was raining and muddy outside and we ran into the store. Before the COVID crisis, there was always someone just inside the doors handing out samples. This time there was a guy in a green Open Market apron and a surgical mask spraying down the carts with disinfectant.

I did my compulsions inside the store and Karhakonha laughed.

"Screw you," I said, adjusting my smiley-face mask and pulling out one of the freshly disinfected carts.

That honking laugh. "What was all that touchy stuff with your face? So cringe!"

"I thought your tribe was matrilineal. Didn't anybody teach you respect for women?"

Karhakonha closed his mouth and didn't say anything.

"Now you ain't got shit to say, like Baby Yoda? Stay that way." I wheeled my cart away.

The store was usually bustling but this time it was fairly empty with all the shoppers keeping a wary distance from one another. Pretty much everyone had on a mask on. There was a group of beefy guys in MAGA hats with N95 masks like my mom had that were supposed to be reserved for health-care workers. I saw one shopper, a senior lady, blowing her nose in the frozen food aisle and I turned right around. I felt like soldiers must have felt like in the trenches in World War I, wondering if and when a gas attack was coming. Someone coughed as I steered through the fresh vegetables section and I jumped. Karhakonha sniggered then stopped himself.

Andy in fresh fruits spotted me. He was wearing a home-made cloth mask with the images of a turtle, a wolf, and a bear. The turtle was shooting out red and yellow rays.

"I love your mask," I said. "What do those symbols mean?"

"It's the seal for the Mohawk Nation," Andy explained. "The red symbolizes the blood that's been shed by past generations and the yellow is the color of life. Who's this with you?"

Karhakonha was looking at his shoes.

"That's my mom's boyfriend's stepson. He's staying with us. He's Mohawk like you."

"Really?" Andy turned toward Karhakonha. "Shay kohn!"

Karhakonha nodded but didn't reply. Then he abruptly turned around and headed toward the baked goods aisle.

Andy shook his head. "You sure he's Mohawk?"

"That's what he says."

"Which Mohawk rez is he from? Tyendinaga? Wahta? Our people straddle the Canadian border. The Akwesasne reservation stretches across Ontario, Quebec, and New York State."

"He didn't say. Is that weird?"

Andy went back to polishing pomegranates. "Hard to say."

"So how's your family doing, Andy?"

"As well as can be expected. Some of the homes on the rez don't have running water so people can't wash up. And the WiFi sucks so we can't spread the word and contact trace. I heard there's more cases per capita on some reservations now than there are in New Rochelle."

"That's terrible."

"For some white people this is a vacation. They can go to their second or third homes and telecommute and wait it out. We have to live with the disease they helped spread. Colonials gave Delaware, Shawnee, and Mingo warriors smallpox-infected blankets during the French and Indian Wars. This is nothing different."

"That's so sad."

"No worries. There's a special on sapodillas today. You should check them out!"

I loaded up the cart with supplies as quickly as I could. Andy's words had made me anxious and I wanted to get out of the store. I got a pound of sliced turkey, a gallon of skim milk, two bottles of lemonade, two bottles of orange juice, four pounds of ground chuck, ten russet potatoes, ten bottles of POM Wonderful 100% Pomegranate Juice, twelve hamburger buns, twenty-four organic eggs, organic baby spinach, organic farfalle pasta, Open Market–brand pop-tarts which were somehow organic too, a loaf of thin-sliced wheat bread, light mayonnaise, a couple frozen pizzas, a couple meal kits, shredded cheese, raisins for Kevin, and persimmon-flavored La Croix seltzer water because they were out of every flavor enjoyed by humans on Earth. I wanted to get more but our fridge is tiny so I knew I'd just have to come back again in a week and do this all over again. Also, my period was starting so I picked up a twenty-pack of Extra Heavy Overnight Maxi Pads with Wings.

Sally was at checkout. She wasn't wearing a mask.

"Sorry about that cruise to Italy," I said as I unpacked my cart.

Sally started scanning my purchases. "What are you sorry about?"

"You didn't cancel it?"

"No way! My boyfriend and I have been planning this for weeks."

"Aren't you worried—"

"The president says he's got it totally under control."

"I think they've canceled most of those cruises."

"I'm sure they'll reschedule them soon. Trish says it's all part of the impeachment hoax."

"Trish?"

"Trish on Fox Business."

"You can't rely on Fox Business."

"You sound like the mouthy guy who was with you last time!"

"Kevin? Well, you have to admit—"

Sally waved a hand. "I've been reading all about this situation on Parler. When the hotter weather comes this is all going to disappear. The virus can't live in hotter weather. Last year 37,000 Americans died from the flu. The flu! Nothing is shut down, life goes on. This isn't going to be anywhere near as bad as that and people are going crazy. Right now there are only five hundred confirmed cases of coronavirus, with twenty-two deaths. Think about that!"

"I think there are more than that . . ."

Karhakonha was back. He slipped a package of apple strudel sticks in with my order.

"That's all you're getting?" I asked.

"I would have gotten more if we had gone to Tradesman Tom's."

Sally leaned forward conspiratorially. "They say someone died at Tradesman Tom's. But I don't believe it."

I swiped my credit card and we loaded everything into the cart. I did my compulsions at the door and started into the parking lot. The MAGA-hat guys in the N95 masks were right in front of us, packing their supplies into an SUV. One of them looked at Karhakonha and pretended to cough.

We tried to walk around them, but the coughing guy stepped right in front of Karhakonha. "You from Wu-Tang?"

Karhakonha was silent.

"All this shit came with you guys from Wu-Tang."

Karhakonha looked the guy dead in the eyes. "You mean *Wuhan*?"

Another MAGA guy came out of the SUV. "Oh, now he can talk."

"I don't care where you came from, I just want you to go back," the first MAGA guy said.

A third MAGA guy got out of the back of the SUV. "You look Mandarin to me."

I stepped in front of Karhakonha. "You guys need to back off. You ever hear of social distancing?"

"My dad's a cop," one of them said. "I go where the fuck I want."

All three started fake coughing right at us.

We walked away, hurriedly packed our groceries into the car, and closed the doors.

I handed Karhakonha an antibacterial wipe and I took one too. I removed my latex gloves and wiped my hands and my face and my neck. I was breathing hard. "We gotta get out of here."

"Hold up."

"Are you kidding? We've got the cast of *Duck Dynasty* about to beat our ass!"

Karhakonha had his eye on the side window. "I said hold up."

"Why?"

The MAGA guys had noticed we hadn't driven off yet and were closing in.

"Turn on the engine—but don't reverse yet," Karhakonha instructed me.

I turned the key.

"Spin the tires—now!"

The MAGA guys were right behind our car. The tires spun to life and spewed a flurry of mud all over them. I pulled away into the road.

As we drove off, there were tears in Karhakonha's eyes, and I thought he was going to cry or something. But instead he started to laugh. Hard. I started to laugh along with him.

"I fucking love something about this pandemic," he said.

"I know, right? What's wrong with us?" I said.

"Nothing's wrong with us. Something's wrong with *them*. The pandemic is bringing it all out, like worms in the rain."

"That's it! It's making everything so clear. The racism is just there on the surface."

"Where you can fight it. Motherfuckers are always trying to gaslight. But now we see you. We fucking see them for who they are. Red hat–wearing MAGA motherfuckers!"

"Oh my god, this is such a relief, hearing you say that. I thought I was the sicko. Because there's definitely shit about this pandemic I love too."

"I spend a lot of time in my room by myself. Now everyone's doing that. Works for me."

"I wash my hands like I'm scrubbing in for brain surgery. Like all the time, even before this. Now that's pretty much the law. It's beautiful."

"What kind of idiots don't know the difference between Wu-Tang and Wuhan? They were capping!"

"Totally capping."

Karhakonha let out a primal scream. "Give me one of those strudel sticks."

Karhakonha was asleep in his sleeping bag and I was up late watching BTS videos.

They tape all of their concert tours but they don't put them out on the same platforms, so if you want to see everything you have to be a detective and track it all down.

I had just come across some footage from their 2014 Red Bullet Tour that I had never seen before and I was so excited. That was their first tour and they only played about twenty-two shows. The group looked so young then, especially RM, who I think is my favorite member today. He writes almost all the songs and starting the group was his idea. The whole K-pop industry is really interesting. They were inspired by American hip-hop and the way Motown manufactured musical groups in the 1960s like cars on an assembly line. But it wasn't about churning out a cheap product, it was about quality control and creating something that stood for excellence all over the world.

K-pop bands are typically named with acronyms or simple words so they translate better in overseas markets, and most of their songs throw in a few English-language hooks so if you don't speak Korean you can still get a general sense of what the song is about. RM speaks the most fluent English of any member of the group, so he takes the lead when the band does interviews in America. A lot of K-pop groups have one member who speaks different languages who's kind of the designated spokesperson/translator. What BTS does doesn't get lost in translation and that's what I think is so beautiful.

The Mad King wants to build walls between people and pit groups against each other. A lot of BTS's songs are about learning to love yourself, and why the education system is so screwed up, and the importance of mental health, and those ideas transcend borders and unite everyone who hears them. You don't have to know the language to love the music. RM was this aspiring rapper in a smallish country and the rest of the Korean music industry thought he was too homely to be a star, and he managed to help build a group and take his vision global. Now they use BTS songs in Korean tourism commercials. I score that as a win.

I put a sticker of RM on my water bottle on top of the Suga

sticker I had placed on top of the Jungkook sticker. I wish someday, at some moment, I could become a true leader just like RM.

Kevin was flipping through channels on the TV.

Welcome back to Harvard Business Review Live. *We're here with David Kessler, the world's foremost expert on grief. Professor, you were talking about how even our emotions about emotions have changed.*

Yes. One unfortunate by-product of the self-help movement is we're the first generation to have feelings about our feelings. We tell ourselves things like, "I feel sad, but I shouldn't feel that; other people have it worse." We can—we should—stop at the first feeling. If we allow the feelings to happen, they'll happen in an orderly way, and it empowers us.

Click.

Think about the two emblematic slogans of the pandemic: "social distancing" and "We're all in this together." In ordinary times, these slogans point to competing ethical principles—setting ourselves apart from one another, and pulling together. As a response to the pandemic, we need both.

But Professor Sandel . . .

Click.

The Senate passed a $2 trillion stimulus bill overnight. Democrats argue that the bill still gives too much money to millionaires and corporations at the expense of ordinary Americans . . .

Click.

The Cuban drug Interferon Alfa 2b, the antiviral therapy Remdesivir, and hydroxychloroquine, a drug with dangerous side effects that's being touted by the president, are all seen as possible . . .

Click.

The toll continues to mount in the United States with more

than 51,970 positive COVID-19 tests and 675 patient deaths . . .
     Click.
     No one saves us but ourselves. No one can and no one may. We
ourselves must walk the path . . .

I cleared my throat. "Can you stick to one channel?"
"Sorry," Kevin said. "I'm just a little worked up."
"About what?"
"L-Boogie. She's supposed to call."
"I thought she was supposed to call yesterday."
"Can you at least pretend to act supportive?"
"This *is* me pretending to act supportive."
"Oh, okay." He shifted in his chair. "Thanks for making Karhakonha feel at home."
"I didn't do anything. What's his real name, anyway?"
"That is his real name. He's Mohawk, and so's his mom. Kanyen'kehà:ka names are given through a longhouse ceremony by a clan mother. Each name gets passed down, two clan members don't have the same name, and each clan has its own names."
"What's his government name?"
"That's not my place to say. You should ask him."
"Is it a secret?"
Kevin turned off the TV. "We're all gonna be together for a while. Do you really want to stir things up?"
"You can just tell me."
"I told you, it's not my place."
"Well, what's in the box?"
"What box?"
"The one with all the wires marked 'This Machine Cures MAGAts.' Is it dangerous?"
Kevin laughed and turned the TV back on.

As you know, Professor Kessler, the Greeks believed in many differ-

ent kinds of love—love of a friend, love for a family member, love
of a romantic partner. Are you saying there are also many different
kinds of grief?

We're feeling a number of different griefs. We feel the world has
changed, and it has. Just as going to the airport is forever different
from how it was before 9/11, things will change and this is the point
at which they changed. The loss of normalcy; fear of the economic
toll; the loss of connection. This is hitting us and we're grieving.
Collectively. We are not used to this kind of collective grief in the
air.

Kevin's phone rang. He seemed a bit jumpy and juggled the
remote nervously before turning off the TV. "Yes? Fuck! Goddamn telemarketer."

"Who were you expecting?"

"Who do you think?"

"L-Boogie? Do you think she's ever going to call?"

"I'm trying to stay positive. I'm not going to lie, I need this
story. A lot of things are riding on it. Like my next job. There's
not a whole lot of freelance work out there."

"Maybe you should get aggressive."

"What do you mean by that?"

"You used to be a city reporter for the *Daily News*, right?"

"Yeah. But I'm an entertainment freelancer now."

"My dad was a school security guard. He told me he never
waited for the cops. He didn't like them, he didn't trust them,
and he figured they were more likely to hurt a kid than help. If
he thought a kid was up to something, or if he heard a rumor
about something, he'd go up to the kid and talk to them. Don't
wait for L-Boogie to call you. Go out and get the story."

Kevin turned the TV back on. "I'll keep that advice in
mind, kid."

We're going to make it because I love New York, and I love New

York because New York loves you. New York loves all of you. Black
and white and brown and Asian and short and tall and gay and
straight. New York loves everyone. That's why I love New York. It
always has, it always will. And at the end of the day, my friends,
even if it is a long day, and this is a long day, love wins. Always.
And it will win again through this virus.

I got ready for a run. I headed out the door, did my compulsions, took a puff from my inhaler, and put on my smiley-face surgical mask. I made it down the road a few yards and circled back to check the faucet in my bathroom twice and the front door locks three times. Then I washed my hands. I was circling a little bit but I felt in control, like when a car starts to skid on snow and you grip the steering wheel hard and gradually guide it back between the white lines. My medications were leaving me a little nauseous but my mind felt sharp.

The air was clear and cool and the sun was out and the road felt hard and good beneath my feet. As I ran I began to realize something was missing—people. People were sheltering in their homes or they had left for their second homes in Connecticut or New Jersey or Massachusetts or wherever people had second homes. Andy in the fresh fruits department was right. Riding out the virus was easier for rich white families. Sheltering in place works out better if the place you're sheltering is at the top. Most of the Black people I know, even the ones with money, are getting by with one house, or an apartment. Must be hard to socially distance yourself in a one-bedroom. For us the crisis is real, for rich white folks it's just real estate.

I ran down North Avenue, the main artery to the heart of New Rochelle, and because there were no cars I headed right down the center of the road. There was nobody in front of me as far as I could see. But when I looked behind me I saw Quade, and he was closing fast. He probably wanted to talk to me about that stupid party. I didn't want to go to his stupid party. Quade was a human subtweet. I just wanted to get away from everyone and everything. People are dangerous. People are trouble. You can't help them or save them. You have to run. You have to keep your distance. My dad had learned that firsthand.

People think that human connection is some sort of absolute good, and it's not. People think if we all hold hands and sing campfire songs we're all going to magically be better people, and it's not true. Facebook brings people together and it sucks. Twitter brings people together and it's evil. All the electronic ways we have of bringing people together are just allowing all the psychos and sociopaths and white supremacists to find each other and build networks and militias and Super PACs and it's turning the world into garbage. Connecting in the electronic age isn't enough. That just gets people electrocuted. Things have to go deeper.

I picked up the pace. I'm not the best distance runner on the cross-country team, but I'm pretty good. I'm inconsistent with my times, though that's mostly because I never know when my asthma is gonna act up. People that don't follow women's sports don't know that when it comes to long-distance running, the best girls are pretty much as good as boys now. If you go to watch a marathon, the first couple runners are men, but there are usually a few women in the top ten or twenty, which means they're beating pretty much every other dude but the super-elite ones. Quade is a football player, but he isn't a runner. I figured I could leave him in the dust.

I was moving fast now, focusing on pumping my arms and gaining speed. North Avenue is mostly straight, with some gentle curves, and it slopes downward in the direction I was going, from north to south. I was moving at a nice clip, but for me it was a sustainable one. I was zipping by houses and driveways and cars and basketball hoops and oak trees. Over the hedges and through the gates and on the lawns I saw some people. I saw a toddler in a mask jumping in a bouncy castle. I spotted two tween girls in lawn chairs sitting six feet away from each other with a bluetooth speaker between them blaring Travis Scott. But I was still the only person on the road— besides the guy running after me. I didn't want to look back to see if Quade was gaining because I didn't want to break my stride. If he was gonna catch me he was gonna catch me.

I ran by the beauty shop. The lights were all out and the place looked closed. I thought of the masked deejay and her/his/their henna tattoo. Was that Doreema? I hoped she was doing okay. I thought of her and Cal and Andy and Sally and Sal and Alvee and Brother Anthony and all the other workers and shopkeepers and preachers and people who have to report to work or need to work to support their families or don't know where their next paycheck is coming from.

Just then I heard the bells from that church on Cemetery Street sounding the hour. In the temporal blur of the pandemic, the only thing anchoring the hours was that bell. I remembered that Ernest Hemingway book *For Whom the Bell Tolls* that I read freshman year. The title comes from a poem by John Donne. I remember googling it.

> *No man is an island,*
> *Entire of itself.*
> *Every man is a piece of the continent,*
> *A part of the main.*
> *If a clod be washed away by the sea,*
> *Europe is the less.*
> *As well as if a promontory were,*
> *As well as if a manor of thy friend's*
> *Or of thine own were:*
> *Any man's death diminishes me,*
> *Because I am involved in mankind,*

And therefore never send to know
For whom the bell tolls:
It tolls for thee.

The church bells were still ringing and I was still running and I couldn't resist any longer. I thought of Orpheus and Eurydice and the musical *Hadestown* and how bad things happen when you look back, but I figured there was no way Quade could be that close now so I could sneak a peek. Just one little glance. So I took a look over my shoulder to see how much distance I had put between me and him. That was a mistake. To my annoyance, I had only put a few hundred yards between us. I should have had faith. Now I knew how Orpheus felt. It's hard to trust in the unseen but sometimes we have to make a decision to go on faith. I thought of poor Persephone. Four little pomegranate seeds and she was stuck four months every year forever in the underworld. I stopped looking back and faced forward again, hoping to go even faster, but thanks to my distraction my right foot plunged into a pothole and I fell flat on my face. I yelled as my knee scraped the road, tearing off skin. "Damnit!"

Before I could scramble back to my feet, Quade was standing over me.

"You okay?" He reached out and almost touched my hand. A burst of static electricity knifed between our fingers.

"Stand back!" I warned.

"Really?"

"We're supposed to be socially distancing."

"I was just—"

"Just stand back, okay?"

I got up and brushed myself off. I looked at my knee. It was all torn up and starting to bleed, but it wasn't a serious injury.

"Why were you running after me?" I asked.

"You don't own North Avenue, Geth."

"Has your dad bought that too?"

Quade laughed. "I'm not going to apologize for having money. My dad started with a million-dollar loan. He turned that into a chain that's worth a hundred times that."

"On Broadway, joining a show that's already a hit isn't the same as originating a role."

"Why are you sweating me? I see you and Tovah at the Ozy Theater all the time."

I stood up and brushed myself off. "You need to screen more Miyazaki movies."

"We showed *Princess Mononoke* a couple months ago."

"But you still haven't screened *My Neighbor Totoro* and that's one of his best. You need a Miyazaki festival."

"I'll take it up with my dad. I'm hoping we can do some cool things when the theaters open back up again and this coronavirus hype dies down."

"You know it's not hype, right? People are really getting sick."

"You're missing my point."

"What was your point?"

"If the government forces businesses like Ozy to close because of the so-called pandemic, my dad has to lay off workers. The workers don't want that and neither does my dad. They need to give people the choice of whether to work or not."

"But if they go to work they'll spread the sickness and nobody can work."

"Unemployment is bad for health too. For every one percent of unemployment, forty thousand people die."

"Is that true?"

"Fuck if I know—I heard that stat in the movie *The Big Short*."

I laughed. "Oh, then it must be true."

Quade smiled. "This isn't a political thing. My dad just wants to get back to showing movies, and I do too. I had this great idea for a film festival. I wanted to show every one of the Marvel Cinematic Universe films in order. I call it the MCU Festival."

"Every MCU movie? Aren't there like a dozen?"

"There are twenty-three. The first in order of release is *Iron Man*. The last is *Spider-Man: Far From Home.* We would show them all, including the post-credit scenes."

"I love post-credit scenes."

"The post-credit scenes are genius! They get people to stay to the very end."

"I don't know though. I thought *Thor: Ragnarock* was funny, and I loved *Black Panther*, but I fell asleep before the end of *Avengers: Endgame.*"

"You fell asleep?"

"They killed off Black Widow and I felt nothing. They brought in Captain Marvel, I still didn't care. I was sitting there thinking, *Why don't I care?* And realized it was because the movies had so much CGI, I didn't care about the humans."

"Have you read the Avengers comics?"

"Some, yeah. I'm more into manga than superhero comics. *Watchmen* was cool though. The HBO series more than the comic book."

"And you act like *I'm* the elitist? Some of the Marvel comics are deep. Thanos is like a character worthy of Shakespeare. He's like Othello or Macbeth. He tries to destroy the universe so he can marry death."

"Are you serious? Thanos wants to destroy half the universe with a finger snap. Standard supervillain stuff."

"But Thanos isn't the villain, he's the hero. If half the universe got killed, think how much better life would be for the other half. No more famine, no more shortages. Everyone would have twice as big an apartment. Everyone would have a job. Diego and I could *both* get into Naverton."

"Or one of you would be dead."

Quade smiled slyly. "You're twisting what I'm saying, but you know I'm right. You ever read Nietzsche? Neither have I. But I heard someone quote him on Joe Rogan's podcast: 'One should die proudly when it is no longer possible to live proudly.'"

"Wasn't Nietzsche crazy?"

"I think he was just infected with something. So, are you and Diego coming to my party?"

"You didn't call it off? Hello? Social distancing."

"That shit doesn't affect teenagers."

"Do you not have a grandmother?"

"You ever heard of herd immunity?"

"I assume you're gonna mansplain it anyways, so by all means."

"If enough people get the virus and become immune, it runs out of hosts. That protects the rest of the herd. We're doing the community a favor by having this party."

"That's quite a rationalization. I can see why you love Thanos so much. You need to start collecting infinity stones."

"So you're not coming?"

"I don't know. This whole thing has made me just want to pull back, you know? I know some people have a problem with social distancing and everything, but for me, it just kind of fits. I have all these anxiety issues anyway, and this whole COVID crisis has confirmed my view of the world. It's like everything I had on the inside is now on the outside. So maybe I was right all along. Being alone is the way to go."

Quade shook his head. "What happened to you, Geth? You used to be cool. You were outgoing and shit. Weren't you like vice president of the Climate Change Club? Now you're like 'Fuck the world' like Tupac."

"I think you know what happened. I'm just watching out for myself."

"I get it, no disrespect. Your family's been through some shit."

"Yeah, we have."

"Well, it's gonna be a legendary party. Just tell Diego that QB2 is looking for him."

I slowed down on my way home as I passed Starbucks. The place had been shut down for a while but there hadn't been any garbage pickup since they closed. The dumpster at the side of the store was crawling with foxes. They looked like furry red worms slithering between the boxes and garbage bags and other trash. I was more than fifty yards away and I could smell a rotting stench like something had died. The foxes didn't make a sound, or at least a sound that humans could hear. Maybe they had their own fox language that was completely different from how regular people speak where up was down and hot was cold and black was white. I wondered what went on in the mind of a fox. Did they really believe in what they were doing or were they just driven by base instinct? Did they feel jealous when they saw golden retrievers chewing on steak bones or labradoodles sticking their heads out of the open windows of SUVs? Did the foxes not understand their fox lives were built on trash or did they just not care? Did they have any sense that what they were doing was trashing the entire neighborhood and wrecking their own ecosystem? As I was considering this, one of them looked right at me. Its eyes were as bright and blank as a dead channel on TV.

When I got home, my mom was lying on the easy chair in her AKA T-shirt and baggy sweatpants with a half-filled mug of wine on the coffee table nearby. Kevin was rubbing her feet.

"Eww," I said, "I don't need to see that."

"Pipe down," my mom responded. "I just came off of an eighteen-hour shift."

"Is that legal?"

Mom turned to Kevin. "What's that military term?"

"How would I know?" he said.

"You were in Afghanistan."

"I worked in *Time* magazine's Kandahar bureau for a month. I only got two bylines."

"You know the military term I'm thinking about."

Kevin thought about it. "FUBAR?"

"Fucked-Up Beyond All Recognition. FUBAR. That's what the whole situation at the hospital is like. I told you how patients are dying alone—now they're expiring on social media. One of my patients was at the end, but we couldn't let her husband or kids in the room. She had to FaceTime them to say goodbye."

"Oh shit," I said.

"*Oh shit* is right. It's a shitshow."

"Tell her about the PPE," Kevin said, working his way up her calves with his massage.

"We have one mask to wear all day."

"One mask? Is that sanitary?"

"Of course it's not sanitary. It's FUBAR. We had a shipment of masks and gloves come in and some feds—I don't even know what department they were from—seized them right in the hallways and said they were taking them to Florida."

"What?"

"Number 45 doesn't care about New York," Kevin fumed. "There's no way he's gonna win here. So he's redirecting supplies to swing states with Republican governors."

"That has to be illegal."

"That call to Ukraine was illegal. The last election was illegal. 45 is trying to cheat his way back into office. Did you hear that he wants them to put his name on the stimulus checks? He needs to put his name on the death certificates for everyone who dies in this crisis."

My mom motioned for him to move back to massaging her ankles. "A little lower, a little harder, and a lot less political."

"Should a child be watching this?" I asked. "I'm a child."

"Tell her about what they want you to do if you test positive," Kevin said.

My mom sighed. "We have to come in even if we might be COVID positive."

"What?"

"What I said. We're so short-staffed that the nurses and doctors are coming in even if they were probably exposed. They figure everyone in the hospital's got it or is going to get it."

"What about the patients?" I asked.

"Especially the patients," Mom said. "The only reason to come to a hospital right now is if you're already dying. And frankly, you'd be safer going straight to the cemetery."

Kevin flicked on the TV.

In a new Gallup poll, 49 percent approve of the job the president is doing while 45 percent disapprove, matching his highest approval . . .

My mom groaned. "Oh my god, turn it off."

In the latest poll, 60 percent of Americans approve of the president's handling of the coronavirus crisis while only 38 percent disapprove . . .

"Turn it off!"

Kevin flicked the TV back off. "Sorry. I was gonna turn to the Hallmark Channel."

Suddenly my mom sat up.

"What?" I said.

"Your compulsions, pom-pom."

"What about them?"

"Clucking your tongue, touching your eyelid."

"I know what my compulsions are. Why are you bringing them up?"

"Because when you came home, you didn't do them."

* * *

Tovah: *Are we ever going to get to see movies again?*

Me: *I'm not going back into a multiplex* 😵 *I'll just get a bigger flatscreen.*

Diego: *Movie theaters are over*

Me: *Time loop movies are over*

Tovah: *They already suck*

Me: *But now we're living in one*

Diego: *What else is over? Roll call*

Me: *Tanning booths*

Me: *Kissing booths*

Tovah: *Salad bars*

Diego: *Singles bars*

Tovah: *Dating apps*

Diego: *Dating*

Tovah: *Fox News*

Diego: *Fox News is not over*

Diego: *My mom is watching right now* 😬

Me: *Public pools*

Me: *Public toilets*

Me: *Public anything*

Me: *Can you believe people used to use public phones?*

Tovah: *So germy*

Diego: *The only person with the metabolism strong enough for a phone booth was Superman*

Diego: *That's why he would change there*

Diego: *Even Batman would be like nah man I'll change at the YMCA*

Me: *Good one Diego* 😅

Diego: *Was that sarcastic*

Me: 😏

Tovah: *Capitalism*

Tovah: *MAGA hats*

Diego: *You wish*

Diego: *Free refills*

Tovah: *Those were always gross*

Diego: *Middle seats on airplanes*

Me: *Any seats on airplanes*

Tovah: *Samples at grocery stores*

Diego: *Massage chairs at malls*

Me: *Malls were already out*

Diego: *Communion*

Tovah: *Why?*

Me: *They use the same wine cup*

Tovah: *Are you kidding?*

Tovah: 😖

Diego: *It's not supposed to be wine. It's the blood of Jesus*

Tovah: *Like that's not grosser*

Tovah: *The guy dies for your sins and you drink his blood? Do you also suck out his bone marrow for good luck? I'm so glad I'm Jewish*

Me: *Communion is pretty gross*

Diego: *Don't take this the wrong way but you guys are going to hell* 👅

Tovah: *The idea of us being cast into eternal damnation gave you an erection?*

Diego: *Finger slipped* 😁 *but yes I am fully erect*

Tovah: *That's the reason we're in this huge mess*

Diego: *My hardons?*

Tovah: *That's only a small problem* 😉

Tovah: *People believing in magic over science*

Me: *I hope it's a wakeup call for global warming*

Diego: *My hardons?*

Me: *Enough with the hardons. We get it--you're a boy*

Tovah: *People are stupid. Religion is magic*

Diego: *Religion is not magic*

Tovah: *Like Stevie said if you believe in stuff you don't understand*

Diego: *If society ended right now could you fix your laptop? Could you build a WiFi router from scratch? Do you even know how an internal combustion engine works?*

Diego: *Technology is so complex that nobody understands anything* but experts. *Just like nobody understands anything in religion but priests. I think that's why people will believe anything these days. High tech forces them to believe the impossible every day*

Me: *That actually wasn't completely nonsensical* 😳

Tovah: *I hope all those things aren't gone*

Me: *What things?*

Tovah: *Movie theaters and hugs and hot tubs and riding in school buses and changing rooms at the Gap and lemonade stands and all that*

Diego: *The past is gone. It's not just people dying it's a way of life. I saw it on TV. We're all going through the stages of grief as a planet*

Tovah: *Now you're really depressing me*

Me: *Don't be depressed. Tomorrow will be a great day*

Tovah: *???*

Me: *We find out if we got into Columbia.* 🛡 *Are you going to check with me?*

Tovah: *[Three dots appear then vanish]*

THURSDAY, MARCH 26, HAD ARRIVED and I was set to find out whether I'd gotten into Columbia on Thursday, March 26. My mind had been traveling in circles all night and I didn't get any sleep because my mind had been traveling in circles. The sun hadn't come up yet and I didn't want Karhakonha to see me up yet and see how nervous I was so I got out a flashlight and grabbed my BTS water bottle and went under my covers. I put a sticker of Jin over RM and Suga and Jungkook. Jin's real name is Kim Seok-jin. He's the oldest member of BTS. He's a great singer but some people think he's the weakest dancer in the group but I think that's unfair and he's working on it. The thing about Jin is that he might have to leave the group and go into the military. In South Korea, every male citizen eighteen years or older has to serve some time in the military before they're twenty-eight. Since Jin's the oldest member of BTS, he'll be the first to have to go. He'll have to sign up before the end of this year, actually, which really sucks.

I read Elvis got drafted into the military too in the 1950s and he agreed to serve in the regular army and not just perform for the troops in the special services, which I guess is brave, but Elvis also started hooking up with his first wife when she was only fourteen, so I'm definitely not okay with Elvis's life choices. Kevin told me once that Jimi Hendrix enlisted in the army and trained as a paratrooper but nobody ever thanked him for his service. I keep thinking about what it will be like for Jin to have to trade screaming fans for screaming drill sergeants, hotels suites for barracks, glittery stage costumes for drab military uniforms. I kept thinking about how sometimes people are called to put their lives on the line to serve others. I kept thinking about that and kept thinking about that until the sun came up and the afternoon came and went and pretty soon it was time to check the website to see if I'd gotten into Columbia. Thanks, Jin.

> Me: *I'm about to check the Columbia website. Want to do it together?*
> Tovah: *[Three dots appear then vanish]*

Whatever. This was a big day for me and I wasn't going to let anyone ruin my big day. When he was in high school, my dad hated bullies so he wanted to study criminal justice and go into law enforcement to help protect kids. But then a cop handcuffed him to a bench outside the principal's office saying he matched the description of a robbery suspect they were looking for. The cops kept him there for five hours like he was in a pillory in a medieval village as teachers passed by, eyes down not meeting his gaze, and kids pegged him with spitballs. By the time cops uncuffed him school was over and my dad was over school. He never finished his education. He worked as a security guard so he could at least be around kids.

It was weird when I was a freshman in high school to always see him there at his post in the art wing where all the art teachers were and where students displayed their work, but I got used to it and pretty soon I appreciated it. He was always there flipping through books on anthropology or nanotechnology or Egyptology that he was going to give to my mom with a bouquet of flowers. He was always there for me and Tovah if we needed money for a school trip or had to get a form signed or just needed an adult we could trust to talk to. He loved Tovah and encouraged us to stay together. He wanted us to go to Columbia together because he had failed to get there himself.

"Everyone needs someone," he'd tell me. "The most important thing in life ain't money or power. It's other people. You gotta go deeper than just connecting. You gotta have genuine interest in them and they'll have genuine interest in you.

People open doors for you. People tell you things. People introduce you to other people. And you do the same for them. Even if they never do a damn thing for you, that ain't even the point. People are just interesting. If there are only angels in heaven, I want to go to the other place. Because paradise is other people. If I had a friend like yours when I was your age, I might have finished school."

I tried, Dad. I tried to make at least one good friend. Maybe I haven't been such a good friend myself. I tried to do well in school. This has been a weird year and school is already weird enough. But I tried. I don't believe in God but I believe in you. That sounds corny when I say it but I guess corny things can still be true. I think you're watching me from somewhere. I hope you're okay with me sitting alone at lunch sometimes or maybe not having a date for the prom. I hope you're happy and proud whether I get into Columbia or not. I have tried my best to try my best. If I don't get in I don't get in. It is what it is.

At eight p.m. I sat down at the kitchen table with my laptop, went to the Columbia application website, and entered my Columbia application ID. My stomach was growling. I hadn't eaten all day. I could feel a headache coming on. I stared hard at the spinning circle at the center of my screen waiting for something to happen. I wondered if Tovah was doing the same thing. I wondered how many seniors were sitting at how many kitchen tables in front of how many laptops about to bear witness to what course their lives were going to take for the next four years.

An image opened up across my laptop screen like a widescreen movie. The camera moved dramatically uptown. 113th Street. 114th Street. 115th Street. The main Columbia campus was unveiled before my eyes. Butler Library. Low Library. Lerner Hall. Cinematic images followed. Aerial shots of blue-topped Columbia buildings. The sun rising over the white-columned campus. Celebratory Sousa-like music. The words "CONGRATULATIONS!" materialized on the screen. Then, beneath that, "Welcome to Columbia University!"

I put my head in my hands.

I had gotten into Columbia.

I heard a high-pitched squeal like a train whistle or a tea kettle boiling over or an Amber Alert and I realized it was coming out of my own mouth. My mom and Kevin were in the kitchen and they were hugging me and hugging each other and jumping up and down and they were yelling too. I wanted to say something but I didn't know what to say and when I tried to talk my throat was all tight and nothing came out except "I can't believe it I can't believe it I can't believe it" and the words were small and shrill and it didn't even sound like me.

A message scrolled across the screen.

Dear Geth,

Congratulations from the Dean of Admissions! The Dean of Columbia University and the members of the Committee on Admissions join me in the most rewarding part of my job—informing you that you have been admitted to the Columbia Class of 2024!

At Columbia, you will surround yourself with friends, faculty, and advisers who bring a world of different talents, backgrounds, and perspectives to our campus. This is just the beginning of your journey, and all of us at Columbia look forward to welcoming you to our community next semester. We feel lucky that you chose to be a Columbian.

Everything was happening. Tovah would be accepted to Columbia as well as we would actually room together at Carman Hall. We'd study together in Butler Library. We'd grab noodles at that ramen place, and coffee at that Moroccan café, attend lectures together, check out student plays together, grab dessert together at the Hungarian Pastry Shop. And we were going to get to raise our rabbit Steinbeck in our dorm room. Everything we had dreamed together was happening.

I don't know. I should have been happier. It was weird but I wasn't. I was feeling elated and deflated at the same time, like a birthday balloon that was leaking air. There's this Japanese slang term *kenja taimu* I've seen in online discussions about K-pop. The literal translation is "wiseman's time" and it's that feeling boys get after all the foreplay when they've finally gone all the way and done it and there's a sense of emptiness and a moment of clarity and they think, *Is this it?* I never understood that term until now. I was feeling *kenja taimu*.

Diego was on the swing set at the hidden playground. "Does your mom know you're here?"

Smiling, I sat on one of the swings leaving another one between us. "Does yours?"

This felt comfortable but strange. I wanted to tell him all about Columbia but I didn't want to boast. I wanted to talk all about me but I needed the focus to be all about us. I guess it was a date even though we had known each other for years. I wanted to get closer but we had to social distance. We were planets circling each other and we could feel each other's gravity.

"My mom is too busy watching Fox News to notice me coming or going," Diego said.

"Oh god."

"They're saying people should go back to work."

"They were saying that the whole thing was a hoax before. Now they want people to go back because what—the economy? I'm not dying for capitalism."

"Well, there is an argument."

"And what's that?"

"Well, living is worth dying for. We can't stay in our houses forever. Wouldn't you have wanted to go to graduation, if they hadn't canceled it? Or prom, if they have it?"

I stopped swinging. "Would you want to go?"

Diego smiled. He had a great smile. It was starting to get dark outside but his smile lit up the playground. "To graduation? That's the one thing my mom would have turned off Fox to attend."

"I mean the prom."

"I don't know, maybe, if they have it."

"People will be disappointed if the star quarterback bails. You might be Prom King."

"Are you going? I mean, if they even have a prom."

"Is that an invitation?"

I thought Diego blushed but I couldn't really tell in the dimming light. "Are you saying you're free?"

"I can't make any promises. I have an active social life."

"Like what?"

"Like Quade asked me to come to his party."

"He's asking everyone to come to that party."

"Is anyone going? It sounds like a health hazard."

"He says it's going to be the party to end all parties. His dad made a lot of money with Ozy Theaters."

"His dad is throwing him the party?" I said.

"Hell to the no. His dad is riding out the pandemic in the Caribbean. Some island where they only have two cases. But Quade has his credit card. A black card."

"It's ironic that black cards are black and we're the last people banks give credit too. So what kind of a party can Quade buy with all his daddy's money?"

"BTS."

"BTS is not playing some high school party in New Rochelle."

"That's the rumor."

"That's *so* not possible. He can't afford them. Elon Musk couldn't afford them."

"I heard he's getting one of them via video," Diego said.

"Which one? RM? Suga? Jin? J-Hope? Jimin? V? Jungkook?"

"I don't know names. Wait—there are seven members?"

"Of course there are seven members!"

"That's a lot of people for one group. Rae Sremmurd gets by with two. So did OutKast."

"Stop hating. There are a million motherfuckers in the Wu-Tang Clan and nobody knows half of them. And Rae Sremmurd is not a real group. You made that up."

"Google it. It's 'drummers ear' backward."

"There's no way Quade is getting a member of BTS to play his party. Besides, they're all isolating together in Seoul and hardly doing any press or promotion."

"I'm just saying what I heard."

"Nobody's going to that stupid party anyway," I said.

"I don't know about that. I mean, don't you feel robbed? No graduation, no track season, maybe no prom, no end of our last year in school."

"Hell yeah, we've been robbed. The Night King is straight-up looting our lives. It's Grand Theft Autocracy. Baby boomers keep taking stuff from us. They destroyed the planet with global warming. Then they destroyed everyone's credit with the deficit. Then they ruined our rep on a global scale. The whole world now thinks Americans are stupid and contagious."

"Quade's throwing this party because he wants to take a shot right back at everyone who stole our future. You gotta fight for your right to party and all that."

"Quade creeps me out. Why does he care so much about whether you're going to Naverton?"

"He asked you about that?" Diego said.

"That's weird, right?"

"Quade's dad went to Naverton. I think Quade always wanted to play there."

"So if you go there . . ."

"There's only one starting QB slot, yeah. He was a big star at New Rochelle High School before I transferred here three years ago. He's been on the bench ever since. He probably doesn't want a repeat of that in college."

"He's like your Salieri."

"Who?" Diego said.

"Salieri. He was this composer who was competitive with Mozart. Salieri was good, but not great. That's why people remember Mozart, but when you mention Salieri they say, 'Who?'"

Diego got off the swing. "We should head back. I think we've violated enough social distancing rules for one night."

I smiled. "Have we?"

"You look like you want to say something."

"So you're not even gonna ask me?"

"About what? The prom?"

"No, silly!"

"About you getting into Columbia?"

"How did you know?"

"I had this dream I was soaring over the campus. Butler Library. Low Library. Lerner Hall. The words 'Congratulations! Welcome to Columbia University' across the sky."

"Seriously, how do you know all this?"

"I knew the second I saw your smile."

We arrived at Diego's house. I could hear the TV playing through the closed front door.

You know, impeachment didn't work, and the Mueller Report didn't work, and Article 25 didn't work, and so maybe now this is their next, ah, their next attempt to get the president.

I stifled a laugh. "Oh my god. Does she believe that shit?"

Diego shrugged. "My mom is very religious. A lot of evangelicals don't believe this virus is for real. Or if it is real, God will protect them like he protected the Israelites when Yahweh sent plagues to free them from bondage in Egypt."

"Is that the way they read that story? I kind of see this coronavirus as freeing us from the cruel Pharaoh in the White House. I just can't believe that we have so many people living among us who believe in magic."

"Religion isn't magic," Diego said.

"That's exactly what it is. Like Tovah said, if you believe in something you don't understand, that's magic."

"I think that's superstition. And that's a Stevie Wonder song."

"I just think if people believe in the Rapture they should do it on their own time and not try to take the rest of us down with them."

"You mean up."

"I mean exactly what I said. These religious nuts are not going to the good place."

Diego frowned. "I know everything's partisan these days and I was willing to let some of what you were saying slide, but you really need to back off."

I didn't feel like backing off. "Nothing I'm saying is partisan. These are just facts. This is on you. How can you just let your mom believe all the shit they say on that channel?"

"You've been an Ivy Leaguer for fifteen minutes and you think you know everything?"

"Don't make this about Columbia."

"My mom was a dental surgeon back in Cuba. Now she's a dental hygienist. She risked everything to come to this country. A cruise ship passenger needed an emergency extraction. She boarded the ship, did the surgery, hid in the laundry room, and never came back. So yes, now she supports people who stand up for a strong defense and for American values abroad."

"You think the Night King and his White Walkers stand for those things?"

"You're so damn judgmental. Jesus said, 'Judge not, lest ye be judged.'"

"We're quoting scripture now, huh? The Bible also says to honor your mom and dad."

"That proves my point."

"You're not honoring your mom if you let her believe crazy shit on TV."

"Back off. My mom lived in a police state."

"And what kind of state are we living in right now?" I said.

"Can't you separate political stuff from real life?"

"No, I can't! Nobody can! And nobody should! Look at how we're living! Look at how we're dying! Because people like your mom believe in the magic and lies they see on TV! Everything we learned in high school taught us to reject that as garbage. The Enlightenment. The scientific method. The Civil Rights Movement. You have to call this out!"

Diego was angry. I had never seen him like this. He couldn't be this worked up about politics and television. Something else was up. His chiseled face was resculpted into a look of fury. "You are such a hypocrite. You point a finger at me, but what have you actually done? When have you ever put yourself out there like my mom did? When have you ever risked everything? You have to respect that! And if you can't . . . maybe we shouldn't be friends."

Dinner was on the table when I got home. My mind was running in circles after the argument and I couldn't stop it. I wanted to call Tovah and tell her about Diego but it was weird she hadn't called me to talk about Columbia so I decided I had to wait to hear from her first. She had to have gotten in because her grades were even better than mine. But the acceptance rates were so low these days, the whole thing was random. The food smelled so good and I tried to put Tovah and Columbia and Diego out of my mind.

"Do you guys always eat so late?" Karhakonha complained.

Kevin put his finger to his lips. "Shhh. We're guests."

"You're not guests, you're family," my mom said, putting a hot dish on the kitchen table. "Sorry, I couldn't cook until after my shift, but I wanted us to all eat together."

I sat down at the table. "Shepherd's pie! I like this."

Karhakonha scrunched up his nose. "I'm a vegan."

Kevin's brow furrowed. "Since when?"

"Since Tuesday."

"It's Thursday now. It takes about four days to fully digest red meat. So you're technically still a carnivore. Eat what she made you."

"I've been studying foodways—how culinary habits and culture intersect. I want to eat sustainably. I'm only eating traditional foods. Pumpkin, squash, beans, and maize."

"Maize?" Kevin said. "Do you mean corn?"

"It's okay," Mom cut in. "I have some baked potatoes. Is that close enough?"

"Next time I'll cook," Kevin said. "I'm actually pretty good."

"I can cook too, Mom," I chimed in.

"I know, I know. I was in the mood to cook tonight. It relaxes me."

"Rough day?"

"Every bed was filled and every patient was a COVID patient and every patient was intubated and almost nobody who gets intubated ever gets off it. You're dealing with a lot of scared sick people all day. And we haven't hit the peak yet."

"Really?"

"There's a lot about the virus we're still learning. A lot of my patients are having heart attacks. We don't know exactly why yet, but the virus could be causing inflammation that leads to myocarditis which leads to a weakening of the heart muscle. It could also be directly infecting the heart. We simply don't know. It's just hard knowing that a lot of the patients I was dealing with tonight are not going to be there when I come back in the morning."

"I heard on the news that some folks from the other side are pushing for the economy to be opened back up," Kevin said.

"How can they say that?" I asked.

"They think it's about a tradeoff. A one percent or two percent death rate is worth bringing the NFL back, or opening up the nail salon."

Mom shook her head. "I would like these people who think that to choose. To decide which one or two or three family members they would pick to die. Or which one of their children they would sacrifice. These aren't percentages. They're people."

Kevin scooped up some shepherd's pie. "Well, the one upside to all this is it's got more people living in the now."

"How do you mean?" I said.

"I'm only speaking for myself. My 401(k) is trashed. My early retirement isn't going to happen. You spend your whole life preparing for this fictional time when you're really going to start living. And you know what? It never arrives. You've got to start living *now*."

Mom poured a glass of wine for Kevin and a mug of wine for herself and they toasted and kissed.

"That's so cringe," Karhakonha said.

"And what did you do with your day?" Kevin asked.

"*Xamaica*."

"What?"

"It's a massively multiplayer video game. It's like *Fortnite* but even bigger. People are dropped into this virtual world with its own industries and farms and jobs."

"Sounds sustainable."

"Actually, it is. Fossil-fueled capitalism has screwed up the planet. We've unleashed unstoppable viruses that have driven us indoors. Yeah, it's ironic that an electronic simulation can teach us to live more in balance with the natural world, but why not?"

"And the people in this *Xamaica*, they fight?"

"It's about more than that. Bet. L-Boogie is doing a virtual tour of *Xamaica*."

My mom sipped her wine. "I like that song she does with Travis Scott."

Kevin smiled. "It's with Kendrick Lamar, but close enough."

Karhakonha grimaced. "That's so cringe that you know that."

"How would a virtual tour even work?" I asked.

"They haven't explained it, but she's got something in the works. There's already two L-Boogie playable characters. She's actually a marketing genius for doing it. It's so smart. It's the first time anyone's doing it, so if it's bust she can just say oh well, I tried. And if it works, she's a genius. *Fortune* magazine just tweeted that she's the first female hip-hop billionaire."

"We live in the very best time to be isolated," Kevin said. "With video games, you kids don't need to leave the house."

"It's by design," Karhakonha said.

"What do you mean?"

"Think about it. The Singularity is coming. But these thinking machines have to learn our ways before they do away with us. What better way to copy what we're doing than to engineer a situation where all human interaction is online? Ones and zeros. Shit the machines can understand and quantify. That's all we're doing these days. We're learning by Zoom. We're playing on the computer. We're ordering on Amazon. The Matrix has got us right where it wants us. And pretty soon it'll be done with us. If we had just kept to the old ways and kept living off the land instead of on the grid, none of these killer robots would have had shit on us."

Kevin finished his wine in a long gulp. "The crazy thing is that doesn't sound crazy."

After dinner, Mom brought out chocolate-chocolate cupcakes with "C" written on each of them in vanilla icing. She smiled. "Did you think we weren't gonna celebrate your big day? I don't know how we're gonna pay for it, but congratulations, my little Columbia student!"

Kevin cheered and everyone raised a toast to me. Karhakonha mumbled something about schools he was waiting to hear from. I put on a happy expression like I was putting on my smiley-face surgical mask. I also ate about a million cupcakes, which seemed to keep on multiplying. But I couldn't stop thinking about Diego. And I kept wondering what was up with Tovah.

'M GETTING A LOT OF POP-UP ADS for masks. This is weird because I've never googled the word mask. I've never posted a photo of a mask on Instagram. But I'm still getting all these banner ads for masks. They always say Alexa isn't listening but that bitch has gotta be reading lips. How many times have you said something like, "I'm thirsty," and suddenly your feed is full of Gatorade ads? Maybe someone else on my WiFi network is searching for masks and triggering these ads, but I don't know. Happens too often to be a coincidence. Big Brother, meet Big Sister Alexa.

I'm seeing ads for masks with tiger stripes, masks with pink floral prints, vintage masks, nylon masks, masks made of sustainable materials, paisley masks, polka dot masks, masks with pleated stripes, organic cotton masks, zero-waste linen masks, tie-dye masks, lavender gingham masks, even masks with characters from Miyazaki movies. If I had $59.99 lying around, which I most certainly don't, I might have ordered that last one.

Instead I just picked up my old smiley-face mask and headed out of the house.

Tovah and I drove separate cars and met up at the parking lot at Lord & Taylor. Everyone was calling it a social distancing playdate. It was kind of a cross between a tailgate at a football game and I actually don't know what. We were trying to be responsible but I don't think anyone told our parents where we were going and one of us brought beer and we all kept an eye out for cops. People had been so good and we had been wearing masks and we had been keeping six feet apart but the general consensus was we deserved a bit of a break. I actually didn't even want to go but I knew this was the only way to find out what was going on with my girl Tovah and Columbia and those three dots that appeared and disappeared whenever the subject came up. We all pulled in and parked six feet apart and sat on the hoods of our cars and talked.

There was Stacey from my track team, Alice and Spencer from AP Gov, and a couple people I just know from around. It was kind of a random collection of people like the featured artists on a DJ Khaled album. Except for Tovah, I hadn't seen any of them since school shut down. Except for Tovah, I also hadn't been dying to see any of them, so that told you how connected I felt to them, which was not at all. I looked around for Diego but he wasn't there and he hadn't sent me a text in a while so I figured he was still angry about me calling his mom a religious bigot and everything. Now that I write that down I can see where he might take offense.

Spencer, a total stoner who's skinny as a vape pen, let out a groan. "It's official—they're gonna cancel prom."

Alice, a strawberry blonde lying on the hood of her father's Jaguar, sighed. "You knew that was gonna happen. They canceled graduation so how were they gonna not cancel prom?"

I was super bummed about prom being canceled but I played it off because it wasn't that cool to act like you were into school traditions like prom. And I wasn't. But I was 100 percent into the idea of Diego asking me to prom. And now that was never going to happen. Just when you thought things couldn't suck any more than they already did, they found new ways to suck harder.

Stacey, who was one of those kids who would ask you what grade you got on a test and not even act like it was rude, said, "Are any of you going to Quade's party?"

"Bet," said Spencer. "I heard L-Boogie will be there."

"Stop playing," Stacey scoffed.

Spencer mimed peeling bills off a stack. "Yo, Quade's dad gets paid."

"I heard it was BTS, or one of them," Alice said.

"That's impossible," I said. "Even Quade's dad couldn't pull that off."

"One of the members is doing like a Zoom drop-in. I heard Quade got RN."

"RM is his name," I said. "No way Quade got him."

"Or maybe he got I-Hop."

"You mean J-Hope."

"Or Huggy Bear-C."

"That name you just made up."

Alice flashed me her middle finger. "Bitch, you ain't my autocorrect."

"We've been good for weeks so I'm down for any party," Stacey moaned. "I'm so bored."

Tovah, who had been silently following the conversation, interrupted: "We're getting used to social isolation and everything, but partying during a pandemic is getting more dangerous, not less."

"Why's that?" Stacey asked.

"There's a formula for it. Imagine that the virus is a rocket, and its velocity is the rate of infection. When you're talking about an infectious disease, the farther it travels, the faster it moves. Do you have a pen and some scrap paper so I can write down some of the variables?"

"Not exactly small talk," I said.

"Yo, I talked to Quade," Spencer said. "Kids our age can't even catch the disease."

Tovah shook her head. "Quade's a doctor now?"

"You have to have an underlying condition to get it."

Tovah laughed. "The underlying condition is living in America."

Spencer waved a hand at her dismissively.

Tovah turned to me. "I didn't want to talk to them anyways." Then she leaned in and whispered. "Stacey is a spoiled rich bitch but she's looking like a snack tonight. I wish I could have asked her to the prom! I would have rented a cheesy white limo, we could have worn matching pink gowns, I would have rented a suite at that hotel downtown with the pool . . ."

I held up a hand and whispered back, "That's great, but I'm pretty sure Stacey's straight."

"You think so?"

"You never know, but yeah. I don't want you to put yourself out there and get hurt."

"That's why I only tell you these things."

"We haven't even talked in a minute," I said at a normal volume. "How are you doing?"

I really wanted to talk to Tovah about Columbia and whether she got in too, but I didn't want to pull a Stacey and get into somebody's business without them bringing it up. I had already alienated Diego. I didn't need to turn Tovah against me too.

"I've been socially distancing myself," Tovah said. "This whole quarantine situation must be driving you crazy with your anxieties and everything."

"You know what's weird?"

"What?"

"I stopped my compulsions."

"No more hops or touching your face or any OCD stuff? That's the opposite of weird."

"I know, right? I thought everything that's going on would make it worse. But what was really driving my anxieties was the fear that everything would go wrong."

"And now that everything has gone wrong, there's no more fear. Genius!"

"I've been cutting back on meds. Well, except meds for my asthma, that's still acting up."

"So your mind is clear but your lungs are still messed up."

"Exactly. Now would be the perfect time for us to hang out and have some fun. If hanging out didn't break social distancing rules and all of that."

"Yes, except for the fact the world is coming to an end, our friendship would be better than ever."

"So what's been going on?"

"Well, I was going to tell you . . ."

"What is it?"

"I got accepted to the University of Melbourne."

I couldn't hide the disappointment and confusion on my face. "In, like, Australia?"

"It's considered the best college on the whole continent. It's the Columbia of Australia."

I wish she hadn't mentioned Columbia because it broke my heart. I thought about that dorm room Tovah and I were supposed to get at Carman. I thought about Butler, ramen noodles, the Hungarian Pastry Shop, all of it. I even thought about that rabbit we were gonna get together. I would never get to feed Steinbeck his goddamn carrots.

"Columbia's the Columbia of Australia," I blurted out. "Columbia's the Columbia of everywhere."

"Wow. Elitist much?"

"I thought we were going to go to Columbia together. Wasn't that the plan?"

"That was *your* plan. My plan was . . . You ever heard of Ramanujan?"

"Let me guess. He's a mathematician."

"Not just any mathematician. He was the Kanye West of mathematicians, back before we had to cancel Kanye. He was totally self-taught, twenty-five years old, flunked out of two colleges, worked as a shipping clerk in a small village in India, and he writes this letter to G.H. Hardy."

"Who's G.H. Hardy again?"

"Author of *A Mathematician's Apology*, and one of the greatest mathematical minds of all time. Hardy reads the letter, can't believe all the original theorems this guy has solved, and brings him over to England to work with him at Oxford. Some of Ramanujan's ideas are used in computer science today and mathematicians are still trying to understand them."

"So your point is travel is good for the soul?"

"Not exactly. Ramanujan went home five years later, depressed and disillusioned, and he died of a liver infection a year after that."

"So what's your point?" I said.

"When someone asked Hardy what his most important contribution to mathematics was, he said it was finding Ramanujan. He called their pairing 'the one romantic incident in my life.'"

"Were they gay?"

"Hardy was what they used to call a 'confirmed bachelor,' and Ramanujan left a young wife behind in Madras, but I don't know. The point is you have to put yourself out there."

"How did Ramanujan feel about how things worked out?"

"Probably not super great. But they did make a movie about him starring Dev Patel."

We were talked out and quiet for a second. The other kids were drinking beers and playing "Never Have I Ever." Of course it was at this moment that my asthma decided to act up. I hadn't even brought my inhaler. My chest felt tight and I couldn't quite catch my breath.

"How are—" I started, then I choked on the words.

"Are you okay?"

"I'm fine . . ." But I couldn't finish.

Spencer looked over at us. "Yo, is she okay?"

Tovah waved him off. "She has asthma."

"You sure it's not that COVID?"

"Yes, and it's not that Ebola either. I'm the hypochondriac, not her." Then quietly, to me, "Dude—you okay?"

I caught my breath. "How are we going to stay friends if we're not in the same hemisphere?"

Tovah, relieved, kissed my forehead. "Think of it as advanced social distancing."

I was getting upset now. I could feel my face getting hot beneath my smiley-face mask. First she drops the news that she's moving to another continent. Then she gives me a flip answer. We've been each other's best friends since forever. This pandemic is taking everything from us. Classes. Track. Prom. Graduation. Now we were going to blow up our friendship without even talking about it? The fact is, she had been acting distant even before social distancing. She quit the track team even though she knew I was gonna be on it. She didn't want to go to *Six* even though she knew it was the show I most wanted to see. When we started quarantining she never expressed any feelings about how we weren't seeing each other face-to-face anymore like we had done practically every day I could remember for forever.

I started to talk but my throat seized up again and nothing came out. I saw the flash of red and blue lights before I heard the siren. A police car pulled into the parking lot.

A red-haired officer leaned out of the window. "You kids have somewhere to be?"

Spencer, Alice, Stacey, and the others put away their drinks and got into their cars.

The officer drove over to me. "I need you to take off that mask so I can see your face."

My chest got tighter like a bra that was too small. I tried to respond but I couldn't get words out. My mask suddenly felt like a gag.

Tovah jumped in: "Why is she the only person you're asking to take off her mask?"

The officer didn't even look at Tovah. "This isn't your concern."

"She's my friend. Taking off her mask isn't safe."

"Just get in your car."

"You let the white kids go," Tovah said. "You didn't ask them anything. My friend's the only Black girl and you ask her to do something unsafe. Anything you do to her you better damn well do to me. And my father's a partner for a major New York firm . . ."

The red-haired officer gave Tovah a long look. Tovah knows math and she's dealt with racial speculation all her life so she knew what was going on. The cop was running ethnic calculations in his head. Melanin math. He knew he could get away with whatever he wanted to get away with when it came to a Black girl. But he was trying to figure out exactly what race Tovah was to decide if he could get away with it with her. He could probably tell she was half something. If that meant the father she was talking about was white, that might mean that harassing her would have consequences. He tapped a finger on the dashboard as he weighed his options.

Then the officer smiled, nodded, and drove away.

I took a moment and caught my breath. Then everything came out in a stream of words: "Oh my god I thought he was gonna pull a *The Hate U Give* on my ass. I can't believe white women can talk back to officers like that. The Caucasity!"

"I'm white and Asian. But yes, whites get a pass. We also get discounts at lululemon."

"What was the lawyer shit? Your dad is an accountant."

"I said a major New York firm. I didn't say what kind of firm. And I'm sure if Officer Redhead had arrested us, my dad would have audited his freckled little ass."

"You are crazy. You belong in the land of kangaroos."

I didn't want to get into it but I was as shaken by Tovah's news about college as I was by that dumbass racist cop. She was the one friend I had who would always stick up for me and in half a year she'd be half a world away. I thought about the song that stupid Kevin had put on my playlist, "So Far Away," about how nobody stayed in the same place anymore. The song was written about a million years ago but it was even more true and tragic and timely now. What was the point of anything if nothing lasted?

English Essay
Isolation and Lord of the Flies

Lord of the Flies *by William Golding tells the story of a group of British schoolboys trapped on a deserted island. In the first few days on the island, they work together, govern themselves, and form friendships. But as time goes on, the boys start to lose their humanity, and they quickly give in to violent behavior. The story ends with all of the boys crying after being rescued. But they don't shed tears of joy; they weep for their loss of innocence, and the chaos that they spread among themselves. Golding's theory was that humans are inherently evil, but the constraints of society, such as laws and cultural norms, help humans maintain order and peace. But when humans pull themselves away from those restraints, they succumb to brutality. The boys in* Lord of the Flies *don't have any adults around to stop them from putting themselves in danger. They symbolize how people would behave if they were free from civilization's boundaries and rules. While the boys are on the island, they act immorally and make choices that hurt themselves. The boys' emotions drive the horrible decisions that they make.*

Jack is the main antagonist of Lord of the Flies. *Jack also relentlessly bullies Piggy, a boy his age who tries to help everyone maintain order. Jack uses the fear that all of the boys have inside to manipulate and control them. His jealousy of Ralph's power is what causes him to act out. The boys' fear causes them to become killers and turn on each other.* Lord of the Flies *basically boils down to white male rage although nobody ever talks about that. White male rage makes pretty much every situation more intense*

*and difficult, from driving in rush hour traffic to the current coro-
navirus crisis.*

*If you listen to the audiobook there's an introduction recorded
by the author, William Golding, where he basically says there are
no girls in* Lord of the Flies *because if there were girls on the island they would have been more reasonable and less evil and* Lord
of the Flies *wouldn't have happened. Golding would have had to
name the book* Ladies of Quiet Island *and it would have been
about one chapter long.*

K EVIN WOKE ME UP just after dawn.

"Do you mind? I need your help with something."

He stepped out of my bedroom to let me get dressed. I didn't want to go. I wanted to sleep in. I should have been excited about Columbia but instead I was bummed about Tovah. And I was confused about Diego. I wanted to avoid everything and everybody and just disconnect. But it seemed like Kevin legit needed me so I pulled myself out of bed. Karhakonha was totally zipped up in his sleeping bag like a caterpillar in a chrysalis and I figured he was either dead or asleep or turning into a butterfly. His mysterious rectangular box with the warning "This Machine Kills MAGAts" lay closed beside him, wires sticking out of the corners.

"I need to take your car," Kevin said when I came out of the bedroom.

"You mean my mom's car?"

"Yes, I need you to drive."

"Why can't you drive? Where's your car?"

"I'll tell you on the road."

We climbed into my mom's Honda Fit. I turned the ignition and it started on the fifth try, which is pretty good for that car. Mom hated this old Honda, but I kind of felt connected to it. It was the only thing in my teen years that was a constant. The engine wheezed and huffed when it got on the road, and as an asthmatic I felt like it was one of my people.

The radio blared the latest: "*There are at least 117,688 cases of coronavirus in the US with more than 2,000 dead . . .*"

Kevin turned off the news and put his iPhone in the holder on the dash and punched in an address.

"Credit Services Inc.? Why are we going there?" I asked.

"You know those stimulus checks they're sending out?"

"You said you weren't gonna cash yours because it has the Mad King's signature on it."

"Well, that was then, this is reality."

"Aren't you gonna get a big payday from the L-Boogie interview?"

"The L-Boogie interview hasn't come through. I need this government cheese."

"So we're going somewhere to pick up the check?"

"I have direct deposit."

"I don't get it. So you have the money already?"

"Not exactly. That's why we're going where we're going."

The address was a drab little office park in Mamaroneck. The place seemed deserted, probably because anyone with any sense was social distancing. I pulled up in front of the automated gate. Kevin signaled for me to roll down the window and he leaned over to shout into the intercom: "I'm here to see Thomas Dale of Credit Services Inc."

"Nobody is on site at the facility this week."

"You're here."

"I'm in Missoula," the voice said.

"Montana?"

"There's another Missoula? Yes, I'm an operator based in Missoula, Montana. Telecommuting is a thing now. It has been for several years. Sorry to blow your mind."

Kevin signaled for me to roll up the window.

"What do you want me to do?" I asked.

"Drive through the gate."

"What?"

"This facility was robbed three days ago," Kevin said. "Another freelancer I know wrote about it on a local news blog. Whoever robbed it knocked out the security cameras. I'm guessing that with the coronavirus crisis, they haven't fixed them yet."

"What about the alarm system?"

"Doesn't work. That's how they got robbed. Drive through the gate and park."

"This isn't that simple. You're a white man. I'm a Black girl. I'm gonna get in a lot more trouble than you when the cops get called. I'm the one who'll get choked out."

"You're right. Forget it. Pull a uey and let's—"

"Screw it. Let's just do this." I put the car in drive and rammed through the wooden plank barring the gate, which snapped like balsa wood. I pulled into a parking space.

Kevin unbuckled his seat belt. "I'm going in. You should stay here."

"What are you going in for?"

"You don't need to know that."

"Maybe let me decide that?" I said.

"I can't get into this now. I'm going in."

"Then I'm going with you."

Kevin walked up to the front of the office building and used a credit card to jimmy the lock to the front door. It popped open with little resistance. "I did this a lot when I was a metro reporter," he said by way of explanation.

The lobby of the building was empty but there was a sign listing the various companies inside and where they were located. A couple dentists, a physical therapy center, a realtor, and on the third floor, Thomas Dale of Credit Services Inc.

Kevin headed up the stairs.

"Are we robbing the place?" I asked.

"I wish. But the previous robber probably got everything they had of any value."

"What are we doing here?"

"Paying Thomas Dale a visit."

"What makes you think he's here?" I asked.

"He lives in Mamaroneck. It's a one-man office. I'm betting he's coming into work."

We arrived on the third floor. The walls were gray and blank and without decorations.

"This place looks like the inside of the Death Star," Kevin mumbled. Credit Services Inc. was in room 303. We walked down the hall and Kevin knocked on the door. There was no answer. He knocked again, harder this time. After a pause, he knocked again, and this time the knocks had a sense of desperation, with a touch of stubborn pride. They were pretty nuanced knocks.

A male voice finally answered: "Can I help you?"

"Can you let us in?" Kevin asked.

"The office is closed."

"You're here. Or are you actually in Missoula?"

"What are you talking about? You're going to have to leave or I'm gonna call the cops."

"I'm a journalist," Kevin said. "Do you want everyone to know what you do here?"

"We don't do anything illegal. You need to leave."

"You fucking seized my car."

"You were three months behind on payments."

"I was going to pay with my stimulus check. But now I find out you're gonna fucking seize that before it's even deposited in my account!"

I put my hand to my mouth in surprise. "That can't be legal."

The voice behind the door was grim: "I'm calling the police."

Kevin pounded on the door again. "I want my fucking stimulus!"

The voice replied, shouting now, "What did you think coming down here would accomplish, dude? I don't make the policies, I just enforce them!"

"I want my stimulus!"

"Talk to the fucking White House! They're the assholes that signed the loophole into law. It's totally legal for creditors to grab your stimulus before you get it! None of this money is going to people like us, dude! My wife has COVID! My mom has COVID! My life is shit too! I'm sleeping in this office, dude! You think I want to fucking steal your stimulus? I don't even want to live in America no more! I want to move to China or Italy or some shit!"

There were tears in Kevin's eyes. He leaned his forehead against the door. "Just open up. Can you just do that?"

Through the door, we heard footsteps and then three muf-fled beeps, which I assumed could only mean the man was calling 911.

"We need to leave," I told Kevin.

We drove back in silence. We pulled into the driveway and I turned off the car. I started to get out but Kevin motioned for me to stay there with him.

"I need a second."

"You need a second?" I said. "I need therapy."

"I'm sorry, I shouldn't have dragged you—"

"This whole thing was white privilege. I actually hate that term, because it's like we're giving you magical powers, but it fits here. Y'all can take whatever risks you want—white water rafting, running with the bulls, bringing AK-47s to Walmart, whatever. I'm Black. I can't fuck with the criminal justice sys-tem. They will bury me under the jail."

"You're right. I apologize. Really."

"So why did you take me with you on this little adventure?"

"Your mother has enough to deal with at the hospital. I want to marry that woman. I've been open with you about that. I don't want your mom to see me as a complete fucking loser."

"What about Karhakonha? Why couldn't he go with you?"

"Do I really need to spell that out for you?"

"You didn't want this getting back to your ex."

Kevin sighed. "You are not seeing me at my best. I used to be a pretty good journalist."

"I've seen some stuff online."

"Journalism used to pay. Back when I was just out of college, the most steady, most profitable businesses were newspapers. They turned out good profits like clockwork. Then the Internet happened. Newspapers started giving away their content for free. Then they realized they couldn't make money that way. So they started putting up paywalls. But walls never work. People had gotten too used to getting the news for free."

"I know, it sucks."

"All people read now are tweets. You can't understand the big stories in 140 characters."

"It's 280 characters now."

"And that's just helped the White House double the number of lies it spreads. That's my point—technological advances should push the world forward, not backward."

"That's not happening? We're in a plague but I'm still able to go to school because of Zoom. I hate it, but technology does some things right."

"People communicate more, but understand less. That's why it's the Information Age and not the Informed Age. That's why 45 is president. That's why he's always going on about fake news. He never would've happened with a functional fourth estate. We would have Watergated his ass. He's getting away with a pandemic. And I can't even fucking get my stimulus."

"I know, it sucks."

"It's weird. One second you're a hotshot in a hot industry and the next you're close to retirement age and you're wondering if you've got enough in your 401(k) to live on. I know I don't look like the best person to take advice from, but take this advice: Don't wait and work for some future day when you're gonna be on some beach. Wake up and live your life. I mean it." Kevin pounded the dashboard.

"Careful," I said. "This car is seven years old. In car years, that's seventy."

Kevin sighed. "I know the feeling."

Mom was lying on the couch in her AKA T-shirt and baggy sweatpants when we got home. She had an empty mug of wine next to her on the floor.

Karhakonha was at the kitchen table stirring a cup of coffee with a stick of butter. "Where were you guys?" he asked. "We haven't seen you in a minute."

"What are you doing?"

"Making butter coffee. Want some? It's mad nice."

"Butter coffee? Is that like Butterbeer?"

"What's that?"

"What they drink in Harry Potter."

"The kids in Harry Potter were low-key alcoholics? That's dumb funny."

"Butterbeer isn't alcoholic. I think. Actually, they never make that clear. Why are you putting butter in your coffee?"

"This is grass-fed butter. It's wavy. Trust."

"I'm gonna need more of an explanation than that."

"This is brain food. It boosts your focus and keeps you feeling full for six hours."

Mom called out from the couch: "We're out of food."

"What?" Kevin said.

"I was hoping you were out picking some up."

"Can't you just order from Instagrocer or Instacart or InstaAmazon or something?"

Karhakonha sipped his coffee. "Peep this. Grocery delivery is low-key terrible because the stores aren't designed for volume. They don't have trained delivery staff—they have their baggers making runs. Then there are the bots."

"Bots?" Kevin said.

"Just like how concert tickets get sold out ten seconds after they're on sale, people are using bots to grab all the delivery slots."

"I once waited in line for nine hours to get U2 tickets," Kevin said. "They sold out right in front of me."

"What's U2?" Karhakonha asked.

"They're an Irish rock band," my mom said.

"You waited nine hours for that? You're capping. That's so cringe."

"How do you know so much about this stuff?" I asked Karhakonha. "The butter and the bots and all of this."

"I've been spending time in the DIYBio community."

"What?"

"I'm living that biohacking life."

"Bio what?"

"The world needs balance. All things new that are sustainable are the ways we used to live by. These are the ways that were taken. Paleo, Keto, socialism, matrilineal, nonhierarchical. I'm learning to hack the body to return us to where we should be. The way forward is back."

"I'm hearing words come out of your mouth and I don't understand any of them."

"Why you gotta be so extra? Let me just enjoy my butter coffee."

Another robocall from the mayor of New Rochelle arrived in my e-mail inbox.

Dear New Rochelleans:

As New Rochelle's public health crisis approaches the four-week mark, all of us are struggling to make sense of an unprecedented challenge and to put our local experience in some meaningful context. I write today to offer my own personal observations about where our community stands, in the hope that these comments might be helpful as you process your own thoughts.

On March 10, Governor Cuomo announced the nation's first "containment zone" in New Rochelle. Although often exaggerated in media accounts, the zone was accurately judged to be a forceful response to an emerging hot spot of COVID-19. Just one week later, each and every one of the zone's restrictions was overtaken and exceeded by new statewide standards. In effect, all of New York had become a containment zone, with all of America not far behind. There is no better illustration of the whiplash speed with which the virus has upended every public health goal, assumption, and expectation, making aggressive action look mild in a matter of days, as we strive to keep up with the virus's relentless pace.

Few of us had even heard the term "social distancing" until a couple of weeks ago; now it rules our lives, forcing us to operate under awkward limitations that would have been nearly unimaginable at the outset of this crisis. The disruption of our personal interactions is matched by an equivalent disruption of our institutions—the closure of schools, businesses, and houses of worship, which has had a profound effect on the rhythm of our city, with far-ranging social and economic implications, particularly for our most vulnerable residents.

And all of us have had moments when it has felt as though we've stumbled onto the set of a movie. For me, it is surreal to wander through a nearly empty City Hall, or see police in protective gear stationed at the perimeter of Glen Island, or learn the names of friends and colleagues who have tested positive. I have had many sleepless nights, thinking through contingencies that, even if not probable, now seem all too plausible.

Keep in mind, these are the burdens carried by those of us who are healthy. For those who are ill and their families, especially those hospitalized, the burdens are exponentially heavier. And there are some in our city already mourning the loss of loved ones. There will be more.

There is no minimizing this challenge. It is unprecedented in its scale and probable duration. It has expanded with astonishing ra-

pidity. And it will be hard in ways that can be only dimly predicted.

Yet if the virus is tough, we have proven ourselves to be tougher. In the face of extraordinary pressure, and in the glare of the national spotlight, New Rochelle's social infrastructure has held firm.

As I write, there are 264 confirmed cases of COVID-19 in New Rochelle, but it would not shock me if one day in the near future this number suddenly spiked by a hundred or more. That would not necessarily indicate some fresh community outbreak, but rather a change in data collection methodology to catch up with the facts on the ground. And, of course, even applying the rosiest interpretation to the figures, a long road still lies ahead.

At a time when everyone is eager for clarity, there is a natural tendency to overreact to every bit of data and to invent trends within mere statistical noise. We should all do our best to resist this impulse, and those of us in leadership positions should take special care to explain honestly what we know and what we don't know.

And to the hackers who stole contact information from City Hall to spam our residents, we will catch you and we will prosecute you.

We'll get through this together. #NewRoStrong

A bunch of seniors decided to have a social distancing get-together. I had no interest in going but I was hoping to see Diego. Plus, with Tovah going to Australia for college, the opportunities I have to hang out with her are running out. I still didn't get her Melbourne choice but maybe if we met face-to-face again she'd drop me some clues. The seniors all decided in a group chat to not meet in the parking lot near Lord & Taylor because the cops were watching that one. So everyone decided to meet at this spot near the highway. Tovah, Diego, and I broke off into our own group chat to discuss.

Tovah: *This sounds dangerous*

Me: *We might as well go by and see what's up*

Tovah: *And dumb*

Diego: *I'm okay with skipping it*

Tovah: *Geth wants to go because we never get invited to anything*
Diego: *I invited you to every football game this season*
Diego: *You came to two*
Me: *You nearly lost one. We're bad luck*
Me: *You're a better halfback without us*
Diego: *I'm a quarterback*
Tovah: *Geth is pandemic popular*
Me: *???*
Tovah: *I'm the same way. We're getting invited to things like group chats because the social order has broken down*
Tovah: *After it's over everything's going to go right back to how it was. But we'll be retronyms.*
Diego: *What's a retronym?*
Tovah: *It's like a word that you have to come up with a new word for because the times have changed*
Tovah: *Like landlines. After cell phones people couldn't just call them phones*
Tovah: *Snail mail*
Tovah: *Conventional oven. Brick and mortar store*
Me: *There's something sad about retronyms*
Me: *It's like being outdated and replaced at the same time*
Tovah: *That's our future*
Me: *Sometimes they just steal the past and don't even acknowledge it*
Me: *Emojis are basically hieroglyphics* 😵
Diego: *Thanks for the Ted Talk*
Diego: *I'm going to drive to the place*

Diego didn't even offer to give us a ride, which was totally not like him. Tovah and I walked to the meeting spot, but a lot of the other kids drove. Tovah didn't mention a thing about Columbia or Australia or our hypothetical rabbit Steinbeck and I didn't either. Diego pulled up in his blue Nissan just as we arrived. The sky was red and yellow and purple. The world was dimming like the coming attractions were over and the feature film was about to begin. There were no clouds and no planes. The exit ramp where we were meeting was off the Hutchinson River Parkway, which at the end of the day is usually packed with traffic. But with all the commuters home because of the pandemic, the road was clear in either direction as far as I could see. The kids who had come to the get-together were racing their cars up to exit 18 and back again. I saw a red Honda Fit and a white Toyota Camry and a black Jeep Grand Cherokee and a silver BMW and a black Tesla and a bunch of other vehicles. The revving of the car engines and the squeal of their tires and the laughter and cheering of the other kids were practically the only sounds on the road. The Tesla was silent.

"QB1!"

"QB2."

Quade came over and gave Diego a bro hug. I could see Diego was uncomfortable with the contact. Maybe because we were still in a global pandemic, but also because it was Quade. Tovah, Diego, and I were standing a few feet apart. Quade offered Diego a beer but he shook his head and nodded to his car.

"We're all driving, bro," Quade said. "Have a sip at least."

"I'm good," Diego replied.

Quade nudged him. "You up for a little race?"

"I've got a 2010 Nissan," Diego said. "You've got a 2020 BMW."

"My Beemer's a sweet ride. My dad bought it before everything went to hell—"

"How's the Ozy?" I interrupted. "After this is over, I wanna go there, order a deluxe Ozy-Man burger, and watch *Howl's Moving Castle*."

Quade took a sip of his beer. "Ozy Corp. is declaring bankruptcy."

"Oh no! I'm so sorry."

"Don't tweet about that or nothing, the news isn't public."

"I'm so sorry," I repeated.

"I know, it sucks. There goes my summer job. I was going to totally transform Ozy's web advertising model. I've really been studying this viral marketing shit."

"That sucks, man," Diego said.

"Sorry to hear that," Tovah added.

"My dad wants to work, his employees want to work, but the goddamn government won't let it happen."

"But it's for the greater good, right?" Tovah said. "If we all stay home now, we'll all be healthy later."

"People are just being pussies. Gushy-ass pussies. How many people die of traffic accidents every year?"

"About forty thousand." Tovah's brain works like that.

"My dad told me that when they reduced the national speed limit in the 1970s from 65 mph to 55 mph, they saved ten thousand lives a year. If they cut it to 45 mph, they might save ten thousand more. You know why they don't? Because at some point you have to call bullshit. People need to drive, they need to work, and yeah, it can be dangerous, but suck it up. This quarantine's gushy-ass pussy bullshit."

"So basically you want workers to die for capitalism," Tovah said.

"People have died for dumber ideas," Quade said.

Diego shook his head. "Ever see that movie *Patton*? I watched it on Netflix yesterday. It's about this crazy World War II general and there's this scene where he says, 'No bastard ever won a war by dying for his country. He won it by making the other poor dumb bastard die for his country.'"

"That sounds about right," Quade said.

"No. No, it doesn't," Diego said.

Quade took a sip of his beer. "You know, I still haven't heard back from my top college choices. I worked hard, I followed the rules, I deserve to get in wherever I want. But they keep moving the finish line. They move it up for some people, they move it back for me. I just want a fair race. Otherwise, burn it all the fuck down." He finished off his beer, crushed the can against his forehead, and threw it into the weeds beneath the exit ramp. "Do you want to race or not?"

I don't know why Diego decided to get into his car and race. Maybe it was because all the people around us heard Quade's challenge. Maybe it was a quarterback thing or a piggyback thing or whatever position he plays. Tovah and I tried to convince him to stay put but he wouldn't listen. He gave me one of those looks that when you know someone for a long time can communicate a lot, and his look told me, *You said something stupid and reckless to me so now I'm gonna do something stupid and reckless, because that's the way guys do.* Guys are idiots. I read somewhere that paleontologists used to believe that stegosauruses had a brain in their skulls and another in their tails. I think guys have the same sort of deal but they don't have tails, so you can guess where that other brain is located. Sometimes it takes over and they get moody or horny or defensive or reckless and they can't help themselves, so women have to step in and show them how to act right. Otherwise they get stuck in a tar pit and fossilized, forever frozen in whatever position they fucked up in. So I climbed into the passenger seat next to Diego, and Tovah got in the back. I felt nauseous and my vision was blurry. I didn't know if it was from anticipation and fear or a side effect of my clomipramine.

"What are you doing?" Diego said.

"Watching out for you," I said. "The guy in *Fast and Furious* died doing shit like this."

"You do realize with the extra weight there's no way I'm gonna win?"

"Are you saying we're fat?" Tovah said. "Weight is not the relevant part of the equation here, it's occupancy. Did you know that if a teenage driver has a passenger, his chances of an accident double? And if he has two, it triples? Those numbers rise when you add in factors like driving at night and speeding."

"Not helping," I said.

Quade pulled up next to us and revved his engine. Alice, laughing and probably drunk, was riding shotgun with him. There was a bumper sticker on the back of his car: *The higher we soar, the smaller we appear to those who cannot fly.* I hadn't seen a bumper sticker on a BMW before.

"The rules are simple," Quade said. "The race is to exit 18 and back."

One of the guys pulled off his shirt and waved it like a flag to start the race. Quade tore off onto the parkway, his tailpipe spewing sparks.

"What's the matter?" I said to Diego, who hadn't moved. "Go! Go! Go!"

"We're way behind!" Tovah cried.

"I have a strategy," Diego said, coolly turning on the GPS on his phone.

"Why do you need directions? It's a straight highway!"

What was he doing? How fast was he gonna have to drive to catch up to Quade now? Plus, Quade was probably drunk. I wanted to support Diego, I wanted to be there to protect him, but this whole thing was too stupid and too risky. He was a dinosaur and his second brain was swinging his horned tail and someone was gonna wind up a pile of bones in the basement of the American Museum of Natural History. I opened the car door and stepped out.

"Where are you going?" Tovah asked.

"This is stupid," I replied. "You guys can get yourselves killed if you want."

I could see Diego's angry eyes in the rearview mirror. "This is what I'm talking about. You criticize other people but you don't have the guts to risk anything yourself."

"There's risk and there's risk. This doesn't help anyone."

"You're spinning in your own little circle. You're in this Ivy League of one. I'm asking you this one time to stop thinking about yourself and take a chance and get in the fucking car. Are you in or are you out?"

Diego adjusted his mirror so I couldn't see his eyes. I shot a look at Tovah but she didn't follow me out of the car. I closed the door.

They pulled onto the highway and drove away in a spray of gravel and dirt.

Did I make the right choice? Here I was, on the sidelines again. I felt like I needed to support my friends. But friendship isn't a suicide pact. And maybe they should have supported me and not done this stupid race. The kids around me were cheering and screaming and lifting cans of beer as Diego and Tovah sped down the road in pursuit of Quade. They didn't look like they were going anywhere near fast enough to catch him. I tried to tell myself I didn't care. I should never have come. School is pretty much over anyways. I'd never see these people again. I just wanted to go off and be on my own island and leave all this mess behind.

Ten minutes later they were back and the kids cheered as Diego pulled up in his blue Nissan. Quade and his silver BMW were nowhere to be seen. Tovah rolled down the window, reached out, and gave me a fist bump.

"What happened?" I asked.

Tovah smiled. "Quade got pulled over by cops a mile down the road. Diego drove five miles below the speed limit the whole time. Classic turtle vs. hare."

I turned to Diego. "How did you know?"

"I have my ways," he said. "Or my Waze, I should say. I just checked the app and saw there were cops waiting. We're gonna go celebrate. Catch you later."

My two best friends drove off, leaving me alone at a party I never really wanted to attend.

* * *

When I got home, I turned on *Text Z for Zombie.*

As the cops close in to seize the vial of germs that can turn Black people into zombies, biracial lovers Mavis and Adele are faced with a choice. Only stomach acid can break down the deadly germ and so one of them is going to have to sacrifice themselves and drink it down to save the world. But they'll only be immune from the zombie-causing effect of the germ if they stop thinking of themselves as Black. Will one of them give up their cultural identity and risk their life to save Black people around the world?

I got all the way to the final episode before I fell asleep.

In the morning I had a message from Diego. It was a playlist.

Diego's Broadway Playlist
For Now, *Avenue Q*
I Know Sometimes a Man Is Wrong/Don't Worry About
the Government, *American Utopia*
Don't Lose Ur Head, *Six*
Piragua, *In the Heights*
Come Down Now, *Passing Strange*
We Dance, *Once on This Island*
You Will Be Found, *Dear Evan Hansen*
Being Alive, *Company*
You Learn, *Jagged Little Pill*
Love Who You Love, *A Man of No Importance*
Wicked Little Town, *Hedwig and the Angry Inch*
Wait for Me, *Hadestown*
Say It to Me Now, *Once*
You'll Be Back, *Hamilton*

I'm pretty certain the playlist was an apology.

My mom was going to church on Zoom.

I sat next to her on the couch in the living room as we both watched the service on her laptop. I kept thinking about what Diego said. How all I did was criticize. How I never risked anything. I thought about my dad in that hallway. I thought about all those terrified kids. I thought about him making the decision to go back. What did it cost him? What did it cost our family? My life was so screwed up. The world was so screwed up. What could I do to take more control? Getting in the back of some guy's Nissan for a testosterone-fueled road race wasn't the answer. I needed to be a driver, not a passenger.

"Food, water, housing, clothing, sanctuary, health care, and freedom from incarceration should be rights, not commodities," Brother Anthony was preaching. "No one should ever have to pay money for things! Listen to your Brother Anthony now, I know what I'm talking about! Scarcity is the devil's work—and so is work. Hold on now. Consider the lilies of the field, they toileth not. The devil works to get us to see only the desert amidst the abundance. Hold on now. Five loaves, seven fishes, and five thousand people! What is to be done? Sharing ensures there's more than enough, and even the smallest example can grow and roll back all the devil's empires. I declare this to be so in the name of the hungry, the thirsty, the naked, the refugees, the sick, and the imprisoned—the least of these. Hold on now!"

I was on my computer only half listening. I wondered what all the people we used to serve at the soup kitchen were doing. I went to the website for the church and there was a notice saying the homeless ministry was closed until further notice, but there were various links to other places that the faithful could go if they wanted to support their community in these troubled times. I clicked on one of the links.

COVID-19 Human Challenge Trials
What is a human challenge trial? It's a controlled method of speeding up vaccine development by testing them on human volunteers. We're a group of researchers who are currently studying whether or not to launch a human challenge trial for COVID-19.

Please click one of the following options:

*I am not interested in being exposed to the coronavirus but I want to support research in safer ways.

*I am interested in being exposed to the coronavirus to speed up vaccine development.

HAD AN IDEA. IT TOOK ME a minute to get it all together. I met Diego at the hidden playground at midnight. There was no moon and the only light was starlight. But I had bought candles and placed them everywhere—on the seesaw, on the basketball court, even on the swing set. I only had a few but it looked like a million.

"What have you done?" Diego asked.

"Well, we're not having a prom, so . . ."

"This is our prom?"

I had brought a bluetooth speaker to connect to my iPhone. I started my playlist.

Geth's Social Distancing Prom Playlist
Not Somewhere Else but Here, L-Boogie
Lucid Dreams, Juice WRLD
134340, BTS
Reasons, Earth, Wind & Fire
The Weekend, SZA
MIA (feat. Drake), Bad Bunny
break up with your girlfriend, i'm bored, Ariana Grande
Ladies, Fiona Apple
Instant Crush (feat. Julian Casablancas), Daft Punk
The Show Goes On, Lupe Fiasco
Time Flies, Drake
The Closer I Get to You (feat. Beyoncé Knowles), Luther Vandross
Lady Stardust, David Bowie
Autumn Leaves, BTS
Summertime Magic, Childish Gambino

That slow song by L-Boogie kicked off the playlist. Diego looked at me. "How are we going to dance if we can't touch?"

We were six feet apart. I hadn't thought about being touched, really touched, in a long time. I thought I could do without it, but it's like food and air and warmth. I wanted to be touched by Diego. I needed to be touched by him. Not in latex gloves. Not behind a mask. Not through a computer screen. A touch screen is the opposite of touching. You don't feel anything. Nobody feels you. My art teacher, Ms. Swanson, once showed our class details from that famous painting by Michelangelo of God creating Adam with a single touch that's on the ceiling of the Sistine Chapel. The cloak behind God is shaped like the hemisphere of a brain. There's a female figure under God's left arm who could be the Virgin Mary or Eve or Sophia, the embodiment of the human soul. God and Adam reach out toward each other with single index fingers, so close, yet still not touching. So much could be communicated in a single touch. Intelligence. Soul. Redemption. All the love that would ever exist between Adam and Eve and every person who would ever fall in love ever. I had to touch Diego. I needed to touch him. But we had to stay six feet apart. I started to sway and he moved in time with me.

"This is probably how our grandparents used to dance," I said.

"I never met my grandparents," Diego said.

"Mine passed away when I was young."

"What was your dad like?"

"You really want to talk about that? This is prom night!"

"You don't have to if you don't want to," Diego said.

"It's okay."

"It's just that I see his photo every day when we go to school."

"I see it too. I'm glad they have the memorial, but it's a little weird. It's like he's gone but he's still here."

"Isn't that a good thing?" Diego asked.

"The best thing he did when he was here was he was always there. He used to come to all my track meets even though I never won a single race—I was the queen of third place. He made dinner every night—he was a way better cook than my mom. He used to give her a foot massage after her shift—it was eww but I knew she loved it. He used to always give her books and flowers. Now he's gone. I hate being reminded that he's gone."

"We can talk about something else."

"No, it's fine. I understand it was his job . . ."

Diego came close and hugged me, still swaying to the music. I gasped a little. I hadn't touched anyone like this in so long. I felt a tingling across my scalp and down my neck and through my spine. It was like ASMR to infinity and beyond. I could hear his heart or maybe it was mine. He smelled woodsy and fresh like a sports body wash. I put my arms around him.

"He was a hero," Diego said.

"He was my hero. That girl that shot up the school that day? I don't even want to say her name. She was in my English class. Everyone hated her. People made fun of her."

"I know. She was in my gym period."

"She was in my lunch period. I used to invite her to sit at my table. All the fucking time. I even invited her to my thirteenth birthday party. That was my dad's idea. That's the kind of person he was, the kind of person he wanted me to be. He didn't even carry a weapon. No gun, no nightstick, no nothing. When she started shooting, he went up to her with his arms raised, just trying to talk to her . . ."

"Shhhh. Shhhh."

The music had stopped for some reason. Diego and I stood there in silence hugging each other on the empty basketball court in the candlelight.

I looked up at him, tears in my eyes. "Do you want to kiss me?"

"We're friends."

"We can't be friends with benefits?"

"Like dental and student loan assistance? That would be useful in this economy."

"I'm serious."

"I'm not the guy you think I am."

"Don't you like girls?"

Diego took his arms from around me and put his hands in his pockets. "Why would you say that?"

"Because you're using this social distancing to keep your distance. Just like Tovah."

"What?"

"We're alone in a playground after midnight. Most guys would take advantage of that."

"I'm not most guys."

"I brought condoms."

"Did you really do that?"

"This is a prom. I'm a traditional girl. Do you like girls? You didn't answer."

"I revere girls."

"You revere girls?"

"Yes."

"That doesn't sound that sexy."

"I don't know what you want from me."

"This whole year has been stolen from us. I just want something we can remember."

Diego turned away. "It's not you. There are some things about myself that I need to work on. I've been talking to my sports psychologist."

"Are you impotent?"

"Not everything is so simple."

"So what is it? We have all night. I don't care that it's a Monday."

"I'm a football player. I'm the most highly recruited athlete out of New Rochelle since Ray Rice. And he went to the NFL. That's where I need to go—my mom is counting on me to get a full ride to someplace like Naverton. You have no idea how many expectations are on my shoulders. When you're the QB it's even worse. People like Quade are gunning for me every day. He would kill to be in my place. I have to lead and not look weak. We didn't lose a single game this season. Not a single one all the way to the state championship. That's the way it has to be. No mistakes. No surprises. I have all this pressure and I have no idea who I really am."

"I don't see what anything you just said has to do with anything."

Diego bowed his head and then looked away. "I think we should go home. I'll walk you."

I was home alone and completely confused. Boys are simple and stupid but they can still be hard to figure out like a long hashtag without any capital letters. You know that feeling you get when someone texts you an alarming article and you get all worked up like there's an imminent threat and it turns out the article is from like two years ago or whatever? I felt like that. Tricked. Flustered. All bent out of shape by something I should have seen coming. I slipped the box of condoms I had bought back beneath my bed and went to the kitchen to get a tube of horseradish-flavored Pringles. Goddamn Instacart. I turned on the TV.

There are at least 160,008 cases of coronavirus in the US and 2,948 people have died from the virus, according to CNN Health's tally of US cases . . .

I changed the channel to the finale of *Text Z for Zombie.* Biracial revolutionaries Mavis and Adele are in love and on the run and the cops and feds and state troopers are closing in. The women are faced with a terrible choice. To destroy the deadly vial of germs that turns Black people into zombies, one of them has to drink it. They will only be immune to its effects if they think of themselves as white. Only it turns out there is too much for just one person to drink. If they want to destroy the serum, they both have to leave Blackness behind in their hearts and drink the contents of the vial together. They kiss once and promise to remain true to each other. Mavis and Adele somehow squeeze in the time for a love scene even as the cops and the feds and the state troopers run up the back stairwell of the hotel to get to the room where the women are getting it on. When all the law enforcement guys finally enter the hotel room, they find two female zombies in a passionate embrace. The police and the feds and the troopers shoot both zombie women in the head. As they stand over the bodies, one cop snarls, "Goddamn nigger zombie bitches."

Turns out *Text Z for Zombie* was a limited-run series. There won't be a season two.

Geth's Post-Prom Luv Sucks Playlist
Fake Love, Drake
thank u, next, Ariana Grande
Boys Don't Cry, The Cure
I Get Out, Lauryn Hill
Be Careful, Cardi B
I Want You to Love Me, Fiona Apple
Just Friends, Amy Winehouse
I Can't Win, The Strokes
Ashes to Ashes, David Bowie
Fuck Love (feat. Trippie Redd), XXXtentacion
This Is America, Childish Gambino
New Person, Same Old Mistakes, Tame Impala
The Long Night of Octavia E. Butler, Sons of Kemet
Dry Leaves Are Blowing, L-Boogie
Cry Alone, Lil Peep
Rag and Bone, The White Stripes
Lithium, Nirvana
Fake Love, BTS

Karhakonha: *Nice playlist*

Me: *???*

Karhakonha: *I would have had more Strokes*

Karhakonha: *"Ode to The Mets." "Between Love & Hate." "Threat of Joy." "I'll Try Anything Once"—the demo version with just Julian and a keyboard*

Karhakonha: *My stepdad started liking them after I did. Facts*

Me: *Where are you? Are you hacking my computer?*

Karhakonha: *You're capping*

Karhakonha: *I'm in the bathroom*

I went over to the bathroom. The door was locked and I banged on it.

Karhakonha: *I'm in the middle of a number 2. I'm at 1 1/2, maybe 1 3/4.*

"Stay out of my computer!"

Karhakonha: *Why are you so extra? You practically invited me*

"Screw you! I did not!"

Karhakonha: *Your password is BTS. That's an invitation. Laminated*

Karhakonha: *I can see everything on your laptop. I can see everything you bought*

Karhakonha: *Mint-flavored condoms? Really? And you put them on your debit card?*

I swallowed a scream. "Are you some kind of fucking hacker?"

I heard a flush. Karhakonha opened the door. "I'm a bio-hacker. There's a difference."

Karhakonha was weirder than I would have guessed. Maybe smarter too. I was burning with anger about him hacking my laptop but I was curious about his deal, so I set my smouldering rage aside, like a lit cigarette on the edge of an ashtray. He humble-bragged that he had been in some sort of gifted program in his old school. He was one of those kids who was obsessed with computers. But he wasn't one of those people who thought robots were gonna get smarter than humans. He had a whole different theory about the future—and the past.

"Ever hear of the Anthropocene?" he asked.

"Vaguely."

"Bet. In Geochronology, every age of the world gets a label. It's like when you cut into a mountain and you see all these layers of rock like rings in a tree. You can tell just when one age ended and another began. There's fires and floods and meteors and shit and the rocks change color and composition."

"What does this have to do with anything?"

"Well, you've heard of *Jurassic Park*. Geologists break up the history of the Earth into eons, eras, periods, epochs, and ages, and they give them names. Right now the epoch we're living in is called the Holocene. Although with global warming and everything, some geologists argue we've entered the Anthropocene."

"Why does this even matter?"

"Because the definition of the Anthropocene is that we're in a geological stretch in which mankind—not meteors or weather or any of that other shit—is the primary change agent on Earth. This shit didn't happen when the Kanyen'kehá:ka were living off the land. Now the world is out of balance. In a million years, when people cut into mountains, the rocks will have changed because of fossil-fueled capitalism, not God or nature. Facts."

"I've heard some of this. I used to be vice president of the Climate Change Club."

"Well, this is why I'm a biohacker. I want to work with nature, not against it. I'm trying to adapt traditional ideologies in an indigenous futuristic way. Butter coffee? That's a hack on my brain. I also slid a microchip beneath the skin of my middle finger and . . . watch!"

He snapped his finger and his computer turned off.

I sighed. "Like Thanos."

"Bet."

"You think coffee and having what basically amounts to the Clapper is going to help you stop pandemics and climate change?"

"This is just the start. We have all we need in our bodies to fight for the future. Trust. Like Crispr. That's this technology that lets you edit your DNA like you edit a Google Doc. It could make you smarter or taller or immune to heat or COVID-19. You know Elon Musk?"

"Of course—the Tesla guy."

"He has a company that's working on neurolinks—combining brains and computers. Mee Corp. is working on some similar tech—a couple rockers and rappers have already bought prototypes. That's the next step. Human and machine together like the chocolate and peanut butter in a Reese's. And I'm gonna be ready for it. Biohacking. That's the future."

"Are you really Native American?"

"That's a racist question."

"No it isn't."

"I peep you a vision of mankind's future like I'm Hari Seldon in the goddamn Foundation Series and you ask me about my race? Yo, that's straight racist."

"My friend in the supermarket seemed to think you might not be Mohawk."

"So some of your best friends are Mohawk?"

"Well, one at least."

"Yo, where is this coming from? We were talking about biohacking."

"I just want to know who I'm talking to."

"You need to know someone's race before you talk to them?"

"I need to know if someone's real or if they're pulling an Elizabeth Warren."

"Yo, I love me some Elizabeth Warren."

"Lizzy's my girl, but she's not Native American."

"Race is a state of mind. People today get to choose their gender. Why not their race?"

"Because people paid a price to be part of certain cultures. I'm Black. My ancestors came over on slave ships. I don't want some motherfucker stealing my cultural heritage because he likes hip-hop. Fuck Post Malone."

"You had him on a playlist."

"Number one, stop reading my shit. And number two, 'Circles' is my jam."

"Don't women pay a price for being women? How come Caitlyn Jenner gets to join the party? That motherfucker loves Agent Orange!"

"Number three, I'm really getting the feeling you're not really Native American. Are you just gonna tell me the truth or do I have to 23andMe your sorry ass?"

"My mom is part Native American."

"What part? I need percentages."

"You mean like quadroon, octoroon, that kind of thing? That's some racist *Gone with the Wind* shit right there. What percentage Black is Halsey? Or Prince?"

"I don't know Halsey's story, but Prince was actually 100 percent Black."

"He was half white in *Purple Rain*."

"That was a movie. That was mythologizing."

"So he can do it and I can't? I don't know what percentage Native American I am. I just know my grandmother used to tell us stories. Did you know almost every skyscraper in New York was built by Native American ironworkers? There are all these stories and legends about us being the only ones who would cross the highest beams without fear. But the truth is we just respect heights. The Empire State Building. The Twin Towers. One World Trade Center. My grandma said we worked on all of those."

"I think there are actually rules to claiming Native American heritage. You have to be part of a tribe and get checked out. You can't just register. It's not Spotify."

"Don't you think I know this? My mom had to have a clan in order to be recognized as Onkwehón:we through a long-house ceremony. I'm legit Mohawk."

"I still have questions . . ."

"What about your boyfriend? He seems kind of confused about what team he's playing for."

"What the hell? Were you—"

"Why can't you just cut people some goddamn slack? This identity shit isn't easy! Nobody is ever one damn thing or another—Black or white or gay or straight. All of these labels are like social constructs. They funnel us into the right bathrooms. You're a girl, you go there. You're colored, you go over there. And you better not sit in the front of the bus! None of this is science. That's why I'm DIYBio, ride or die. Science is the only damn thing that will save us!"

We were both quiet for a while.

I spoke first. "Is there something you wanted to show me?"

Karhakonha brooded for a beat. "You know my stepdad's in trouble, right?"

"Yeah, I kinda got that sense."

"And trouble for him is trouble for your mom, cause they're together—you get that, right?"

"I can do basic math."

"I heard what you said to Kevin a couple days ago. How he had to go after the story, be as hungry as he was when he was a city reporter. I think I have a way we can help."

From beneath his sleeping bag, Karhakonha pulled out that box marked "This Machine Cures MAGAts." He opened it and attached some wires and plug-ins to his tablet. Then he waved a hand over it and everything sprang to life.

"What are you doing?" I asked. "Am I going to be subject to a federal indictment after this?"

"Chill. Last summer, I was an intern at Mee Corp. I worked in the neurolink division. I helped do some of the coding."

"You still haven't explained—"

"L-Boogie has a Mee Corp. neurolink."

"L-Boogie is bionic?"

"This isn't sci-fi—it ain't that deep. The prototype's just basically a high-tech tiara that sits on your head and taps into your brain waves."

"That sounds pretty sci-fi to me."

"You can't like move metal with your mind or something. This isn't an episode of *Black Mirror*. All it does is it helps you turn on and off your hardware, log into your e-mail and apps, easy stuff like that. L-Boogie apparently hates trying to remember all those passwords so she got Mee Corp. neurolinks for her technical stuff."

"I can't remember half my passwords."

"I know—that's why half your passwords are BTS. I've been using your Netflix account since I got here. The thing is, since I know this system I can hack it. Once we do that, we can get a message directly to L-Boogie. "

"So what do I have to do?"

"This is a two-person job. Just stay with me. You'll know when to jump in."

Xamaica, like I said earlier, is a massively popular multiplayer online video game. I've never actually played it myself because I'm not into gaming, but most of the boys I know at school, except for Diego, are totally into it. Tonight was the night that L-Boogie was supposed to give a virtual concert in the game. Usually the game is a free-for-all battle with guns and swords and phasers and I don't know what else, but a general truce was called for the night and every player was gathering in this huge steampunk stadium that looked like a mix of the Roman Colosseum and a set out of *Star Wars*.

Karhakonha slipped fingerless gloves on my hands.

"What am I now, Fagin from *Oliver*?" I asked.

"These gloves have built-in microchips in the palms. When the time comes, they'll give you control with a wave of your hand."

We were watching the big event on Karhakonha's tablet screen. There must have been thousands of players gathered in the stadium. They all appeared as their in-game avatars— unicorns with human arms, dragons with huge eagle wings, knights in diamond-encrusted armor and flaming swords, and a lot of other Harry Potter–like mythical creatures that I had no idea how to name or even describe.

The music rumbled in like an earthquake. The ground began to shake and then everyone slowly realized it was just the rhythm section. There was a massive meteor sparking across the sky. It grew brighter and brighter. Then the Earth split in two and a stage rose up. The meteor struck the stage and an avatar of L-Boogie stepped out of the flames, mic in hand, rapping her hit song "Truth and Dread." Her shoulder-length dreads were on fire, her eyes were shooting lasers, and she was a hundred feet tall. She strode off the stage into the crowd, rapping, stomping, dancing, and occasionally flying up into the air and landing again.

Karhakonha was moving his fingers like he was typing away at an imaginary keyboard. "Get ready for the switch."

"I have no idea what I'm doing."

"You'll know. This shit is intuitive like a Mac. One . . . two . . . three . . . we're in!"

Suddenly, I was in control of the L-Boogie avatar. When I shifted, she shifted. I began to bounce with the beat, moving with the music. The crowd moved with me. I realized I could control the crowd the way a conductor conducts an orchestra. I had them moving left and right and up and down and when I jumped into the clouds, the avatars that could fly—the dragons and the pegasi and the hippogriffs—they soared right into the sky with me. The light show was incredible—the clouds, the Earth, even the air around us changed from green to blue to yellow according to the rhythm of the song.

"Who the fuck is this?" A rough male voice came through the speaker on Karhakonha's tablet.

Karhakonha laughed. "We're the motherfuckers in control of your L-Boogie avatar."

"Man, you don't know how much trouble you're in."

"Maybe not, but I know how much trouble *you're* in. You've got banners from Coke and Mee Corp. and Twitter all over your stage. I read this concert has brought in millions in sponsorships. How much of that are you gonna have to give back? We could ransomware your ass right now."

There was a silence. "What do you want?"

"I don't want money. I just want you to put L-Boogie on the line for five minutes."

"Why?" the voice asked.

"I got a reporter friend who's looking for an exclusive," Karhakonha answered.

"L-Boogie ain't give interviews. That shit is known."

"I'm not playing. You let me talk to her, and I give you back control of your concert. It's a win-win. Just put her on the line."

Another silence. "We can't do that."

"Can't or won't? Cause your concert is about to be low-key ruined."

"Can't. She ain't here, brah. Nobody's seen her for three years."

"Who's doing the rapping?" Karhakonha said.

"That's old shit she laid down five years ago. We're not playing. She ain't here."

"Turn on your camera. I want to see the control room."

"Will you give us back—"

"Pull back the curtain and let me lay my motherfucking eyes on you!"

At that moment, it looked like I was seeing everything. We had some sort of admin-level clearance. You know that moment at the end of *The Matrix* where Neo can see the underlying code for the entire world and everything is made up of 1s and 0s? That's what I was looking at. For every player, I could see their phone number and home address. I could see the instant messages they were sending out and the ones they were receiving. I spotted a cluster of players in New Rochelle, and one in particular with a home address on a street that wasn't far away from where I lived. I focused in and I noticed the bulk messages this one user in particular was sending out to every player with an address in his zip code. I opened one up.

We have team meetings every morning at seven a.m. and film meetings right after school. My practice starts before practice because I've got to sit down with the coach and go over everything we'll do that day and learn all the plays for my position and everyone else's position too. I have to memorize route combinations that receivers will run, how defenses may react, what read to make so I can make the right throw, or call the right protection for the offensive line, or call the right audible. Then we have practice after that, walk through the plays, and we are on the field for three hours. After all that I have to shower, study the playbook more, eat a good dinner cause I've burned off all these calories, and then do three hours or more of homework. All that for just being on the bench all game every game because I'm QB2 not QB1. It's the same for all of you. You have skills. You have training. You worked all your life and now these gushy-ass pussies won't let you work. America has put you on the bench while foreigners get to play. I say it's time to get off the bench and start throwing touchdowns. #diegoisoverparty

The message had to be from Quade. He was blasting it out dozens, hundreds, thousands of times. Each note was only slightly different than the last. His message was a living, evolving, mutating thing. Suddenly the concert feed went dead. Karhakonha's tablet was blank for a few seconds and then, with a flash, blinked back to life. There was a pixelated image that sharpened into view. We saw a cramped office with three middle-aged white men in T-shirts and tiaras. The office was strewn with empty pizza boxes and energy drinks and cigarettes. Nobody seemed to be social distancing. One of the men stuck up his middle finger at the camera.

"Satisfied?" the man said. He was balding and paunchy. "Give us back the avatar."

"Who are you guys? L-Boogie is supposed to be real shit."

"Grow the fuck up!" the man said. "Nobody is who they appear to be. This isn't a game—this is reality."

"How do I get in touch with L-Boogie?"

"If we knew that, do you think we'd be doing this?"

Karhakonha snapped his fingers and the music stopped and the screen went dark.

"That was wild," I said.

Karhakonha rubbed his eyes. "I need some fresh air."

We went out to the porch. The sun was setting and the sky was clear and it was hard to believe we were in the middle of a pandemic. Karhakonha looked genuinely upset.

"So we're not getting that L-Boogie interview for Kevin?" I asked.

"Doesn't look like it."

"So why do you care so much?"

"He's my stepdad."

"I know lots of stepkids that don't care about their step-parents."

"I have three other dads and I don't see any of them—including my biological dad. You know, a couple years back, I tried to use DIYBio to track down my bio dad."

"Did you find him?"

"Yup. Turned out he was more of a deep fake than a father. My bio dad fucking sucked."

"I'm sorry to hear that."

"Kevin has his issues but he's for real. Did you know that even after he and my mom separated, he went ahead and finished the adoption paperwork for me?"

Karhakonha wiped his eyes and handed me something.

"A watch?" I said. "That's old school. I thought you were some sort of advanced hacker."

"I'm a biohacker. And that's not just any watch. It can monitor your vitals when you run. And if you get lost, we can track you down and find you."

"Are you giving this to me?"

"Yeah. Thanks for helping me with my stepdad's problem."

"I wasn't much help. But I learned some things. This kid Quade from my school is plotting something against my friend Diego. He was sending out messages: #diegoisoverparty."

"Do you or this friend of yours Diego need my help?"

"I don't know yet. I'm not even talking to Diego right now. But thanks for the watch."

"It's your first step into the world of biohacking."

"How did you get into it anyway? I mean biohacking?"

Karhakonha looked out over the neighborhood. The sky was darkening and the streetlights were blinking on one by one. "We used to live in Southern California, back when my mom and Kevin were married. He was freelancing for the *Los Angeles Times*, and Mom had a studio on the beach. You ever heard of sea sparkle?"

"No, what's that?"

"There's this kind of plankton that floats in the ocean. It's gross if you swim through it, but at night it gives off a kind of bioluminescence. It's an evolutionary thing, to scare off predators. In the dark, when sea sparkle gets riled up by dolphins leaping through the waves, it lights up all the water near the shore this incredible electric blue. Yo, it was mad nice."

"That sounds amazing. Like that scene near the end of *Ponyo* where the queen of the ocean moves beneath the surface of the water and everything just glows."

"Yo, you're into Miyazaki? I'm Studio Ghibli too, ride or die! Yo, this plankton light show was straight *Ponyo*. When I first saw it, I thought to myself, *Biological organisms are mad nice. If a one-celled piece of plankton can do that, what can humans do? You feel me?"

A white woman walking in the street waved to us. It was #KKKaren.

Karhakonha and I both waved back.

"Hey, you need to wear a mask!" #KKKaren shouted.

"We're not breaking any laws!" I shouted back.

"Maybe not yet," she replied. "But do you really want the law to settle this?"

#KKKaren was wearing an N95 mask. She looked like a middle-aged Nausicaä from that '80s film *Nausicaä of the Valley of the Wind*. Karhakonha and I were on our own property, on our own patio, fifty yards away from anyone else. #KKKaren needed to mind her business.

"Are you allowed to wear masks like that?" I asked. "Aren't those reserved for first-responders and health-care workers?"

Karhakonha joined in: "Are you a first-responder or a health-care worker? If you are, thanks for your service. If not, get the fuck out of here."

#KKKaren walked away.

"She sure left in a huff," I said. "How come nobody ever arrives in a huff? Huffs are kind of a one-way trip."

Karhakonha looked ashamed. "I shouldn't have cursed or raised my voice at that lady."

"I thought it was funny."

"We have a different kind of respect for women in our culture. Everything's matrilineal with natural balanced roles and responsibilities. Respect and peace are mad important. If you lash out even at someone who is hurting you, stooping to their level is disrespecting yourself. Even yelling at some racist-ass white woman. My mom taught me better than that. I'm sorry for everything I said to you too."

"I'm sure nothing's gonna come of any of this," I said. "Let's go inside."

Thematic Essay
Ms. Gray
English B

The novel The Catcher in the Rye by J.D. Salinger describes the journey of a teenager who is struggling with something tragic in his past. The novel explores teen angst as a theme. Teen angst is seen as a phase for young people that is characterized by angst, anxiety, and inner conflict. This theme is also prevalent today, which is a time in which mental health, especially among teens, is a big focus. Teenagers often choose to bottle up their feelings and deal with them on their own. Suicide is one of the leading causes of death for people ages fifteen to twenty-four in the United States and because of that mental health and stability have become issues that people increasingly focus on in our society.

In The Catcher in the Rye, there are many examples of teen angst. Over the course of the novel, Holden, the protagonist of the book, frequently mentions that he is depressed although it is often hard to believe him because he comes from a rich family, has a loving sister, and he is an unreliable narrator. But we also learn that his brother Allie tragically died of leukemia at a young age. We see how this has had an effect on Holden and has caused him to be very bitter toward the world and not connect with others. One instance where Holden's depression and emotional problems are apparent is when he is packing to leave for New York. He is describing how he feels when he is packing and he says putting things away makes him depressed. Holden also says, "Almost every time somebody gives me a present, it ends up making me sad" (page 58). If someone bakes you a cake and you can't even taste it because you're too caught up in your own issues, that's really tragic.

Holden is not purposefully trying to appear to be unhappy, he is just really affected by his past. This is seen very often in today's society, especially in high school where many young people are afraid to share their innermost thoughts and feelings. Because of the prevalence of social media, teenagers often feel as though they should not open up or ask for help for fear of being made fun of. Nobody wants to tweet something personal that could generate a negative and embarrassing online backlash with friends and even strangers. In today's society, tragedies such as school shootings, bombings, and terrible acts of all kinds have often torn communities apart. We had a shooting at New Rochelle High School that impacted the community and my family specifically. In The Catcher in the Rye, Salinger uses the character Holden to portray how teens deal with grief and tragedy. Salinger shows the journey a young boy goes on in which he identifies his problems and finds himself. Death haunts the book, but by the end the teen hero finds out a little more about life.

‖ WENT FOR A RUN in the morning.

The streets were empty. I prefer it that way. I was alone with my thoughts and the road. There were no cars, no dog walkers, no couples out for a stroll. I didn't even see any other joggers. When I'm really into it, I can lose myself in a run. It's like when you drive along an interstate highway and you enter a zen state and you're not asleep but you kind of come to miles and miles later and you can't even remember passing that many exits or what you were doing or thinking about for all those miles and you're a bit surprised you're still alive. My mom and me took a road trip to Santa Fe once and I got to drive for a long stretch and it was totally zen like that for hundreds of miles along the I-40 West toward Amarillo. Except for the moment on my car trip with my mom when a cop pulled us over for going five miles over the speed limit. Other than that it was zen all the way to Amarillo. Running for me can be amazing like that.

I found myself in front of the Ozy Theater. I never run that far. I was already exhausted and I had an equally exhausting distance to go just to get back home. That's always a weird feeling when you realize that as far as you've come, you have just as far to make it back. There were no movies advertised on the marquee and there was no lineup of coming attraction posters mounted outside. All the posters had been stripped down. The whole scene felt like that moment in *Titanic* where Jack and Rose are at the prow of the ship and she goes, "I'm flying, Jack," and he sings in her ear and they kiss and we hear the instrumental version of "My Heart Will Go On" and the camera swirls around the lovebirds and it all fades to the present day and the *Titanic* is a wreck at bottom of the North Atlantic and the older Rose looking back says, "That was the last time *Titanic* ever saw daylight." I actually saw *Titanic* at the Ozy three years ago and I remember standing outside looking at the poster of Kate Winslet and Leo. There had been a life-sized statue of a king between the posters and the parking lot, but someone had looted it, leaving just the king's boots, positioned wide apart like the Colossus of Rhodes astride some harbor entrance in antiquity, or a manspreading dude on the F train.

I tried the door of the Ozy Theater and was surprised to find it was open, so I slipped in. I had seen my favorite Miyazaki movie, *Kiki's Delivery Service*, at this theater for my sixteenth birthday. It's a great movie about a young witch who leaves her family to go out into the world to find her place and make her living with her magic. There was something about it that I found to be intensely melancholy—that's the only way to describe it. It was a fantasy but it felt real, like it captured what it meant to be young and thrown out there into the working world and having to get by with your wits and your skills and having nobody there to help you but your talking cat who eventually stops talking.

Inside the theater, they had already stripped everything down. There had been a bar against the wall, now there was just plaster. The bathroom door had been taken off its hinges. The seats in the screening rooms had been pulled out, leaving bolts where they used to be attached to the floors. The screens were gone too, exposing jagged brick walls. There had been a fake sidewalk grate with a fan underneath where moviegoers could reenact that scene from *The Seven Year Itch* where Marilyn Monroe gets her skirt blown up by a passing subway car, but the fan and the grate were gone now. That scene is crazy sexist so maybe that's for the best.

I left the theater and stepped into the parking lot. I ran across the empty asphalt back to my house.

* * *

When I got home, Kevin and my mom were watching TV in the living room.

> Dr. Anthony Fauci, head of the National Institute of Allergy and Infectious Diseases, is drawing media attention as the truth-telling member of the administration's coronavirus task force. But with fame comes attacks from the right, especially online. A post that falsely claimed he was part of a conspiracy to overthrow the president has been shared millions of times on social media. A New York Times investigation has identified more than seventy Twitter accounts promoting #FireFauci, all belonging to right-wing political groups . . .

"This is what I'm talking about," Kevin began to rant. "This is an Only Fans presidency. It's obscene and it only performs for paying customers . . ."

My mom turned off the TV. "Ready for dinner?"

"You know how you can tell a society is civilized?" Kevin asked, between mouthfuls of mac and cheese.

"When they start farming?" Karhakonha answered.

"Nope."

"When they start having marriage ceremonies?"

"Nope."

"Just tell them," my mom said, sipping a glass of red wine. "I read the same article you did."

"Margaret Mead said this . . ." Kevin began.

"Who is that?" Karhakonha asked.

"Famous anthropologist," I said. "She's in every book I have about science sheroes."

Kevin continued: "Mead said the first sign of civilization is when you find a femur that has broken and then healed."

"What's a femur?" I asked.

"Thighbone," my mom said. "It's the longest bone in the body."

"I don't get it," Karhakonha said.

"If you're an animal living in the wild and you break your thighbone, it's over," Kevin explained. "You can't hunt, you can't move. A lion is going to eat you. Hell, rats may eat you. You're easy pickings."

"But if your thighbone has broken and healed, it means someone has your back," my mom said. "Someone nursed you back to health. Someone made peace and not war. Someone had compassion. If you start letting the old die, or the weak, or the outcast, you're not a civilization, it's survival of the fittest, and you might as well be living in the forest. Like Jesus said, 'Blessed are the peacemakers, for they shall be called sons of God.'"

"You stole my punch line," Kevin complained.

"You were taking too long to tell the story," my mom said. "Plus, I'm the nurse."

"So healing is a sign of civilization?" I asked.

"Exactly. If you let people die, you might as well be a pack of hyenas."

"Isn't this basically the story of The Lion King?" Karhakonha said.

There was a knock at the door.

"Who the hell is that?" my mom said.

Karhakonha and I looked at each other.

Mom's eyes narrowed. "What's going on?"

I cleared my throat. "We kind of hacked into L-Boogie's concert."

"How is she even holding a concert during a pandemic?" my mom asked.

"It was all online," Karhakonha said. "We were trying to help Kevin out. It was more of a biohack than a hack."

Mom threw up her hands. "I don't even know what that means."

The knocking continued.

Kevin got up. "This could also be about my credit."

"What?" my mom said.

"They were trying to steal my stimulus check before I even got it. Geth and I had to pay a visit to the collection company."

"Why is my daughter—"

The banging was louder now, and then we heard a voice: "Open up! Police!"

My mom got up and pushed past Kevin. "It's my house. I'll get it."

We all went to the door but Mom got there first. She looked through the little stained-glass window. "How may I help you, officer?"

I could see a little bit over her shoulder. It was Officer Redhead. "I know that guy. He's an asshole."

"Shh!" my mom cautioned.

Officer Redhead knocked again. "I need to come in."

"We're social distancing. Can you ask whatever you're going to ask from out there?"

"Ask him if he has a warrant," Kevin said.

Officer Redhead's face was as red as his hair. "I'm not going to ask again."

Mom was getting angry too. "It's not healthy for us to just have you come in! What's this about?"

The door burst open and the corner hit me in the forehead. Officer Redhead pushed inside, knocked my mom back, and drew his gun. "Everyone on the floor—now!"

I was already on the floor and my head was throbbing and everything sounded like it was underwater and far away. There were flashing red and blue lights. I remember hearing a muffled struggle. Maybe Karhakonha, maybe Kevin, maybe both. Officer Redhead was shouting something but I couldn't understand any of it. I tried to catch my breath though I couldn't quite take air into my lungs. I tasted something salty and warm in my mouth and I realized it was my own blood. I felt like I was going to throw up. I closed my eyes. I wanted this to all be a nightmare so I could wake up.

Then I heard another voice in the room.

"What the fuck, Charlie?"

"They failed to comply with a lawful order."

"Why are we even here?"

"A neighbor called in a complaint. The boy and the girl were seen without masks."

"Not wearing a mask isn't against the law. You're not even wearing one."

"They failed to comply—"

"We need to get the hell up out of here."

Footsteps. A door opening.

Officer Redhead's voice: "Stay safe."

The door slammed, and sirens faded into the distance.

I opened my eyes. "Are they gone?"

"I think so," Karhakonha said.

"Everyone all right?" Kevin asked.

My mom began to cough.

"Is she okay?" I asked. "That fucking pig wasn't wearing a mask."

"You can't catch it that fast," Kevin said.

"There are a lot of things they don't know about the virus yet," Karhakonha said.

"I'm pretty certain they know you can't get it that fast," Kevin said.

"Mom, are you okay?" I asked.

She pulled herself to her feet.

"Honey, where are you going?" Kevin asked.

She coughed. "To the bathroom."

"Mom, are you sick?"

"I'm going to self-isolate," she said. "You should all go wash your hands."

Karhakonha was pissed off and his fists were clenched. "Those goddamn pigs. They had no right to bust into our home. They had no right."

I followed my mom into the master bedroom where she picked up a pillow, a stool, and a fuzzy purple bathrobe. The bathroom in her bedroom was her one indulgence. It was bigger than the kitchen and had a walk-in shower with a floor-to-ceiling sliding glass door. Mom went into the shower and pulled the door closed behind her.

"You can't be serious," I said. "You're going to self-isolate in the shower?"

"I'm probably perfectly fine. I'm going to get a thermometer and take my temperature as soon as you guys leave me in peace."

"She couldn't have caught it that fast," Kevin said as he and Karhakonha came into the bedroom.

"She could have been asymptomatic and the stress triggered it," Karhakonha said. "Those pigs had no right to mess with us like that."

My mom was in nurse mode. "Chronic stress can trigger the release of cortisol, a hormone that boosts your heart rate, blood pressure, and triggers inflammation. If it goes on too long it can limit your immune response. I could have caught something from that cop, but it's much more likely he just triggered something. I've been stressed for weeks."

I pressed my palm against the clear shower door. "I should take you to the hospital."

My mom coughed. "I know better than anyone that they can't do anything. And if I don't have it, I could catch it there. I'm sure I'm fine. But better that I stay here."

Kevin had his cell phone against his ear. "I'm calling to try and get you a test."

"Don't bother," my mom said. "It's impossible to get one unless you're on Wall Street or in the White House or both. There's a lot of overlap these days."

Karhakonha poked his head into the bathroom.

"Now it's a party," my mom sighed.

"Yo, ain't you even gonna call the police on that pig?" Karhakonha asked.

"Listen to yourself," Kevin said. "Calling the police on the police makes no sense."

Karhakonha punched the wall. "This is how they do us. It's like we have no rights in our own country. We have to do something."

"You guys should finish dinner," Mom said. "I'll be fine."

"Dinner's all over the floor," Karhakonha said. "The dishes are broken. Fucking pigs."

"You have a bleeding bruise on your head," Kevin cautioned. He wiped the blood off my forehead with a towel, got a Band-Aid out of the medicine cabinet, and put it on over the bruise.

"Thanks," I said.

Kevin nodded toward my mom. "I learned first aid from a professional."

"I'm just going to get some rest in here," my mom said. "Geth, you and Karhakonha should go get some takeout. Clear your heads. I'll be okay."

"I want to stay with you," I said.

"We're all shaken up," she replied. "Some fresh air and food will do you good. And a little peace and quiet in my own bathroom will be good for me too."

Karhakonha and I walked up the street to Alvee's sandwich shop. There was a misty rain but it wasn't too bad. My head was ringing and I could still taste blood in my mouth. I was more messed up than I thought. I took a deep breath of the cool night air.

"I think I have PTSD," I said.

"I thought I had gotten an STD once."

"That's not funny, Karhakonha. Not even a little bit."

"It's a fucked-up night. I'm just trying to lighten the mood."

"Look at my hands. They're still shaking."

"You should see my underwear. I think I crapped myself when that pig took out his gun." Karhakonha shadow-boxed with the night air. "Somehow, someway, we gotta get payback for this. Pigs have been doing this to us for too long. Facts."

I sighed. "We're in a quarantine. The Mad King is president. It is what it is."

Alvee's was all locked up when we got there. But one light was still on and I could see Alvee's daughter Erica inside.

"Hey!" I called through the window.

Erica mouthed the words *We're closed.*

"I thought you were open for takeout."

"We just want a couple sandwiches," Karhakonha said.

Erica came closer to the window so we could hear her. "I'm here all alone trying to clean up. My whole family is self-isolating. We had to close the shop."

"Oh no! Is everyone okay?"

"My dad is home resting. But my sister . . . she's on a ventilator."

"What? She's like in her twenties, right?"

"Lisa and I both have asthma. Really bad since when we were kids. I'm not positive, thank god . . . but she's got it bad . . . I'd do anything to trade places . . ." Erica put her head in her hands for a few seconds.

"It's okay," I said. "She's young, she'll pull through."

"Like 50 percent of people on ventilators stay on ventilators," Erica said. "I'm really worried. And they won't let us in to see her. She's sharing the ventilator with another patient. They don't even have enough for everyone."

"That's terrible. But she's going to be okay. We'll pray for her."

"Thanks," Erica said. "Sorry we're not open. Stay safe."

In the darkness, the place reminded me once again of that Edward Hopper painting.

We walked home. The streets were empty. There were no pedestrians and almost no automobiles. But the night echoed with the sounds of police cars, ambulances, and fire trucks.

"You know why we're hearing so many sirens?" Karhakonha said.

"Why?"

"I saw this online. In a typical day in New York City, about twenty-five people die at home. Falls, old age, natural causes mostly. You know what they're seeing now?"

"I'm afraid to guess."

"Two hundred home deaths a day."

"COVID?"

"Pretty much all of them, yes. Hospitals are renting refrigerated trucks to hold the overflow of bodies. I read that if you go into cardiac arrest, the EMTs don't try to revive you anymore. Too many patients."

I shook my head. "What happens if you break a femur?"

"I don't even want to think about it."

"I can't believe what happened to Alvee and his daughter. You know, I have asthma."

"Really? I haven't heard you cough or anything."

"I take stuff for it. But I guess it would still count as an underlying condition."

A pack of foxes scampered across the road in front of us snapping and clawing at each other. Their eyes were like little lasers, like the night-vision goggles SEAL teams wear on secret missions. The foxes were a blur as they rolled around scratching and biting. I couldn't tell what they were fighting over or why or even who was winning.

Karhakonha and I walked the rest of the way back home in silence.

* * *

I was in the dark and I couldn't fall asleep.

I never knew death until my dad died. After that, I'd think about death all the time. Driving in the car. Standing in the shower. Sipping a caramel macchiato in Starbucks. Death was always one thought away. Now it's like that for everyone. Death isn't some distant family relation that only shows up for funerals. Death isn't a substitute teacher. Death is always there, feet up on the coffee table. Death is discarding dental floss in the bathroom sink and leaving the toilet seat up. Death is making himself at home. Death has the spare key and the WiFi password. Death is living with you now. You know that feeling you have when you see someone famous and old is trending on Twitter and you're worried it's because they died and then you click and it turns out they're totally healthy, they just have a sex tape out or something? That fear is what I now have all day every day about everyone, multiplied by however many people have died of COVID-19 this week. That fear is spreading faster than the virus.

Another robocall:

> *Dear New Rochelleans:*
>
> *Let's make some noise!*
>
> *Health-care and emergency service providers have been on the front lines in the fight against COVID-19, demonstrating extraordinary dedication, stamina, and bravery.*
>
> *To honor the dedication and bravery of health-care and emergency service providers, we're joining other communities to "Clap Because We Care." At seven p.m. this evening, please stand outside your house or open your window and applaud as loudly as you can. You can also use a whistle, blow a horn, bang a pan, or whatever works for you.*
>
> *Even apart physically, we can stand together in spirit and express our gratitude to those on the front lines in the fight against COVID-19.*
>
> *And remember to make some noise tonight at seven p.m.!*
>
> *Sincerely,*
>
> *Your Mayor*

Tovah: *Dude. I just heard what happened. Are you okay?*

Me: *It would have been nice to have heard from you yesterday*

Tovah: *I'm sorry. I was trying to reach my friend. This must be some other bitch*

Me: *I don't even know what to say right now*

Tovah: *I'm trying to console you after a horrible incident of police brutality*

Tovah: *They profiled you before when you were at Lord & Taylor*

Me: *There's other things going on. Quade is planning to*

Me: *ambush Diego at his party*

Tovah: *With what?*

Me: *I don't know but it's something bad. All Quade's messages have*

Me: *#diegoisoverparty*

Tovah: *We should go down there and stop it. A lot of people are talking about that party. It's more than just a party. I think something bad is going to happen.*

Me: *My mom's sick. We don't know with what but still*

Me: *You know I have asthma. I can't risk getting sick at some party to prevent who knows what from happening when my family is already dealing with*

Me: *too much shit*

Me: *Did you hear about Alvee the sandwich shop guy? He and one of his daughters have it. She's young but she has*

Me: *asthma too so*

Tovah: *I'm sorry but Alvee is dead*

Me: *No I talked to his daughter last night*

Tovah: *He's dead. It was just on the local news. I'm sorry*

Me: *Oh my god that sucks. His two daughters are around our age*

Tovah: *Our whole town is falling apart*

Tovah: *That's why we have to go to this party and stop whatever is happening*

Tovah: *Sometimes you can't think about yourself*

Me: *You think me and my family don't know that?*

Me: *You think my dad didn't know that?*

Tovah: *I'm sorry that came off wrong*

Me: *I'm thinking about a lot of things*

Me: *I'm thinking about my mom and*

Me: *hoping she's not sick and thinking about*

Me: *you and me and*

Me: *why we're not as close as we used to be*

Tovah: *Blame the pandemic*

Me: *The pandemic at least has us talking. You stopped having lunch with me*

Tovah: *We have lunch*

Me: *Not regularly*

Tovah: *Where is this coming from? I said I was sorry*

Tovah: *I know you're not thinking about yourself*

Me: *I've just had a lot of time to*

Me: *think. Anyone could die at any moment. I just want to be*

Me: *honest. Ever since that bitch shot my dad it hasn't been the same*

Me: *between us. I don't have a lot of friends. And you're my only old friend. Like they say you can't make old friends. It just makes me sick that we're not like we used to be because I know that can't be replaced. We lost prom. We lost graduation. We lost senior year. We lost four years of high school to the Mad King. Fuck the Great Gatsby we're the real Lost Generation. We're not even going to the same*

Me: *college on the same continent. I really needed you after my dad died. I couldn't talk to Mom about it because it just made her sadder. And then Kevin was there and I couldn't talk to her at all. I was having nightmares about that bitch shooting my dad. I'd see all the faces of the kids that used to tease her like the Hall of Faces in Game of Thrones. The alarm bells in the school would be ringing and my dad would be walking down the corridor with his palms up pleading for her to put down the gun. Then she'd just shoot him and I'd*

Me: *wake up. Same dream every night. My OCD and anxiety and depression got even worse. I was in whatever hell is beneath the sunken place. I know the sunken place is like a racial thing but you know what I mean. You know how they say Inuits have many words for snow but that may or not be true it may just be a story white people made up because they don't know any indigenous people? I think there should be a thousand words for loneliness. There's loneliness from not having a boyfriend or girlfriend. There's loneliness from not having any friends at all and nobody welcomes you when you enter a room and nobody gives a shit when you leave. There's loneliness from being in an outsider group like being gay or Black or Latinx or whatever in a place where there's nobody like you anywhere. There's existential loneliness where you don't even know what your purpose is and how you fit into the universe. We're all feeling a thousand kinds of loneliness and we don't have the words. There are divorces and suicides and PTSD and loneliness is at the root. Now that the whole world is literally in a depression I can see clearly. Loneliness is a virus. Social media can't cure loneliness any more than hydroxychloroquine cures COVID. Untreated loneliness is deadly. I have to vaccinate myself first or I'll infect the world. My dad didn't think about himself*

Me: *and it got him killed*

Tovah: *I used to tease her too*

Me: *Why do you say that*

Tovah: *Because I used to tease her too. I'm not proud*

Me: *No we were like the only ones who would sit with her at lunch. I even invited her to go to the Ozy with us to see a Miyazaki movie. Porco Rosso--that one about the flying pig*

Tovah: *You were nice to her. I was like the fucking mean girl from a Taylor Swift song*

Me: *I don't remember you ever being*

Me: *mean*

Tovah: *I only did it when you weren't around. When I was around other girls*

Tovah: *I used to tease her too*

Tovah: *Maybe if I didn't she wouldn't have brought that gun to school*

Tovah: *I'm sorry I never told you but I teased her too*

Me: *Why?*

Me: *Why?*

Me: *Why?*

Tovah: *Because I didn't want anyone else to know I was different like her*

Tovah: *That's the first time I've written that*

Tovah: *I didn't even write it in my diary*

Tovah: *You always told me other people might not understand like you did*

Tovah: *I was going to wait for college to come out to the world*

Tovah: *I figured if I moved far away I could be whoever I wanted*

Tovah: *Columbia isn't far enough. Australia is*

Tovah: *Till then I just wanted to fit in*

Tovah: *When the girls said she smelled I laughed with them. When they tossed tampons at her I tossed some too. I put a gerbil in her locker. I don't even know why. One of the girls from the lacrosse team told me to do it. She was throwing a party and I wanted to get invited*

Me: *I can't believe this*

Tovah: *Maybe if I had been a little nicer she wouldn't have done what she did*

Tovah: *It's been hard for me to look you in the eye since that day*

Tovah: *Maybe if we stop that party I can start to make up for it*

Me: *I can't believe this*

Me: *I can't believe that shit about Alvee*

Tovah: *I know I know I know*

Tovah: *I'm a bitch I'm a shit I suck I'm a bad friend*

Tovah: *Can u love me anyway*

Tovah: *Can u love me anyway*

Tovah: *Can u love me anyway*

I started writing something but then stopped. Tovah would have seen three dots appear and disappear. That was enough.

NEVER THOUGHT I'D SAY THIS but I miss school. I'm a good student, but I'm not a nerd. I'm not a teacher's pet. I only go to extra help after school when I absolutely need extra help. I've never been to one of my teacher's houses. I only occasionally raise my hand in class. I'm not a school spirit person. I've only dressed up on spirit day once, maybe twice, and that was only because Diego said it would help get him fired up. I run track but I only wear my jock gear on meet days. I've only ever belonged to one club and that's the Climate Change Club and I joined that because, well, the Earth.

But I miss school anyway. I miss walking into the cafeteria with a full tray and that warm feeling you get when you see your friends at the table waving you over. I miss coming home on the bus with the track team after a big win and the pressure's finally off and the music is on and you can just relax with your teammates the whole ride back. I miss the crowded halls between periods and literally bumping into someone and being a bit flustered before you realize you know them and you're gonna meet at Alvee's after school or maybe hang out in the park. I miss the satisfaction of getting a 100 percent on a test that I studied really hard for. I miss the feeling of being in a room of thirty people and knowing the name of every single person in it. I miss the feeling of people missing me when I miss class and giving me a hug or a "How are you feeling?" when I come back. I miss looking across the room at Tovah or Diego and with one glance knowing they got some joke nobody else in the room or even the world would have understood.

Maybe I don't miss school at all. I don't miss the standardized exams and the teaching to the test and the teachers who don't teach and give too much homework. I don't miss the sexist dress codes where girls get detention for showing too much leg but guys can dress in shorts too short for 1980s NBA teams and teachers don't say shit. I don't miss the droning announcements in the morning and the boring meet-the-teacher nights every semester and the principals and vice principals who stay in their offices all day making rules to govern our lives but don't know the first thing about how we live them. I don't miss the old, outdated textbooks or the classrooms or the uncomfortable desk seats or the smelly rat-infested building or the smelly rat-infested buses. I don't miss the girls who talk about lip gloss or the boys who boast about sports or the teachers who have checked out mentally or the substitute teachers who stare at your tits or the dirty windows or the tampons in the toilets or the condoms in the parking lot or old computers or old stairwells or old teaching methods or the old school building.

But I miss all the kids who just like me don't want to admit they're missing anything.

I poured myself a glass of lemonade, pulled out my phone, and sent Tovah a long text.

Me: *I'm sorry I wasn't a better ally and a better friend. Looking back I realized that when you came out to me in middle school it made me feel special that I had a gay friend and I should have let you share that specialness with the world. I realize now that every time you talked about a girl you liked I got in your way like one of those content filters on school computers that stop you from going to Pornhub but also lock you out of YouTube. You deserved a chance to find what I was always looking for. Dates and kisses that meant something and that thrill of waiting for your cell phone to buzz with a text from someone you love and who loves you right back. There were maybe girls you could have dated but I never supported you to take that chance and ask them out because I didn't want you to get embarrassed.*

I always told you I didn't want you to get hurt but now I realize I wasn't protecting you I was protecting myself. Love's a risk. Love's an unlocked door. You might get hurt. We all get rejected and confused. But if you don't take a risk looking for love you can never find yourself. I love you love you love you and no matter what school or continent you wind up on I hope we can always be friends

Tovah: [*Three dots appear then vanish*]

I woke up to the sound of coughing.

I wasn't really sleeping. I was in that half-sleep mode that's more exhausting than actually staying up. I was too worried about my mother.

Karhakonha was up watching TV.

There are more important things than living.

    Click.

    There are at least 273,880 cases of coronavirus in the US and 7,077 people have died, according to Johns Hopkins University's tally of cases in the country . . .

    Click.

    Listen, I will tell you a mystery! We will not all die, but we will all be changed . . .

Karhakonha noticed I was awake and turned off the TV. "Let's go check on your mom."

We went into the bathroom in the master bedroom. Kevin was sleeping on the tile floor and Karhakonha sat next to him on the closed toilet seat. My mom was sealed off behind the glass sliding door of the shower. She had stacked up like a dozen pillows. She must have been trying to sleep standing up. That book *Medical Apartheid* was discarded at her feet.

"How are you doing?" I asked.

She coughed. "Not good. Sorry I sent you out before. I didn't want you to see me like that. I was hallucinating. It was like Dad was standing right where you are. It felt as real as that." She took a thermometer out of her mouth. "I've been sucking on this all night and it's not giving me numbers I like."

Karhakonha opened his eyes wide. "That's an oral thermometer?"

"I'm just gonna pretend I never heard that," my mom said, then groaned. "My ribs are killing me. I feel like I coughed out my lungs last night."

"Karhakonha gave me a watch that can measure your vitals. Do you want that?"

"I think I know all I need to know," my mom sighed. "I'm officially sick."

Kevin woke up and stretched. "You ready to go to the hospital now?"

My mom shook her head. "There's nothing they can do for me there unless I need a ventilator. I do think you all should let me isolate in the bathroom by myself."

"You're behind glass," Kevin said. "The air vent is on. Besides, if you have it, we probably already caught it."

My mom began coughing again and this time didn't stop for a long time.

"Mom?"

"I'm feeling chills, and my muscles ache. These are COVID-19 symptoms all right. And this fever is something else. It feels like I'm being burned at the stake. Having a little trouble catching my breath. I wish you would all just let me alone for a second."

Kevin motioned for Karhakonha and me to step out of the bathroom. He closed the door behind us. "You and I need to talk," he said, pointing to me.

He drew closer and pulled out a ring from his pocket.

"Really?" I said. "You think this is the time?"

"I already told Karhakonha."

"My mom already turned you down twice," I said. "You

think the third time's the charm? Or are you hoping she's hallucinating so much she thinks you're my dad and says yes?"

Kevin put the ring back in his pocket. "Don't you get it? Yes, I love her. Yes, I'm doing this for me. But I'm also doing this for her and for you."

I laughed. "You're doing this for *me*? Explain that one."

"You're all she's got in this world, and she's all you've got. She doesn't want to leave you alone. Now, I'm thinking positively—she's gonna pull through. But you don't have any close relatives. I know the thought of leaving you alone is weighing on her. If there's anything I can do to unburden her mind so she can focus on getting well, I'm gonna do it."

"If you found a fucking job, that would probably make her a little less anxious, you ever think about that?"

What I said was harsh and totally uncalled for. But my emotions were running high. I couldn't control them. I could feel my anger starting to circle and feed into itself. But Kevin didn't get upset or flustered with me, he didn't even look hurt. All I saw was love in his eyes. Love for my mom. Love for me.

Karhakonha held up his tablet and Brother Anthony called in on Zoom.

My mom was coughing bad now. I could see her chest convulsing beneath her fuzzy purple robe. "We need to keep the vows short. I think I broke a rib."

"Let's get to it then," Brother Anthony said over Zoom. "Do you take this woman to be your lawfully wedded wife, to have and to hold, until death do you part?"

Kevin smiled. "100 percent, I do. You bet."

"And do you take this man to be your lawfully wedded husband, for richer or for poorer, in sickness and in health, until—"

"I do. And I hope you're serious about the 'in sickness and in health' part," my mom said.

"Then by the power vested in me by the Creator and the State of New York, I pronounce you husband and wife."

Karhakonha handed Kevin the ring. "You sure this is all legit?" Karhakonha asked.

"The only thing we have to do is get an appointment with the city clerk to take care of the paperwork," Brother Anthony declared. "Right now, you just need to kiss the bride."

Kevin held up the ring and pressed his lips against the glass of the shower door. Mom pressed her lips against the glass on the opposite side.

I threw some New Orleans–style dirty rice to celebrate. Instacart had substituted that for Uncle Ben's white rice last time we ordered groceries. It kind of added a festive Mardi Gras air to the whole thing. Karhakonha and I cheered and clapped.

My mom collapsed on the floor of the shower and began to spasm. She coughed up blood.

I ran into the other room and called the ambulance.

Brother Anthony insisted on staying on Zoom and praying while we waited for the EMTs to arrive. As they wheeled the gurney into the master bedroom, I could hear his voice calling out from Karhakonha's tablet: "*Behold the voice of the cry of the daughter of my people because of them that dwell in a far country: Is not the Lord in Zion?*"

My mom, holding a towel over her mouth, motioned for me to stand a few feet away and listen to her. "You can't come with me to the hospital."

My eyes filled with tears. "Of course I'm going!"

"The least healthy place in America right now is a hospital. I'm a health-care professional, I know. If you don't have COVID, if you go there, there's a good chance you'll get it. Stay home."

"Mom . . ."

The EMTs were outside the bathroom now. My mom held up her hand.

Brother Anthony preached on: "*Is not her king in her? Why have they provoked me to anger with their graven images, and with strange vanities?*"

"I need to tell you something," my mom said to me. "I know you've been eating yourself up since Dad died. I know you blame him for getting himself killed."

"That's not true."

"I was angry too. Before it happened, every time there was a school shooting, he and I would get into an argument. I always told him if something happens, run away. They don't pay you enough to get yourself shot. You know what he used to tell me?"

"*. . . The harvest is past, the summer is ended, and we are not saved . . .*"

"He used to laugh and say there are only two possibilities. If there isn't a God, then when I die there's nothing, and none of it matters anyway. It'll be just like it was before I was born, and how bad was that?"

"*. . . For the hurt of the daughter of my people am I hurt; I am Black; astonishment hath taken hold on me.*"

"But if there is a God, and I got killed trying to save somebody, he's gonna put a gold medal around my neck like Usain Bolt at the Olympics."

"*. . . Is there no balm in Gilead; is there no physician there? Why then is not the health of the daughter of my people recovered?*"

One of the EMTs cleared his throat. "Ma'am . . ."

"Just one sec," Mom said, then turned back to me. "Your father used to say to me—I'll never forget it—that living is . . ."

She began to cough. Horrible dry coughs, like sandpaper on steel. I didn't think a human body could make sounds like that. There was blood on her fuzzy purple robe. The EMTs put an oxygen mask on her and wheeled her out.

"Mom? Mom?"

When we got outside I was surprised to see a lot of our neighbors were standing outside of their houses. I felt like my family and I were actors putting on a play at the theater and our neighbors were the audience. They were standing in front of their front doors, on their front porches, on their front walks, in their driveways. I realized it must have been seven p.m. They had gathered for the nightly tribute to health-care workers. My neighbors began to clap and stomp and cheer. Children banged on pot and pans. Someone was blowing a damn vuvuzela.

The world's a stage, I thought. *My mom is a nurse and she's dying and you're cheering.*

The EMTs put my mom in the ambulance and turned the siren on. The night was filled with flashes of red and blue light. As the ambulance sped away, I couldn't tell if the sound in the air was the siren or my neighbors' cheering or my scream. Kevin hugged me and said Karhakonha and I had to wait at home but he was gonna drive Mom's car and wait outside the hospital and he didn't care if some cop stopped him for driving without a license. As he pulled out of the driveway and followed the ambulance away, I couldn't hold back the tears anymore.

Tovah called me on my cell. She never calls me on my cell.

"If you're calling about that text I sent you, now is not a good time," I said.

"I appreciated the note but this is not about that. How is your mom doing? I'm sending her R'fuah Sh'leimah, a prayer for healing."

"How did you hear about it?"

"I learned Hebrew for my bat mitzvah. Geth, you were there."

"I mean about my mom being sick."

"Some guy named Karhakonha texted me? He wanted to make sure you were okay."

"My stepbrother."

"This is your mom's boyfriend's stepkid? I thought his name sounded familiar. He's your stepbrother now?"

"It's a long story."

"That's connected to what I was calling about. Quade's party."

"Did you not hear what I said? My mom is sick! I'm not thinking about a goddamn party."

"You don't understand. We have to go down."

"I have asthma. That's an underlying condition—if I catch COVID that could kill me. I can't even go with my mom to the hospital! Everyone at that party has a death wish."

"That's kind of what Karhakonha and I discussed. Have you ever heard of A/B testing?"

"That's like advertising, right?"

"It originated as a way to study cures for diseases like scurvy. The idea is you give person A one treatment, and person B a slightly different treatment. Then you repeat the process with another set of two people using whichever treatment worked best. Businesses adopted the approach to fine-tune advertising. On the Internet, where you can test billions of people, A/B testing is incredibly powerful. Google once A/B tested shades of blue to find out which one customers liked best in ads and they boosted revenues by millions of dollars!"

"What does this have to do with anything?"

"A/B testing manufactures the most effective lies in the history of the world. It's just one part of this algorithmic assault on truth. The Internet's this lab of lies. They know how to keep you watching and clicking and buying. They know how to tell you the perfect lie. That's why right-wingers keep talking about doubling down, because they're caught in this extremist wormhole and the only option is acceleration. And the whole world is getting sucked in."

"Why are you telling me this?" I asked.

"Quade has been manufacturing lies on the Internet. You know the whole #diegoisoverparty? I found out exactly what Quade could be up to. You need to hear this."

I didn't have a car. I couldn't call an Uber. I didn't know if the buses were in service or if there even was a bus to that part of town at this time at night. Because of my mom, I had to isolate, but I had to act. I just knew I had to get down there, and get down there fast.

The streets were empty at first. Taymil Road was clear—not a jogger, not a stray dog, not a car. The moon was full and the stars were out and there were no clouds in the night sky. I was wearing my walking shoes and not my running sneakers, but it didn't matter. I was running full-out, race speed, opening my stride and pumping my arms. After what Tovah had told me, however fast I got there wouldn't be fast enough.

When I hit Quaker Ridge, I began to see other people on the street, so I slipped on my smiley-face mask. If my mom was sick, I didn't want to expose anyone else. Since I was running, it was hard to breathe as deeply as I needed through the mask, so my breaths came in huge heaving gulps. The people I passed weren't wearing masks but their faces looked like masks. They were frozen in extreme expressions like comedy/tragedy masks in Greek plays. In the moonlight, they looked like zombies. Pale faces, stumbling walks, all heading in one direction, but still seemingly aimless. Some of them were holding bottles of beer or flasks of alcohol. There were men and women, old folks and young ones. Many were wearing MAGA hats or cowboy hats or those German helmets with the single spike on top. One guy had a helmet with long curved horns like Loki.

Some of the people on the street were carrying signs saying things like *#Diegoisoverparty* and *#Diegoiscanceledparty* and *Adiós Diego*. But most of the signs weren't about Diego. Whatever

Quade had started had metastasized, mutated, and morphed into something else. As I ran through the streets I saw signs with other messages: *Quarantines Are for the Sick* and *My Virus My Choice* and *No Nanny State* and *I Am Essential* and *COVID-19 = COVID-1984*. Some signs lashed out at science: *Corona Is a Lie* and *The Cure Is the Disease* and *Science = Death*. Some hit economic themes: *Kill the Virus Not the Economy* and *Flatten the Curve Not the Job Market*. Some attacked the media: *The Press Is the Disease* and *Fake News Is Fatal*. Some were religious: *Jesus Is My Vaccine* and *Even Pharaoh Freed the Slaves after a Plague*. Some were absurd: *We Demand Haircuts* and *Don't Cancel My Golf Season* and *Use Both Sides of Toilet Tissue* and *Legalize Hugs*. Some were grim: *Give Me Freedom or Give Me COVID* and *Live Free and Die* and *Liberty Over Safety* and *Sacrifice the Weak*.

A river of people flooded off the road and into the woods. The woods were full of shadows. I could hear the steady pulse of music coming from somewhere deep in the dense forest of trees up ahead. There was the sound of laughter, a few piercing screams, and the smell of something burning. Nobody was wearing masks here either, but more than a few people were carrying guns. The shadows were long and deep and it was hard to see but it was easy to feel. All the things people had been hiding were silhouetted in the shadows. I saw the shadow of a big boy striking a small one. I saw the shadow of a man urinating into a bush. I saw the shadow of a couple groping each other against a tree. The forest was alive with cowardice and carelessness and jealousy and greed. I didn't know what was going on but I had to stop whatever was about to happen to Diego. I was getting closer to the heart of whatever this was.

"Geth?"

"Sally?"

I was face-to-face with the cashier from Open Market. She was spinning in between the trees with a blank look on her face. Her brown hair was matted with sweat and grass and twigs. She had a spliff in one hand and a handgun in the other. She was naked from the waist up. She was swaying back and forth like she was at an outdoor music concert. Her face was lined with shadows.

"I am lost in a forest of night," Sally babbled. "But if you're not afraid of the dark, you might find rosebushes under my cypresses."

"Are you okay?" I asked. "Do you need me to get you somewhere?"

"I got the COVID," she replied. "I'm good."

I took a step back.

Sally laughed. "Social distance all you want. It's not contagious. And if you do get it, it's not real. And if it is real, it comes from China. And China's a long way from here so we have nothing to worry about."

"Why are you here?"

"Most people aren't nuts, but groups, parties, countries, and eras go crazy all the time."

"Do you even know Diego?"

"Who?"

"This isn't the Diego-is-over party?"

"Honey, I just know I don't have a job anymore and I couldn't sit at home. Everyone who dances looks crazy to people who can't hear the music!"

Sally began to spin faster and faster. She moved toward me. I didn't want to touch her. I didn't know what she was capable of. I felt ashamed of my own response. I stumbled away from her and headed deeper into the woods toward the music, following the river of humans. I was lost now. There were people all around me; some of the faces were vaguely familiar but I couldn't put names to them. They seemed to take on the faces of animals. Racoons and squirrels and bears and bats. Red embers floated through the trees and I imagined they were the virus floating through the air to sear my lungs.

I didn't know if I should go forward or backward or stand still. I tripped and skinned my knee. I was turned around now and people were heading in different directions. I didn't know which way I should go. I started one way and then, thinking better of it, headed the other. Women looked at me with anger. Men leered at me. A boy laughed and threw a stick at my face. I started to run. Someone grabbed me from behind.

"Stay away!" I said. "My mom could be sick."

I found myself looking right into Diego's eyes.

I was standing with Diego, Tovah, and Karhakonha in a dark wood and I had no idea where we were headed next or what we were going to do. They had driven down and had arrived before me.

Diego was furious. "You guys shouldn't have come."

"We had to come," Tovah said. "We're friends. Plus, I wasn't going to miss *Lord of the Flies: The Live Edition.*"

"How did you locate me?" I asked.

Karhakonha tapped my biohacking watch. "There's a tracker on this, remember?"

Diego nodded at me. "Now that we've seen each other, you can all leave."

"We're not leaving without you," Tovah said. "What does Quade have on you? You can trust us, we're your friends. And by the way, since we're sharing—I'm gay."

Diego hugged Tovah. "I already knew, Tovah. I'm happy for you."

Karhakonha smiled. "I met you five minutes ago and I got that."

"So what's your secret, Diego?" I asked. "Quade plans to tell the whole town something major about you tonight. Is it about sex, steroids, HGH, cheating on your admissions form, smoking crack, abusing animals, dumping toxins into public parks, kidnapping children, S&M with circus clowns—what?"

Diego looked a little stunned. "You think all those things are possibilities?"

"I was just presenting some options."

"The only secret I have is I'm quitting football after high school. I was never a football player anyway, I was just good at it. I want to go to Columbia and major in Theater."

"That's why you knew about the admissions video!" I said. "We're both gonna be Lions!"

Diego leaned toward me. "I was going to tell you. I was going to tell everyone. Until I decided where I was going, I couldn't figure out where *we* were going. As a couple, I mean. Now I know we have a shot." He winked and flashed me that Christmas-tree smile that I love. Then he pulled back and addressed everyone: "Quade can have the QB gig at Naverton. If he wants CTE, that's on him."

I felt a warmth spread across my face as Diego's words sunk it. He thought we had a shot? As a couple? But I had to keep my focus. "You've got to tell Quade you're out. Stop him from doing whatever he's going to do."

Diego waved us all away. "Don't you get it? I don't care what Quade says about me. I appreciate your concern, but this isn't your fight. I came here to face up to whatever he's got."

I shook my head. "My mom's in the hospital because she didn't run away from other people's problems. My dad's in the ground because he didn't run from other people's fights. It would be a hell of a thing if I was the first coward in my family."

Just then the music cut off.

"I think the show is about to begin," Tovah said.

We walked into a clearing. Protesters and partygoers mixed, with no distinction between them. People mingled and laughed and chanted and threw footballs and beach balls and Frisbees. I saw a few guys from the lacrosse team. I spotted

Alice from AP Gov dancing in the firelight. At the center of the clearing was a huge bonfire, and in front of that, an open metal drum. A bare-chested man with red hair gripped a baseball bat with two hands and stirred whatever was in the drum. I recognized the guy—it was Officer Redhead. As he stirred, whatever witches brew he was preparing bubbled and he threw his head back and howled at the stars.

All at once, everyone's phones buzzed and chirped and rang.

"What's going on?" Tovah asked.

Diego looked at his phone. "It's a clip from my Zoom session with my sports psychiatrist. Quade must have gotten it somehow. But how the hell did he hack my Zoom account?"

"What's your password?" Karhakonha asked.

"I'm not gonna tell you that."

"You're capping. The horse has left the barn, bro."

"QB1," Diego said.

"Your Zoom password is QB1?"

"Yes."

"I don't think we're gonna need Veronica Mars to crack this case," Karhakonha said.

The clip was short. In it, Diego was talking about his mother coming to this country from Cuba: "*No money, no papers, things were rough for her.*"

"This makes your family look good!" Tovah said. "You came from Cuba and manifested from nothing!"

Diego looked grim. "You're missing the point. My mother is an undocumented immigrant. Now that this is out there, she'll get deported—and I'll be forced out too."

"Quade did all this just so he could go to Naverton and steal your job as humpback?" I exclaimed.

"I'm a quarterback, but yeah, looks like it."

Karhakonha looked up from his tablet. "It's about more than that. I've been tracking the messages your boy Quade has been sending out online. This started off as a party where he was gonna leak some info so he could get that QB gig. Now he's turned it into an antiquarantine rally to take down the whole town. He thinks if he can get everyone riled up enough, they'll have to open up all the businesses again—including his dad's movie theater."

A cheer went up at the front of the crowd, as Quade stood in front of the bonfire and the metal drum/cauldron. He had a megaphone in one hand. He surveyed the audience, put the megaphone to his lips, and roared, "Bat soup!"

A line of shirtless guys approached the cauldron, which had started bubbling over. I could see now that there was a gooey foaming brew inside, thick with what looked like bat parts—bat heads, bat wings, entire bat bodies. As the red-haired cop stirred the pot, each shirtless guy stuck two hands into the cauldron and, screaming in pain, scooped the soup into their mouths, chomping down on whatever parts they had come away with.

Diego began murmuring something to himself: "'Alas, poor country! Almost afraid to know itself. It cannot be called our mother, but our grave.'"

"What's that from?" I asked.

Diego smiled sadly. "Something I memorized from an old production."

Quade raised his arms above his head. The shirtless guys lifted their arms yowling and screeching. Rioters raised a Confederate flag, a red MAGA banner, and a yellow pennant reading, Don't Tread On Me, with an image of a coiled snake. Among the trees, foxes had gathered, silent and wary, eyes glittering like yellow lights. The sky was clear and the stars were out and there was no rain, but two lightning bolts knifed across the sky.

"We're here to talk about hypocrisy!" Quade declared. "People saying one thing and doing another. Hypocrisy is why we're all here, right? Well, like my man Nietzsche said, 'No power can be maintained when it is only represented by hypocrites!'"

The crowd cheered, holding up hands and fists and foot-balls and Frisbees.

Quade raised an open palm and quieted the crowd. Two of the shirtless dudes dragged a crate in front of the bonfire and Quade stepped on top of it and lifted his megaphone. I noticed something scrawled in German across the planks of the crate: "Blickt der Abgrund auch in dich hinein." From the forest, the eyes of the foxes burned bright.

"They called him All-American. He was your football hero for three years. I was born right here, and he got the glory. You all got the clip, right? He wasn't even supposed to be here!"

The crowd jeered.

Quade continued: "It's unfair, isn't it? We work hard, we play by the rules, and other people cheat and steal and they get everything. The system is rigged. I don't even recognize America anymore. I used to wear a mask. My iPhone's got face ID, and when I used to wear the mask, when I turned my phone on, it didn't recognize me either. Because the mask isn't us. The mask isn't America. And now they tell us to stay home. They've got the jobs where they can Zoom or telecommute or day-trade. They've got three or four homes to choose from in New York or New Jersey or the Hamptons. We have to leave our living rooms if we want to make a living. We can't get paid unless we go outside the house. If you're asking us to not make a living, you're asking us to die. Is that fair? I'm telling you, it's a rigged system. Then they want to say that *we're* the ones who don't believe in science. Well, I believe in econom-ics. Ain't that a science? And economics tells me if you can't make enough money to pay your bills, you die. More people will die from economics this year than will die from corona-virus. That's a scientific fact. Hypocrisy, that's all it is. And that's why we're here. We're not going to stay in our homes. We're not going to social distance ourselves. We're gonna get close enough to see the whites of their eyes. That's right, I said it. We're at war with this virus and you can't win a war sitting at home with Netflix and chill. They are lying to you about the dangers. No teenagers are dying from COVID-19. That's why it's called COVID-19. Cause nobody nineteen and under needs to give a fuck.

"The people who are getting sick have underlying conditions. They have diabetes or heart disease or some other fucking thing. You know what the basic underlying condition is? They're not fucking healthy to begin with. Or they're old. Or they're on some gushy-ass pussy bullshit. We can't let a few people who are dying anyway kill the whole country. That's why we're here. We're fighting hypocrisy. We're fighting for freedom. We're not running from the virus anymore—we *are* the virus. We're gonna spread it around our town, around the country, around the world. We're literally going viral. If everyone's sick, then everyone's healthy. Infect as many people as you can. Hug someone next to you, kiss them, cough on them, I don't give a fuck.

"This whole thing started with some fucking Chinaman eating bat soup in Wuhan. That's why it's the Chinese Flu, though it's not politically correct to call it that. That's why I call it the Kung-Flu, though it's *definitely* not politically correct to call it that. We're gonna take it back to where it started. That's why we made enough bat soup for everyone. *Double, double, toil, and trouble; fire burn and cauldron bubble. Cool it with a baboon's blood, then the charm is firm and good!* Bat soup for everyone! Soup for you! Today is our day. Whoever accuses us of something, we accuse them of the same thing. Whenever they say we're lying, we repeat what we just said a hundred more times until they get sick of correcting us. Whatever they say we're doing wrong, we do it right out in the open, because if everyone can see what we're doing it can't be wrong, can it?

"This isn't about tomorrow—I don't care about deficits or global warming. This isn't about yesterday—I don't give a damn about reparations or universal basic income or any of that gushy-ass pussy bullshit. This is about us being young and strong and in the majority. At some point, they're gonna take over. But not today. The people outside the wall. The people in the welfare lines. They're gonna leave the lines and leap the wall. But not today. We need to take all we can get and lock in our gains. Nietzsche once said, 'What is the truth but a lie agreed upon?' He also said—"

"Hey QB2!"

A football whizzed through the air in a perfect tight spiral and slammed Quade right in the face. He collapsed into the dirt between the cauldron and the fire.

"Touchdown!" Diego called out, raising his arms in the air after his throw.

The crowd began to surge toward Diego.

"Somebody better do something," Tovah said.

"What can anyone do?" I asked.

"We need to get out of here," Karhakonha said.

"Geth," Tovah said to me, "you need to keep in mind the most important thing I learned after studying every speech ever written to write a valedictory speech I never got to give."

"What?"

"The most original thing you can be is yourself."

I pushed my way through the crowd toward the bonfire. I picked up the megaphone from the dirt where Quade had dropped it.

"Hello?"

There was a blast of feedback. People in the crowd covered their ears.

"Sorry. I'm Geth. Gethsemane Montego. Some of you know me. I'm sure a lot more of you knew my dad. He was that security guard at New Rochelle High who disarmed that school shooter three years ago. He saved some of you. Or maybe he saved one of your kids, or one of your cousins, or one of your neighbors. He couldn't save himself, though, cause you all know he died from his wounds at the scene. The TV and the papers called him a hero. I even got a call from the governor. I got one from Beyoncé, which was even bigger. I've never said this before, but for a long time I was angry about what my dad did. I mean, who goes running toward an AR-15 when everyone else is running away? I was a teenage girl—I needed him at home. Why wasn't he thinking about me? But now, seeing all of you, I realize he *was* thinking about me. He was thinking that he loved me so much, he wanted to make sure all the other boys and girls got to go home to their parents. Do you see what I'm saying here? If this virus has taught us anything, it's that we're all connected. The things that we do can help other people or they can hurt them. When you act by yourself and for yourself, you're just so small. But when you act together, you can do anything. New Rochelle had an outbreak of COVID-19 that was maybe worse than anywhere in the world, but we have acted together and have started flattening the curve. People think their lives are charted out, that we have to be this or that. We *can* flatten the curve. We don't have to be what charts and graphs say we're gonna be. But if we want to be our best selves we can't just be about ourselves. That's why my dad ran back into that gunfire. That's why all of you should go home."

The crowd began to murmur.

"Please, just go home."

Just then, everyone's phones started going off again. A number of people, mostly teenage boys, pumped their fists and ran off. As the crowd began to thin out, others followed. Very soon, the clearing was all but empty.

"What happened?" I asked.

"Great speech," Karhakonha said. "I sent everyone a little incentive to go home. Free credits to spend in *Xamaica*. I got them when we hacked in. They're only good for tonight."

Even the foxes in the forest had begun to scatter.

"This has been a long night," Tovah said.

"This has been a long spring and it's only early April," Diego said.

I sighed. "It's definitely not over yet."

HAD A DREAM last night.

Zero o'clock. Empty halls. Empty classrooms.

Through the windows I see fires in the distance. Overturned cop cars. Fists in the air.

When I turn the corner I see a pool of water.

I look into the water and I see a star.

That's when I woke up.

'VE BEEN WRITING LESS and thinking more.
You may not hear from me for a minute.

<u>Geth's Post-Pandemic Playlist (to be played when this is over)</u>
To Practice Only This, L-Boogie
Euphoria, BTS
Alright, Kendrick Lamar
Someday, The Strokes
Good as Hell, Lizzo
I Don't Need Your Love (feat. Izuka Hoyle), *Six*
Do What I Want, Lil Uzi Vert
Please, Please, Please Let Me Get What I Want, The Smiths
Final Hour, Lauryn Hill
Look Back at It, A Boogie Wit da Hoodie
Just like Heaven, The Cure
I Do (feat. SZA), Cardi B
Thank U, Alanis Morissette
Across the Universe, Fiona Apple
First Day of My Life, Bright Eyes
Work (feat. Drake), Rihanna
My Queen Is Nanny of the Maroons, Sons of Kemet
The Morning of Our Lives, Jonathan Richman & the Modern Lovers
Selfless, The Strokes
Time Will Tell, Bob Marley and the Wailers
Feast on Your Life, L-Boogie

THEY KILLED HIM with a knee to the neck. I started shaking when Tovah sent me the video. The sting of tears came to my eyes and I felt a cold knot in my gut. I started shaking because I had seen it before. I thought of Officer Redhead who had profiled me outside of Lord & Taylor and broken into my home and bruised my face and terrorized my family. Now cops had killed another Black person, with a knee to the neck. I thought of that one line from George Orwell's *1984*: "If you want a picture of the future, imagine a boot stamping on a human face—forever." This felt like that— brutal and infinite. There had been so many incidents of cops brutalizing Black people and it had gone on for so long I had to google to keep the details all straight in my mind.

Eric Garner, forty-three, July 2014. Cops in Staten Island sat on his head and choked him out. His final words: "I can't breathe."

Michael Brown, eighteen, August 2014. A cop in Ferguson, Missouri, fired twelve shots at him, striking him six times and killing him even though a witness said his hands were raised. His final words: "I don't have a gun. Stop shooting."

Tamir Rice, twelve, November 2014. A cop saw him playing with a toy gun in a public park in Cleveland and in less than two seconds made the decision to shoot and kill him. He didn't have time for any last words. "I feel you when I breathe," his mother said about Tamir after his death.

Sandra Bland, twenty-eight, July 2015. After landing a new job, she was stopped by cops for an alleged traffic infraction and was found hanged to death in a jail cell in Hempstead, Texas. Her last words: "How did switching lanes with no signal turn into all of this?"

Christian Taylor, nineteen, August 2015. Cops caught the Angelo State University sophomore inside a car dealership and shot him dead. One of his last tweets: "I don't wanna die too young."

And now George Floyd, forty-six, May 2020. They killed him with a knee to the neck. His last words were the same as Eric Garner's six years ago. "I can't breathe."

All the victims were Black and unarmed. All the killers were white cops. The police and the press like to call killings like these "officer-involved" but that's some Orwellian garbage because the officers aren't just involved, they're doing the killing. I don't even want to go into what the Black victims were accused by cops of doing because it was bullshit. Like cops said Eric Garner was selling untaxed cigarettes, which may or may not have been true but in any case was some bullshit. Sandra Bland got pulled over for failing to signal a lane change, which is not even a thing for white drivers and may not even have happened. George Floyd was killed because cops suspected he was trying to spend a fake twenty-dollar bill. Again, that sounds like some bullshit. And number two, you're telling me a human life is only worth twenty dollars?

Diego was as furious as I was about the killing.

Diego: *Remember when they were going after my man Colin Kaepernick for kneeling at football games to protest police brutality?*

Diego: *Now cops are kneeling on our necks. Is anybody gonna go after them for that?*

The list of Black victims of police brutality goes on and on. Trayvon Martin. Philando Castile. Breonna Taylor. I can't even list all the victims of racial violence in this country because every single Black person in America has been a target of racial violence in this country. Slave ships were racial violence with sails. Plantations were racial violence on land. Wealth inequality is racial violence in the pocketbook. Sean Bell. Kendra James. Amadou Diallo. The only reason why we're talking about it more now is because cell phones are documenting it. You can't gaslight us anymore. That Ingrid Bergman shit is played out. Atatiana Jefferson. Michael Stewart. Freddie Gray. We've always known racial violence is real. But now America sees it's real because it's trending.

ZOOM MEETING
Ms. Swain is inviting you to a scheduled Zoom meeting.
Topic: AP Gov - Period C
Time: June 1, 2020 12:30 P.M. Eastern Time (US and Canada)
Join Zoom Meeting
Meeting ID: 985 127 8765
Password: newrostrong

Ms. Swain: "A week ago, a gentleman by the name of George Floyd was arrested by police in Minneapolis. When I saw the video I couldn't believe I was watching what I was watching. Usually police shootings happen in a finger snap. Then maybe they can say it's an accident or something. In this situation, the white police officer was kneeling on a Black man's neck for six, seven, eight, almost nine minutes. It was basically torture. I know we're studying FDR and the New Deal, but I wanted us to break away and focus on the history that we're living through right now. I want to talk about the incident and the reaction, with all the people who have been looting and rioting. What do you think? You can unmute yourself."

Diego: "I want to say two things. It's always Black people and people of color getting killed. And I feel like if it hadn't been filmed, people would have excused it and said, 'Oh, he was resisting arrest.' Because it's on video they can't say that. But if it wasn't, they would start saying that."

Ms. Swain: "I agree with you one trillion percent if there was such a thing. Back when I was a kid, these things happened and the cop's word always won out. Now we have some objective proof at least. It doesn't always help, but they can't just gaslight us and say cops would never do that. We can see what they're doing. We can rewind it. We can pause it."

Spencer: "I think we have to separate the looters from the protesters. Protesting is your right as, like, an American. The looters, in my opinion, have nothing to do with the protesters. I was reading an article yesterday or the day before that said the riots were started by right-wing groups who want to take away the message from the protesters."

Ms. Swain: "Do you think the officer killed George Floyd on purpose or was it an accident?"

Alice: "I definitely think it was just an accident. Being a cop is a difficult job."

Ms. Swain: "What makes you say that?"

Alice: "My uncle is a cop. The fact is, most of the suspects are colored people."

Diego: "People of color."

Alice: "That's what I said."

Me: "That's not what you said. And I saw you at that crazy event that Quade threw."

Alice: "I wasn't there."

Diego: "I saw you too."

Tovah: "So did I."

Alice: "I'm telling you, I wasn't there."

Diego: "You and Quade and the rest of them think you can get away with everything because his father has all those lawyers—"

Ms. Swain: "I don't know what this is about, but let Alice speak."

Alice: "Thank you. Cops get called names when they're just doing their job. Most people of color are killed by other people of color. People need to talk more about that."

Tovah: "And most whites are killed by other whites. Talk about that."

Me: "Anyone who would kneel on someone's neck for almost nine minutes has done this before. You wouldn't do that to a dog. Did you all see that clip of the white lady who called the cops on a Black man bird-watching in Central Park? They ended up taking her dog away because it looked like it got a little strangled in her leash while she was dialing 911. Dogs get better treatment than Black people. Look at that cop's face when he gets off George Floyd's neck. A Black man is dead at his feet and the cop has zero emotion. The cop's not wearing a mask but he *is* wearing a mask, you know? This isn't a bad day for him. It's just another day."

Ms. Swain: "So what's the solution? How do we stop deaths like this from happening?"

Diego: "There's no solution. This has been going on for four hundred years. It's like AIDS, or maybe COVID-19. There's no cure. You just have to manage the condition."

Ms. Swain: "That's bleak."

Tovah: "I disagree. The solution is obvious. We have to get psycho cops off the street, and educate the police and the public about things like profiling and excessive force. Maybe if the police force was more diverse, with more women and more Black and brown people, this wouldn't happen."

Alice: "Cops aren't bad people. They're just dealing with bad people and bad things are gonna happen. But we need them there or we have rioting and looting like you're seeing now."

Ms. Swain: "That sounds like this old movie, *A Few Good Men*. Jack Nicholson plays this crazy general who justifies his abusive behavior by saying that society needs guys like him to keep the country safe."

Diego: "I saw that movie on Netflix. He gets arrested in the end, right? He's the bad guy."

Alice: "Cops are not the bad guys. All lives matter, especially blue ones."

Me: "Alice, you are a racial Nell."

Ms. Swain: "Okay, okay, I want you guys to be civil, but I'm going to allow that comment from Geth because it's the first pop culture reference I've understood in this class in a long time."

Me: "Alice, I know Quade's your boyfriend now and everything, but you don't have to drink the Kool-Aid."

Alice: "Quade didn't do anything wrong. That's why he didn't get in any trouble."

Diego: "ICE came to my home. That's on Quade. And that's on you if you believe his side."

Alice: "Who would you have us believe? These so-called activists? They're hypocrites. The same people who told us to social distance and shut down our businesses and turn our lives upside down are now in the streets violating all the restrictions they told us we had to follow."

Ms. Swain: "Okay, I didn't quite follow all that but we have to move on. I know you guys read *The Plague* in English. You know the hysteria that a plague can cause. Do you see a connection between the virus and people acting out? Not cops, I'm talking about looters. We've been cooped up for a few months now. I know you also read *Lord of the Flies*. Same kind of thing. People get isolated and they turn on each other. Is that what we're living through now?"

Me: "I don't think it's about isolation. It's about race. The cops are racist. The system is racist. Racism is why the president got elected. Racism is why Black and brown people are getting infected and dying from COVID more than whites. Racism is why that officer sat on that guy's neck for nine minutes. He wouldn't have done that if Reese Witherspoon had passed a fake twenty-dollar bill by mistake in Beverly Hills. There aren't a lot of clips going viral of cops choking out blondes. I guess that's why that movie was called *Legally Blonde*. Cause it's always legal to be blond. Being Black is a felony waiting to happen. We know it's about race but we don't want to talk about race or deal with it and so it keeps happening."

Ms. Swain: "Geth, we're almost at the end of class and you are the first person to really bring up racism. So what's the solution? What can we do to solve our problems?"

'M GOING TO MARCH.

But first I'm going viral. But not viral in a bad COVID-19 way viral.

A couple weeks after my speech in the woods, a clip of me started getting some attention on the Internet. The clip didn't go BTS viral with millions of views or anything, but it went Westchester viral. People around the county saw it and took note. I began to hear from groups that wanted to hear my voice, wanted me to help organize. At first I resisted the resistance because I didn't think that speaking out was really who I was. Then I decided even if it wasn't, it was who I could be. The woods had made that possible. I felt a little bit like a low-key Malala or Greta Thunberg or those Parkland kids. When I saw the George Floyd video I knew I had to get involved, and Tovah, Diego, and Karhakonha were all in too.

We called everyone we knew. I asked everyone from the track team and the Climate Change Club and English class. Tovah asked friends of hers from Beth El Synagogue. Diego recruited players from the football team. Karhakonha called kids from his old school. I thought people would be too scared to go out because of the virus. I thought they'd be worn down from the quarantine and the fact that our whole senior year had been trashed after prom and graduation got canceled. But it was just the opposite. There was a ton of pent-up energy. People all around the world saw the video of that white cop kneeling on that Black neck and they were angry. People saw the other protests on TV, in Philadelphia, Boston, Tulsa, Tallahassee, Los Angeles, and New York City. People saw the structure fires, the overturned cars, the smashed store windows. I saw smug commentators on Fox screaming about the looting. I nearly screamed back at the screen: *You all looted us from Africa! Every Black person here is stolen property. And the crime is still in progress. You're stealing our rights. You're stealing our jobs. You're stealing our health. You're stealing our lives! So now we're going to march.*

We got a great crowd. This is the part you're not going to believe but it's absolutely true. The BTS Army helped give us an army. K-pop fans around the world realized early on that they had the best network for raising awareness about anything. So we stopped with hashtags like #btsfanart and #armyalwaysloveBTS and started up with #GeorgeFloyd and #BlackLivesMatter. When the FBI and local police asked people to snitch on each other and send them photos and videos of protesters so authorities could monitor them, K-pop stans crashed their websites with BTS concert footage. BTS and K-pop social media accounts that used to follow concert dates and video drops started blasting out times and locations for protest rally meetups. This wasn't exactly the same army that General Patton beat back fascists with in World War II, but it was the army we had and we went with it.

So we marched. We marched up North Avenue from midtown to in front of City Hall. There were young people and old people in the crowd. There were Black, brown, Asian, white, and every mix you can imagine. Everyone seemed to be there. I saw Stacey from my track team and Spencer from AP Gov. The mayor showed up, and my high school principal. I saw Cal from the barbershop and Doreema from the beauty shop and Sal from the pizza place. A few cops joined the protesters and held up signs and wore T-shirts supporting the march over their uniforms. Alvee's Caribbean Sandwich Shop had a booth set up and Al's daughter Erica sold sandwiches with proceeds going to victims of police violence.

My mom was back from the hospital and recovering at home but she didn't have her strength back yet, so she couldn't come to the march. She told us she had been getting texts and e-mails from white classmates from college, not asking about her health, but wanting to talk about their own white guilt about race. "It's like talking to me is the eleventh step of some twelve-step program of racial reconciliation they're on," my mom said. "I tell them they need to stop just talking and start really acting." That's why she wanted all of us, including Kevin and Karhakonha, to go to the march.

We had filed an official complaint about Officer Redhead but he was still on the force. "I still see that cop's face when he busted down our front door," my mom told me. "If we can't stop him, maybe we can stop others like him."

At the march, there were spray-painted signs and printed signs and signs written in magic marker. There were wordy signs:

A riot is the language of the unheard —MLK
That's not a chip on my shoulder, that's your foot on my neck
—Malcolm X
Those who make peaceful revolution impossible will make violent revolution inevitable —JFK

There were simple signs:

Black Lives Matter
Never Again Is Now
Enough

There were signs from a white perspective:

White Parents for the Prevention of Karens
White Silence = White Violence
I will never understand but I will always stand

There were funny signs:

Never Liked Pigs, They're Haram Anyway
I'd like to speak to the manager of systemic racism, please.

And there were signs that made you think:

Racism Is a Pandemic Too
We're not trying to start a race war, we're trying to end one
Racism is so American that when you protest it people think you're protesting America.

People say protesters are angry, but I wasn't angry. I was feeling something bigger than that, and more righteous. Rage might be the right word. But there was something more than that too. There's a joy in protesting that I had to feel to understand. You hear it in *Les Misérables* when they're marching through the streets belting out "Do You Hear the People Sing?" You see it in *Rent* when the characters dance on the tables and sing "La Vie Bohème." You witness it in *Hamilton* when Hamilton and his rebel buddies raise a glass to revolution in "The Story of Tonight." I know those are just Broadway musicals and this is real life, but two of those three shows are based on history.

Standing shoulder to shoulder with my friends and classmates and neighbors and like-minded strangers, I was alive in a way I never had been before. I had lived life so anxious about school and money and whatever. Now I had placed myself in maximum danger from the cops and the virus and the Night King and there was nothing for me to worry about anymore because all my fears were right there in the open. When you share your life, even just a little bit, with other people, your life becomes theirs and theirs becomes yours and for a moment you're a multitude and you're bigger than you've ever been before.

Brother Anthony gave a speech at the march that had people raising their hands and jumping up and down like they were in church. Maybe it was a little extra but I liked it a lot.

"Since this pandemic began, billionaires in America have gotten more than half a trillion dollars richer. Hold on now! Since this pandemic began, Black and brown people have disproportionately been unemployed, incarcerated, and infected. Hold on now! What does the prophet say about profits in the book of James? 'Come, you rich, weep and howl for the miseries that are coming upon you. Your riches have rotted and your garments are moth-eaten. Your gold and silver have corroded, and their corrosion will be evidence against you and will eat your flesh like fire. You have laid up treasure in the last days. Behold, the wages of the laborers who mowed your fields, which you kept back by fraud, are crying out against you, and the cries of the harvesters have reached the ears of the Lord of hosts. You have lived on Earth in luxury and in self-indulgence. You have fattened your hearts in a day of slaughter. You have condemned and murdered the innocent one, who was not opposing you!' Hold on now!"

After that Brother Anthony led everyone in prayers, and after him there was a long roster of speakers who said forgettable things on a memorable day. I don't even remember what I said. I didn't speak long. But I remember what I felt. I remember what I saw. I was happy to look out over the hundreds of people in front of City Hall and see that everyone was wearing a mask. There were bandannas tied over mouths and noses, N95 masks, powder-blue surgical masks, dust masks, paisley masks, you name it. Yes, coming together was a risk, but the greater risk was not coming together and letting everything keep going to hell.

People used to wear masks to conceal themselves from other people. Now we were wearing masks to reveal ourselves. We had masks on so we could come together as a community after being quarantined for so long. I can't quite remember, but I think when I was giving my speech I said something like that. It's kind of trivial I know, but seeing my friends and neighbors and family in masks made me think of that great TV show *Watchmen*. We were all masked avengers now. Going out into the world was now an act of bravery. Comic book heroes always have an origin story, where some experiment goes sideways and gives someone superpowers. COVID-19 was supposed to kill us but it has made us stronger, and made us wear masks. We've used the virus to become superheroes.

COVID-19 Human Challenge Trial
Human challenge trials deliberately expose volunteers to diseases in order to test new vaccines and other treatments. Over the years, they've been employed to study such maladies as malaria, typhoid, and cholera. Many researchers believe that human challenge trials could accelerate the development of a COVID-19 vaccine, which would potentially save millions of lives. We're putting together just such a challenge trial and we are actively looking for volunteers. Please sign up below if you would be interested in participating. The risk will be substantial, but the reward could be a better and safer world for billions of people.

A lot of people, including white people, have concerns about vaccines. Most of those people are being stupid and they should just listen to the science. But some Black people also have concerns about vaccines. They have their reasons and some of them are good ones. But they're not good enough to give up on science.

That book my mom had been reading called *Medical Apartheid* broke it all down. When I picked it up, a dried, flattened rose fell out of the pages into my hand. There was an inscription on the inside cover in my dad's handwriting: *To Phillis.* He loved giving books and flowers. I had to read it after that. I found out that during slave times, white physicians in the South experimented on enslaved Black people. Then, starting in the 1930s, white government researchers studied Black men with syphilis in Tuskegee, Alabama, without treating them or even letting them know they were sick so doctors could follow the course of the disease—and the twisted experiment went on for forty years. The so-called Tuskegee Study became like this infamous thing. I remembered there was even a reference to it in *Text Z for Zombie*. Then there's Henrietta Lacks, a Black Baltimore stay-at-home mom and cancer patient who died in 1951. Without her knowledge or consent, white doctors used her cells to develop life-saving medicines, including the Salk polio vaccine, which made lots of drug companies rich but didn't make her a cent.

What a lot of people don't know is that Black people invented vaccines, and we're still leading the way in the area. Back in the 1700s, this enslaved African called Onesimus told Cotton Mather, a plantation owner in the Massachusetts colony, that when he was a kid in Africa, the pus of a smallpox victim had been pricked into his arm with a thorn and that now he was immune—and that vaccination was a thing back where he was from. Mather urged his fellow colonists to try the technique, and years later George Washington had his entire army inoculated. I saw online that one of the National Institutes of Health's scientists leading the search for a COVID-19 vaccine is a Black woman—Dr. Kizzmekia Corbett. She was named after Kizzy, an enslaved woman fighting for her freedom in that book *Roots*.

I love Doreema, but I remember getting my hair done in her shop last year and hearing her say she didn't trust vaccines because white people did Black people dirty in the Tuskegee experiments. "I'm not letting the government inject anything into me and mine except a tax refund into my account. Mmmm-mmm!" she had declared. I'm sure she's going to feel the same way about the COVID-19 vaccine whenever it's ready. I remember what Quade said about that German philosopher Nietzsche, about how there are no facts, only opinions, and how there is no truth, only the say so of whoever's in power. Fuck that. There is science. And if we are going to beat this pandemic, we need to follow the science. We don't need to blindly follow scientists—they can be as racist as politicians and cops—but we need to trust that the scientific method, which my mom told me was pioneered in ancient Egypt, is worth following.

Maybe there *is* something I can do to help.

M Y PERIOD WAS STARTING and I was feeling a little crampy and I needed some fresh air. I figured a run might help.

My mom was still getting her strength back and spent most of her days and nights recuperating in the master bedroom.

I actually hate that term *master bedroom* now that I think about it. It probably goes back to slavery and it's one of those words that should just be retired, like *niggardly*. I know if you look it up it says "alteration of earlier *nigon*, probably of Scandinavian origin." But you know that shit's straight up from slave times. And don't get me started on the word *denigrates*.

Anyway, moneywise, things are tight. The hospital is threatening to cut off my mom's salary unless she comes back to work soon, and Kevin still hasn't found a job. But Karhakonha and I got paying gigs pitching in at Alvee's Caribbean Sandwich Shop until Erica's sister Lisa has fully recovered, and maybe after that too. I'm nervous about working in a restaurant because those places are pretty much ground zero these days, but I've got to make that cash money some kind of way.

"It feels like the world is upside down," I said to Karhakonha as I got ready for a run. "Our parents are unemployed but we're starting jobs."

Karhakonha smiled. "You know the Kanyen'kehà:ka have this legend about the first person on Earth. She used to live in the clouds in a world above our world. But then she got pushed through a hole in the sky. She grabbed at the roots of the strawberry and tobacco and corn as she fell, which is why we have those plants today."

"That's like a scene in *Castle in the Sky*. Why are you telling me this?"

"Because it's a cool story. And because it kinda shows even when you're falling you can grab onto some stuff you can use when you finally hit the Earth."

I needed to get some air. There was a mountain of laundry by my bed and I needed to get out. I put all my BTS stickers all over my water bottle: RM, Jin, Suga, J-Hope, Jimin, V, and Jungkook. Every BTS member has a role. RM is smart, awkward, nice—and he's the captain of the ship. Suga is cold and distant but sweet. Jungkook is a troublemaker, goofy, and the youngest. V is cool and weird and funny. Jimin is adorable and brings sweetness to the group. J-Hope is the best dancer—they're all amazing dancers—and he's the sunshine of the group, always energetic. Jin is the oldest one, but acts like the youngest, always telling dad jokes, the kind of wisecracks that are embarrassing and corny but actually kind of cute. They all became stars together, they toured together, they have self-isolated in Seoul together. They are a true group—a kind of misfit family—and I wanted to have them all together on my water bottle.

I looked on my phone and saw the band's official Twitter had tweeted something new.

@BTS_twt: *We stand against racial discrimination. We condemn violence. You, I, and we all have the right to be respected. We will stand together. #BlackLivesMatter*

I took a swig from my bottle, grabbed my mask, and headed out for my run. The air was cool but the sun was out. A pair of Nikes hung by their laces on a telephone wire. My compulsions were back and I clucked my tongue three times and touched my left eyelid twice as soon as I exited the front door of my house. Then I looped back twice to check the lock. OCD makes me a human GIF sometimes. It is what it is but I can live with it. I ran down North Avenue past the pond in front of the high school. On the right side of the street there was a line of ducks and swans. I've read that all around the world animals are returning to cities now that the cars are parked and the pollution has disappeared and the people are gone. There are pink flamingos in the heart of Mumbai. There are herds of horned mountain goats in the township of Llandudno in the north of Wales. Wild boars are grazing out of flower beds in Ajaccio, the capital of Corsica. Prides of lions are roaming black tar roads outside of Kruger National Park in South Africa. I dodged a fawn nipping at flowers at the roadside. There was a rain cloud on the horizon but I could run faster. I heard echoes in the woods yet life goes on.

My phone buzzed. A message from Tovah. She was feeling a little better these days. A bunch of student coders at our school had taken New Rochelle High and recreated it down to the last brick inside of *Xamaica*. So now graduation was back on, but it was going to be virtual. She'd get to give her valedictorian speech after all, at least a digital version of it.

But this wasn't about that. Tovah had forwarded me a "NowThis" clip. I read as I ran.

January 20 was the first confirmed case of the coronavirus in the US. It was also the first confirmed case of coronavirus in South Korea. Within two weeks of that case, South Korea implemented nationwide testing and the US had tested virtually nobody. The US population is six times that of South Korea but the US coronavirus death rate swelled to hundreds of times that of South Korea. With their health crisis swiftly put behind them, South Korea opened up for business months before the US and the South Korean mega-band BTS, which had been isolating together, resumed releasing new songs and music videos.

The president of the United States had delivered on his "America First" promise in the most terrible way as the US overtook the entire rest of the world in cases of the novel coronavirus. Obama

had left the new president a sixty-nine-page Pandemic Playbook
to respond to just such a crisis—which the new administration ig-
nored. Obama had left his successor the Pandemic Preparedness
Office to deal with such emergencies—but the new administration
closed the program. Obama had left the new president a global
monitoring system called PREDICT to track precisely these kinds
of outbreaks—but the new administration cut its funding by 75
percent. America makes up just 4 percent of the world's population
but accounts for some 25 percent of the world's COVID-19 deaths.
Analysis of data from the Institute of Health Metrics and Evalu-
ation suggests that 90 percent of the US deaths could have been
prevented if the president had issued physical distancing guidelines
even two weeks earlier than he did.

The clip vanished. Everything was temporary. Tovah
would be moving half a world away soon, and maybe we'd
remain friends, maybe we'd never see each other again, maybe
I'd manage to match her up with a hot freshman at Barnard.
Diego's family had hired an immigration lawyer but nobody
knew yet if he'd get to stay in the country and go to Columbia
with me or if he'd be sent to Cuba with his mother. Nothing
lasted. Not school. Not friendships. Not even life. But once
something has happened, it's happened forever. There's a kind
of satisfying permanence to that. Like all those ghost adver-
tisements that haunt the brick walls of the buildings in downtown New Rochelle. As long as I remember my friendships I
can treasure them. That isn't forever but it is enough for now.

I ran by the beauty shop. The place was boarded up and someone had spray-painted across the wood planks, *It's not who you*
are that holds you back, it's who you think you're not. —Basquiat. I'd
heard Doreema had gotten a new gig as a deejay at Starbucks,
which had reopened to serve to-go customers only and had a
turntable set up to attract business off the street. I hoped that

was true, and I was gonna call her to check in. I hated that her shop was closed, but I loved the idea that someone could re-mix their life. I ran by Cal's Barbershop. He was sweeping the sidewalk in front of his empty establishment. Maybe custom-ers would be coming back or maybe they'd be cutting their own hair at home. He looked up at me as I ran by and he held a fist in the air to cheer me along.

I took a right turn on Cemetery Road. BTS has a song called "Jamais Vu." The title is a kind of remix of the phrase *déjà vu*, which means having a weird feeling you've been some-where before even though you know you never have. *Jamais vu* is knowing you've been someplace before but having it some-how still seem new and unfamiliar. Imagine walking into what you know is your own home and not recognizing the furniture or your family. I hadn't been down this street since the funeral and I was feeling jamais vu. I remember it had been raining hard that day and even with the umbrellas we had all gotten soaked, but that was okay with me because with all the rain nobody could see my tears. Today it was bright and sunny and the grass around all the gravestones was green. Maybe after months of isolation everyone was feeling jamais vu. Maybe it was a good thing. Maybe it was a second chance.

I jumped the low iron fence that separated the sidewalk from the cemetery. My parents had gotten married in the church across the street, which is why my mom decided this was where she wanted my dad to be buried. The funeral was supposed to be small and private but the whole town had turned out anyway, even in the rain, and there had been TV cameras and a news copter and the mayor had given a speech. But the only words I remembered were from Brother Anthony, who read some verses from the Book of Matthew.

"'And Jesus went forth, and saw a great multitude, and was moved with compassion toward them, and he healed their sick. And when it was evening, his disciples came to him, saying, *This is a desert place, and the time is now past; send the multitude away, that they may go into the villages, and buy themselves victuals.* But Jesus said unto them, *They need not depart; give ye them to eat.* And they say unto him, *We have here but five loaves, and two fishes.* He said, *Bring them hither to me.* And he commanded the multitude to sit down on the grass, and took the five loaves, and the two fishes, and looking up to heaven, he blessed, and brake, and gave the loaves to his disciples, and the disciples to the multitude. And they did all eat, and were filled: and they took up of the fragments that remained twelve baskets full.'"

I looked around at all the tombstones in the graveyard. There were many that were so new the grass hadn't yet grown over the brown dirt over the caskets. There were some that were so old I was sure that anyone who still knew the person that had died was probably buried somewhere else in the cemetery. Weird that the place didn't have a depressing feel. There were yellow flowers sprouting up between the graves. Red butterflies floated in the air above. There were no cars on the streets, no buses bussing by, no planes in the sky. Not far away, I heard the sound of children playing. Maybe it was some small family going out for air.

I stood in front of my father's grave. The tombstone read, *Egbert Gustavus Montego. Born Kingston, Jamaica, 1966. Died New Rochelle, New York, 2017. Living Is Giving.* I've often thought about what he meant by that phrase. I've often wondered if he thought about that as he ran down the corridors unarmed to confront a girl with a gun.

There are powers in this world that pit us against each other. They have us fighting for scraps, for jobs, for college admissions, for toilet paper, for Instacart delivery slots, for bat soup. But it's a lie. We don't have to fight each other. The best things in life, the things we really need, they're not scarce, they're infinite. Like love. A parent can have a dozen kids and there is always enough love. You can have a million friends or two and there's always enough love. You can marry once and get married again and there's always enough love. You can love anyone of any sex or any race and there's always enough love. The government always says they have no money, but the minute they wanted to they came up with trillions in pandemic relief. The things that really matter aren't fossil fuels that run dry. They're like sun and wind and love and they never run short or run out. They're like loaves and fishes. There's enough for the multitudes.

I want you to know, Dad, that I'm not angry anymore. I'm not scared anymore. I signed up for that trial online and if they take sixteen-year-olds, I'm gonna do it and I don't care how dangerous and dumb it is. I'm helping to organize more protests against police brutality and wealth inequality and presidential mendacity and I'm going to keep speaking out no matter what they throw at us. I'm probably always gonna have OCD and depression and all the other issues I have to deal with, but that's just life and other people have it worse. There's always someone who has it worse. It's like they said at the end of that book I read for school. I have no idea what's coming but there are sick people who need saving. I'm doing something that's better than anything I've ever done and that feels right. I want you to know that I know what you were trying to tell me with your life. With your death. It's crazy that it took a virus to get the message home to me. But how many plagues did God have to throw at Pharaoh before the guy realized he had to let Moses and his people go? The things that mattered before, they don't matter as much anymore. I want to do well at college, make some good money, I won't lie about that. But now I know all that stuff can fall away and none of it matters. I can be alone in my house with my family with no jobs and no schedule and no nothing and be as happy as I've ever been in my life. Loaves and fishes. We always have everything we need because living is giving.

I closed my eyes and listened to a breeze in the tree branches above my head. I was floating in a warm salt lake. When I opened my eyes I noticed a stream full of fish flowing at the edge of the graveyard. I didn't have a flower to leave so I planted a warm kiss on my father's cold headstone, jumped the iron fence, and went running up North Avenue back to my life.

Even when we have nothing, we have something to give.

The End

Acknowledgments

All robocalls in the novel were inspired by public government and school communications but they don't reflect any government or school official, living or dead.

Brother Anthony's sermons were inspired by the legal writings of Anthony Paul Farley.

Thanks to Dr. Jonathan David Farley for checking my math.

The fictional TV interview with Dr. Larry Brilliant is based on "The Doctor Who Helped Defeat Smallpox Explains What's Coming" by Steven Levy, March 19, 2020, *Wired* magazine.

The fictional TV interview with David Kessler is based on "That Discomfort You're Feeling Is Grief" by Scott Berinato, March 23, 2020, *Harvard Business Review*.

The quotation from Michael Sandel is drawn from "Finding the 'Common Good' in a Pandemic" by Thomas L. Friedman, March 24, 2020, *New York Times*.

The high school essays in this novel are based on actual homework assignments.

A few lines of dialogue in this book are actually quotes from Friedrich Nietzsche. Blame him.

I didn't make up the dad joke Kevin tells, I heard it on the street in New Rochelle.